I0527481

Accused

Sharon C. Cooper

Copyright © 2018 Sharon C. Cooper

All rights reserved. No part of this book may be used or reproduced in any manner without written permission except in the case of brief quotations embodied in critical articles and reviews. For permission, contact the author at sharoncooper.net

ISBN: 978-1-946172-11-2
Paperback

Disclaimer
This story is a work of fiction. Names, characters, and incidents are either products of the author's imagination or are used fictitiously. Any resemblance to actual events, locales, organizations or persons, living or dead, is entirely coincidental.

Acknowledgements

Special thanks to my amazingly supportive husband, Al! You're the best! I love you more than I could ever express!

Yolanda and Claire, you ladies ROCK! You're always there to push (or threaten) me when I feel like giving up. I can't imagine my writing journey without you!

And to my BBR, Brenda S – BLESS YOU for your bravery of being willing to read this story in its roughest state! Love you!

Chapter One

Kenton Bailey's gaze darted around at their surroundings as he circled the cemetery one more time. "I don't like this."

"I agree," Agent Quaid Morrow said from the passenger seat. He was on his cell phone, on hold, waiting to talk to someone out of the FBI D.C. field office. Their supervisor had given the okay for the quick detour. "Where is the other team? They should've already been in position."

Kenton wondered the same thing.

"We'll be too exposed," he mumbled more to himself as he drove slowly. The early morning sun had just made its appearance, and no one was milling about. That didn't mean there weren't threats nearby.

The towering office buildings in the distance and oversize oak trees scattered throughout the cemetery provided too many shadowy spots where people could easily hide. The tall headstones weren't much help either.

There was too much Kenton couldn't see despite the open area near the gravesite.

Too exposed.

Kenton continued along the winding cemetery drive but stayed near the area they needed to be in. He didn't want to park until he knew what was happening with their back up. "We might need to reconsider—"

1

"You promised, Kenton," Santana grumbled.

He glanced in the rear-view mirror at his long-time confidential informant and met her glare. Her long braids hung loosely around her shoulders, while a few covered her golden-brown face. Santana had helped him on numerous cases. Now she was vital in helping the FBI put away one of the leaders of the DeLevese gang who had orchestrated a hit on a judge.

Santana had been an eyewitness to the killing. Kenton hated that she was in this position, knowing that her life was in serious danger, but getting Snake-eyes off the streets would cripple the gang. Which was something his team tried to achieve for years. The DeLevese crew had already started spreading into other territories, but taking one of their leaders down would be a big win for the FBI.

"I know I agreed to this visit, Santana, but my number one goal is to get you to that courthouse and keep you safe. I can't—"

"I have been threatened, shot at, and now you're telling me that I can't get this one thing? I should've just disappeared like I had planned."

Kenton huffed out a breath. She was his best CI. She was also good at disappearing. Their case would fall apart without her. "I'm glad you didn't."

"If I have to testify and give up my whole life for you and the frickin' FBI, this is the least you can do for me before forcing me into WITSEC!" she snapped, before turning her attention to stare out the window.

Considering she would have to leave her life in D.C, all she had asked for was to stop at her father's grave before she was scheduled to testify. Part of Kenton felt that was the least they could give her. The moment her testimony was given, she'd be whisked away by the U.S. Marshals and placed in the federal witness protection program.

All things considered, she was handling the situation well and had only broken down a couple of times during her few months of being in protective custody. Kenton's biggest concern from day one was the target on her back. Testifying against one of the most dangerous gangs on the east coast was a death sentence.

He knew it, and she knew it, too.

"We have a problem," Quaid said the moment he disconnected his call.

"What's that?"

"The agents who were supposed to shadow us on this little detour got delayed. We're going to have to forfeit this idea or do this solo."

Kenton shook his head before Quaid finished his sentence. "No way. This case is too big. We can't take the chance."

"Please, Kenton." Santana gripped the front seats, pulling on them. "All I need is five minutes. I don't know where I'm moving to, but the marshals told me I can't return to D.C. as long as I'm in the witness protection program."

"Come on, man. We got this," Quaid encouraged. "You've circled the area a hundred times. There's no one out here this early in the morning, and I won't let anything happen to your girl. Besides, you did promise her."

"Yeah, listen to Agent Morrow. We can do this," Santana pleaded, sounding hopeful.

Kenton glanced at her again. Santana had become more than just a confidential informant to him over the years. She was like a sister to him. He helped her get off drugs, and she'd finally landed a full-time job. Trouble used to follow her, but she'd stayed clean and out of trouble for almost three years. Kenton didn't want to see anything happen to her. He'd never be able to forgive himself.

"Five minutes," he finally caved. "And if trouble breaks out, you have to do everything we taught you before leaving the safe house. Your life might depend on it."

"I know. I know. I'll stay close. I promise. I only need a few minutes with my father. We're actually near his grave site. The closest we can get is near that huge oak tree on the left-hand side." Santana pointed to a tree nearly fifty yards in front of them.

Kenton parked as anxiousness curled inside of him. He still didn't feel good about the idea. They were all outfitted in bulletproof vests, and he and Quaid were strapped, but it wasn't enough protection as far as he was concerned. Granted, he knew someone at the agency would come looking if they were delayed, but his gut was still uneasy.

He removed his dark shades and faced Santana. "Okay, let's go over the procedure again."

She sighed loudly and dropped back against the seat. "Come on, man. We've gone through the drill a hundred times. I know it already. I'm supposed to stay alert at all times. Do whatever you and Agent Morrow tell me, stay close to you two, etc, etc. Oh, and I'm supposed to make this quick. I got it."

Quaid smirked and shook his head. "I don't know how you've put up with her all of these years."

"He loves me," Santana said good-naturedly.

She was right. She was like family, and Kenton didn't like putting her life at risk any more than he already had.

"Sweetheart, I want you in one piece so that you can live your life to the fullest. I can't help worrying about you."

Santana didn't say anything, just stared out the window at the headstones. She had reservations about joining WITSEC, but the guy she was testifying against was bad news and had a long reach. It had taken some doing, but she had finally been accepted into the program. All he had to do was make sure he got her to the courthouse in time.

"Sit tight. I'll open the door for you," he told her. "And remember, stay close to us at all times."

She rolled her eyes but did as she was told as they made their way to the middle of the graveyard to her father's tombstone.

While they waited, giving Santana some privacy without being too far from her, Kenton stayed vigilant, glancing around at their surroundings. He didn't like the idea of being in the open like this, but he was glad they seemed to be the only ones out there. Except for chirping birds, and the sound of traffic in the distance, it was very quiet.

That didn't mean that they were alone, though.

Kenton's attention went back to Santana as she swiped at her eyes, then turned to them. "Thank you. I'm ready," she said swallowing. Kenton's chest tightened, and it took all of his restraint not to pull her into his arms and hug her tight. She had no family that he knew of and very few friends. He was the only person she had in this life, and soon she would be back to having no one. Even he wouldn't know her location.

Instead of offering her a shoulder to cry on, he and Quaid fell in step, one on each side of her as they hustled toward the SUV.

"You okay?" Kenton asked, a hand at the small of Santana's back as he kept her moving forward.

"I guess so. I'm just ready to get this over with."

"I know...soon."

Unease crept through Kenton. He slowed, unsure of the weird feeling that suddenly overcame him.

Something's not right.

That thought rattled around in his mind while the stirring in his gut increased. Quaid glanced around as well. Was he picking up the same vibe? His friend walked a step ahead of them, and they both stayed alert and kept moving. There was still no one in sight.

"What?" Santana asked, easing even closer to Kenton. "What is it?"

"Just keep moving and remember everything we taught you."

With his free hand, Kenton pulled his gun from its holster and kept it at his side. Without a word, Quaid pushed a button on his cell phone. No doubt sending the distress signal to their supervisor. He held his weapon in his opposite hand as they scanned the area while hurrying toward the vehicle.

Quaid glanced at him. "Maybe we should—"

5

Quaid's body jerked and fell back, hitting the grassy ground with a thump. A bullet hole in the center of his forehead.

Kenton's heart slammed against his chest as his gaze darted around.

Shit! Sniper.

Santana screamed and ran toward the vehicle. Kenton jerked her to the ground, covering her shivering body with his. His pulse raced. Anxiety raged through him. He looked from a huge oak tree, twenty yards out, and back to the SUV that was just a little further away, trying to gauge their best option.

A bullet pinged off a small tree less than two feet away.

"We gotta get to the truck!" Kenton ground out, his pulse pounding loudly in his ear. He grabbed Santana's hand and jerked her up, her sobs growing louder. Panting, they ran in a zigzag. Outrunning a sniper was nearly impossible, but if they wanted to stay alive, they needed to take cover. They needed to move faster.

"Keep running!"

Twenty feet. Just twenty more feet.

Tires squealing and a revved engine snagged Kenton's attention. A dark sedan came zooming down the narrow road and...*gun.*

"Get down!"

Pushing Santana to the ground, Kenton lifted his 9mm and fired off two shots. Glass shattered. The driver swerved. But the muzzle of a gun appeared through the back window.

"Ooomph," Kenton gasped, a bullet slamming into his shoulder. "*Shit.*" He stumbled back but stayed on his feet and got off two more rounds despite the pain radiating down his arm.

"Kenton!"

He could barely hear the sirens in the distance over the ringing in his ears and Santana's screams. She ran toward him.

"Get down!" he yelled and fired off another round toward their attackers. "Stay down!"

6

Her body jerked. Her eyes grew large, and she grabbed the top of her bulletproof vest.

Blood.

No. No. No.

Kenton lunged, hoping to catch her, but she staggered then dropped hard to the grass. "Hang on, baby! Hang on!" Before he could get closer, he felt a pinch near his ear. Unbearable heat coursed through his neck, his shoulder, and his knees went weak sending him crashing to the ground. Pain gripped his body, clawing through him like a scalpel scraping across his bones.

Hang on. He couldn't lose her. He had to hang on.

Santana stretched out her arm, reaching for him as tears flowed down her face, and her chest heaved. Kenton crawled toward her, his vision blurring as he fought to keep moving. He had to keep moving.

"K-Ken…" Santana's body shook. Once. Twice. And then…nothing.

No! No! No!

"Santana!" he yelled, barely recognizing his gravelly voice as heavy darkness descended over him.

Hang on. I have to hang on. I have to save her.

Santana! Santana! Santana!

Chapter Two

Five years later…

Kenton jolted awake and bolted upright. His hands fisted the sheets as his heart pounded wildly against his ribcage like a caged animal trying to break free. His gaze darted around, slowly adjusting to the dimly lit room. Pale blue walls. Bathroom a few feet away. Semi-closed blinds revealing that it was almost dark outside.

He huffed out an exhausted breath and rubbed his sweat, slicked forehead with the back of his hand. *It was just a dream.* The fog in his mind slowly started to clear.

Atlanta.

Supreme Security.

Crash room.

He was safe.

Blinking several times to clear his vision, Kenton squinted at the digital clock sitting on the bedside table. Four hours. He'd slept for four hours. Not nearly long enough to feel rejuvenated after the assignment he'd been on for the last two days.

Dropping back onto the pillow, he draped his forearm over his eyes and sighed as his heart rate slowly went back to normal. It had been months since he'd dreamed about

Santana, Quaid, the shooting, and the day that changed his life forever.

Why now? Why had the dream invaded his sleep again?

Slowly sitting up, Kenton rubbed the side of his neck, making contact with one of the puffy wounds from where he'd been shot all those years ago. If only he had listened to his gut. Guilt still plagued him that he had put all of their lives at risk.

His ringing cell phone jarred him out of his musing, and he snatched it up from the small table next to the bed.

A slow smile broke through when he saw who was calling. "Hello, Dee."

"Kenton, where are you?" she asked by way of greeting.

He blew out a breath and chuckled, placing his feet on the floor. "You do realize you're not my wife, right? There's only one man you get to ask that question to, and it *ain't* me."

Dakota had married Kenton's boss, Hamilton Crosby, almost a year ago. With that union, she became like a sister to him, and he loved her to death even if she was bossy as hell.

"I know who I married. Quit being a wise-ass and listen. I'm trying to help you here. So answer the question."

"All right. All right. I'm at Supreme. What's up?"

He stood and slid into the dress pants that he had discarded earlier. Since the drive to his house often took an hour due to traffic, occasionally, after an assignment, it wasn't unusual for him to sleep at work instead of driving home. The converted warehouse that Supreme Security, an agency that provided personal protection to a high-end clientele, had all the comforts of home. Including crash rooms for security specialists.

"I just talked to Egypt, and she's getting ready to leave the office."

"Yeah, and?" Kenton usually made it a point to stop by and see her whenever he was in the building, but he'd had to work a double shift. All he had wanted to do when he returned to Supreme was get a little sleep, and then he had planned to go and see her.

"Your woman is about to go on another blind date with someone she met online. You have to stop her."

Damn.

He didn't like Egypt dating anyone other than him, but really hated the idea of her dating guys she met online. If she stopped shooting him down every time he asked her out, she wouldn't have to settle for the chumps she met on the internet.

"Oh, so now you don't have nothin' to say? Kenton, you need to step up your game with Egypt if you want her. Otherwise, she's going to end up with someone else, and neither one of us want that."

Dakota was right. The last thing Kenton wanted was to lose his chance at making Egypt his. He'd been attracted to her from the moment they'd met years ago. Since then, their relationship had grown into a special friendship, but he wanted more. He knew she felt the same. Except, she was still singing the same tune: *I can't go out with you.*

"Dee, I'm going to catch you later." He slipped into his shoes and finished buttoning his dress shirt, leaving off the tie and suit jacket.

"I hope that's code for: I have to hurry and get off the phone so I can go see Egypt before she leaves the office. If it is, stop her from going on this date. It's not safe."

"Yes, ma'am," he mocked. "I'll see what I can do. Now can I go?"

"Yeah, but call me later and let me know how it turns out," she said before disconnecting.

Kenton chuckled, shoved the phone into his pocket and strolled to the bathroom to relieve himself and freshen up. A short while later, he headed up one level to Egypt's office, slowing as he approached the opened door. He had no idea what he would say to convince her to stop with the online dating, but he had every intention of trying to change her mind.

He pulled up short when he spotted Egypt across the room. She was standing behind her desk at the window, holding onto the wand used to open and closed the blinds. As she stared at something outside, he took the opportunity to study her profile.

Gorgeous.

At some point in the day, she must have changed clothes, because she wasn't currently wearing her usual business attire. Sure, she always wore bright colors, but nothing like this orange, one-shoulder, long-sleeved blouse that showed off her long delicate neck, smooth brown shoulder, and emphasized her full breasts. His gaze went lower to the multi-color skirt that stopped just above her knees. With the various patterns in the garment, it reflected her artsy style and fit her curvaceous hips and butt perfectly.

Egypt was a stunning woman on any day, but this was the second time in a matter of weeks, that he'd seen her looking like an Egyptian goddess. Her long dreadlocks were piled on top of her head, with a few locks hanging loose and framing her face.

Closing the blinds, she turned suddenly and startled when spotting him at the door.

Those eyes.

Those dark, exotic doe-like eyes that made him weak in the knees whenever she looked at him, zoned in on him like a laser beam. His body stirred as he took in the whole package.

"Hello, Beautiful," he finally said and moved farther into the room, closing the door behind him.

Egypt smiled and batted her eyes demurely before directing her attention to the immaculate desk. Her gaze eased back up to him, a sexy grin on her tempting lips.

"Didn't you guys just go through a sensitivity training? I'm pretty sure you can't address any woman here by the name, Beautiful."

His body tightened with need as he stood in front of her desk. Everything about her turned him on from her attractive face to her sassiness, to that enticing fragrance she wore. The thought of her going out with someone else made him want to punch something, but he planned to remain cool. He didn't know when or how, but one day she would be his.

Kenton planted his palms down on the desk, bringing him closer to her. "You're the only one here or anywhere, that I call by that name. As far as I'm concerned, it belongs to you. So no harm done, right?"

Egypt shook her head and smirked.

Kenton never had a problem getting the attention of the opposite sex, but he wanted her more than he had ever wanted another woman.

"But I have to ask. Will I need to take another sensitivity training if I tell you that you look absolutely gorgeous today?"

Now she laughed, the sweet sound washing over him like a powerful wave, forcing his need for her to grow.

"You are such a flirt, but don't worry, I won't tell anyone." She sat in her desk chair and pulled a large handbag from the bottom drawer. "I would love to hang around and let you continue to pay me compliments, but I need to get going."

"I take it you have another date," he said, unable to keep the distaste of the idea out of his tone.

"As a matter of fact, I do. And if I don't head out now, I'm going to be late."

"Is this a first date or someone you've been out with before?"

"First date."

"Did you do a background check on him?"

"A preliminary one, yes."

"Does anyone here know him?"

"I hope not. You guys would scare the bravest man away. Now if you're done with the interrogation, can I leave?"

She stood with her bag and moved from behind the desk. Kenton watched the smooth sway of her hips in the tight skirt, and his shaft pressed uncomfortably against his zipper.

Damn. This woman and her fine ass. I can't let her get with someone else.

12

Kenton diverted his attention. First, he needed to get himself back under control. His body always betrayed him whenever they shared the same space. After a few slow breaths, he turned back just as Egypt was slipping into a short, burnt orange jacket. Before she could get to the door, he stepped into her path.

"Where are you guys going?"

Sighing loudly, Egypt glared at him. "Like I would tell you. The last time I told your spy," she said of Dakota, "where I was going, she told you. I don't need you showing up again, Kenton."

"That only happened one time. I promise I won't show up this time." He was glad that she took precautions and usually let Dakota know where'd she'd be and with who, but he still didn't like the idea of her dating.

"Why do I always have to go through this with you, Hamilton, and Angelo? Don't get me wrong, I appreciate you guys looking out for me, but I'm a big girl. I don't need my *big brothers*, going all *He-Man* whenever I have a date."

"You know not to include me in the *big brothers'* scenario," Kenton said in a low voice close to her ear, his hand moving to her hip.

Had he not known for a fact that their feelings for each other were mutual, he wouldn't have made such a bold move. He was close enough to feel Egypt shudder against him.

"I definitely don't see you or consider you as a sister. In fact, the things I'd love to do with you would not fall into the brotherly love zone."

Her hand went to his chest, and her touch scorched his skin right through his shirt. At 5'9" she was tall for a woman, but even with her high heels, the top of her head only came up to his nose. He had always been attracted to tall, curvy women and she didn't disappoint.

"Kenton, I…we," she started, but stopped and dropped her gaze. When her tongue slid across her bottom lip, an uncontrollable growl rumbled in his throat.

"Cancel your date, and go out with me," he said,

caressing her soft cheek with the pad of his thumb.

Egypt glanced up at him, and the urge to kiss her was stronger than ever.

"I already told you. I can't go out with you."

"You can't or you won't?"

She stepped out of his hold but didn't move away. "Is there a difference?"

Kenton shoved his hands into his front, pants pockets to keep from touching her again. "Yeah, there is a difference. Have you ever seen the movie, *Pretty Woman*?"

Egypt's brows shot up. "Are you kidding me? There's not a woman alive who hasn't seen the movie, at least twice. Question is, have *you* seen it?"

"I have three sisters, two who are older. It was impossible for me not to see it and every other chick flick that exists. The point is, toward the end of the movie, when Edward asks Vivian to stay with him for one more night, she gives a teary-eyed *I can't*. That's how you say I can't, but without the tears."

Egypt stared at him with her mouth hanging open but didn't say anything.

"When you tell me you can't go out with me, that speaks volumes. It means you can't go out with me because you're afraid, or it's because of something that has happened in your past. Deep down, you really do want to date me."

She shook her head, and Kenton didn't miss the soft smile spreading across her lips. "You're too much. You know that?"

"Tonight, there was something else behind your words, and I can't put my finger on it. Have I done something to make you think that you and I *can't* date? And don't give me that shit about fraternizing. That rule is *not* included in our employee handbook."

"Kenton…"

He grasped her arm gently and pulled her close. "If you told me that you *won't* or will never go out with me, I would've backed off a long time ago. You haven't done that.

So which is it? You *can't* go out with me, or you don't want to?"

Egypt folded her bottom lip between her teeth as if debating on whether to tell him the truth or lie. As a former undercover FBI agent, he'd been good at reading people, and he already knew the answer. She wanted to be with him as much as he wanted to be with her, but something was holding her back. He didn't know what, but he had every intention of finding out.

"Sweetheart, your silence tells me everything I need to know." Kenton cupped her face between his hands and lowered his head.

"Wha—"

His mouth covered hers, effectively cutting off her words and he savored the softness of her lips. He had wanted to kiss her like this for months, and finally, he was getting the chance to taste her sweetness.

He nudged her lips apart with his tongue, and a wave of heat instantly spread through his body when he slid into her mouth. The quick pecks on the cheek and the chaste kisses on the lips that they'd shared on occasion was nothing compared to this. This…this was special. Memorable.

Hot.

Soft.

Sweet.

The kiss was everything he knew it would be and more. Egypt's sensual moans and the way she fisted the front of his dress shirt, served as encouragement. Kenton savored every lap of her tongue and the warmth that encompassed him. He adored this woman. The eagerness in the way she kissed him back let him know that he'd been right. She wanted him as much as he wanted her.

Even so, his mind screamed—*Stop!* Let her go before you scare her off. The rest of his body wasn't in agreement. Seeing her all dolled up for another man did something to him. Even though taking the liberty to kiss her had been risky, Kenton was determined to prove to her that she and he belonged together.

His hands traveled down the sides of her body and stopped on her curvy hips. He pulled her closer, deepening the kiss. His body was on fire. No doubt she felt the effect that she was having on him pressed against her stomach.

Damn. She felt good.

If he didn't stop soon, he wouldn't be able to, and he *really* didn't want to. He also didn't want to totally scare her off. Knowing that, he slowly pulled his mouth from hers and lifted his head.

Egypt gasped and stepped back as if just realizing what they'd done.

"W—Why'd you do that?" she asked quietly, lust brimming in her eyes and her fingers hovered over her lips.

"Because I wanted to make sure you're thinking of me while you're out with another man." He brushed the back of his fingers down her cheek. "Stay safe, and have a good evening."

Even though it was hard to leave after what they'd shared, Kenton opened the door and walked out. He left her standing there, knowing that he gave her something to think about.

This was all a part of his plan. He was determined to show Egypt why he was the better choice out of any of the jerks she was going out with. He just had to figure out how to get past the walls she had built around herself.

One way or another...

Chapter Three

Crap! I can't believe he kissed me. Really kissed me.

Egypt hurried up the concrete stairs to the restaurant trying to tap down her nervousness. She always looked forward to her dates before they happened, but when it came time for them, she started second-guessing her decision. Meeting someone online and then agreeing to go out with him made her a little leery. This time was no different. Except it was different.

Kenton had kissed her.

Her fingers went to her lips. It was as if she could still feel his luscious mouth on hers. She couldn't believe they had actually kissed. Their first *real* kiss. It was even more amazing than she had imagined it would be. But now his words played on a loop in her head, screwing with her mind.

I wanted to make sure you're thinking of me while you're out with another man.

He had ruined everything. All it took was that frickin' kiss and those words to throw her off balance, making her even more unsure about going on a blind date. Egypt had no doubt that he knew what he was doing. He knew she wouldn't be able to stop thinking about him.

"Urgh, he gets on my damn nerves," she mumbled to herself as she strolled into the restaurant. She and Kenton

17

were good friends with a great working relationship. However, the last few months, something had shifted between them. He'd been more touchy-feely, and attentive. And she enjoyed every minute of the flirting and had even gotten used to him asking her out every other day.

At first, Egypt thought she was just lonely for some companionship, but something was going on with him too. But no way was he lonely for company. The man attracted women without even trying, probably because he was tall, muscular, and *fine* as hell. He was one of the most requested security specialists at Supreme, and those requests weren't only because of his protection skills. The man was the total package. Witty, charismatic, and had the compassion of a saint. Add those traits to his rugged sexiness that fueled her fantasies, and you had an irresistible man. The perfect catch.

Too bad they could never get together, no matter how many times he asked her out. It couldn't happen.

Just stop thinking about him.

"Hi, I'll be right with you," the hostess said to Egypt when she rushed back to the stand and grabbed a few menus. "Conner party of four your table is ready." The small group stepped forward and she escorted them to the dining room.

Egypt glanced around the waiting area. The buzz of conversation and soft jazz sifting through the overhead speakers mingled together. There was a large group of people in business suits talking and laughing quietly near the hallway that led to the restrooms. Closer to the hostess station stood an older couple patiently waiting to be seated, while two other people sat on a bench near the door she had just entered, taking a selfie.

So far it didn't look as if her date had arrived, but Egypt glanced to her right, toward the bar area, checking to see if Devonte might've been there. She spotted a few men sitting alone, but none resembled the profile picture that he had uploaded to the dating site.

Egypt inhaled a long, steadying breath and released it slowly to tap down her anxiousness. Hopefully, she and

Devonte hit it off. She'd been on three dates with guys that she had met through the dating site, but none had resulted in second dates.

Maybe tonight will be different.

Dakota, one of her best friends, told her she was probably giving off some type of vibe, insisting that Egypt was too into Kenton to open herself up to anyone else. Which was probably true. Egypt compared every man she met to him. If he knew how often she thought of him when on a date with other men, his ego would swell even bigger than it already was.

Shoot.

Egypt shook her head. She was falling right into the trap Kenton had set. Making her think about him all evening.

Nope. Not gonna think about him. I have a date, and I'm going to enjoy myself even if it kills me.

"Hi, sorry for the wait. Party of one?" the hostess asked when she returned. Egypt looked around, surprised the woman had already seated the smaller groups that had been standing nearby.

Egypt glanced at her watch. Devonte was almost ten minutes late. "Actually, I'm meeting someone here, but I don't see him. I believe he made a reservation. The name is Devonte Abernathy."

Pushing her long blond hair out of her face and behind her ear, the hostess studied the list on the wood podium. "Ah, yes, here we are. Abernathy for two. He hasn't arrived yet, but would you like to be seated?"

"That would be great. Thanks."

The woman grabbed a couple of menus and a wine list. "Follow me, please."

Egypt trailed her into the dining room, and the intoxicating scent of fresh bread, basil and a host of other scents wafted past her nose. She hadn't eaten since lunch, and her stomach chose that moment to grumble.

"Is this okay?" The hostess stopped at a small booth. "When your party arrives, you should be able to see him from here."

"This is great."

Once Egypt was seated, the hostess handed her a menu and set the other one on the table, along with the wine list.

"Your server will be right with you."

"Thank you." Before Egypt could look over the menu, a server was at the table.

"Hi, I'm Monica and I'll be your server this evening," she said as she filled the water glass that was in front of Egypt. "Will anyone else be joining you?"

"I'm expecting one other person. Can you give him about five more minutes?"

"Sure, no problem. May I get you something from the bar in the meantime? Maybe a glass of wine or a mojito?"

"A glass of Sauvignon Blanc would be great."

"Good choice. I'll be right back with your drink."

Egypt scanned the menu and narrowed her choices down to two entrees and heard her phone chime. Setting the menu down, she pulled her cell from the side pocket of her handbag and glanced at the screen.

Devonte: Sorry I have to cancel on dinner. Maybe another time.

Are you frickin' kidding me?

Egypt growled under her breath, debating on how to respond. Part of her wanted to tell him to lose her damn number, while the other part of her was thinking—good riddance. Before she could decide what to do, the server returned with her drink.

"Here you go."

"Thank you," Egypt said, deciding not to respond to the text, and blocked the jerk's number. She shoved her phone back into her bag and lifted the menu. "It looks like it's just going to be me tonight."

"Oh…okay. Well, let me tell you about our specials."

Egypt listened as the woman described one dish after another, making each one sound more delectable than the last. Though disappointed her date had canceled, she was looking forward to dinner.

Once she placed her order, and the server walked away, Egypt pulled her ereader from her purse. It had been a long time since she'd taken herself out to dinner, and it was a good thing she enjoyed her own company.

By the time she finished her meal, she had made a decision. No more online dating. She hadn't been too thrilled about the idea of finding love through an online dating site anyway, but at the time, it seemed like a good starting place.

What was a girl to do when she was tired of living life alone and was ready to fall in love, get married and have a family? It had taken her years to finally drum up the courage to date again after her last relationship, though brief, had ended badly. Now that she was ready to date, she kept meeting losers.

Dakota's words from earlier that day filtered into her mind.

You'd be able to stop dating these assholes if you'd just give Kenton a chance.

If Egypt was honest, she could admit that it was getting harder and harder to keep distance between them. But she had to be strong and diligent in her decision not to get involved with a coworker. She had too much at risk to get involved with Kenton.

"Was everything to your satisfaction?" the server asked, seeming to come out of nowhere.

"Yes. Thanks for recommending the chicken puttanesca. It was excellent."

"I'm glad to hear that. Can I get you anything else? Maybe dessert? Coffee?"

Egypt patted her stomach. "Oh, no. I think that's it for me."

"All right then. I'll leave this right here." She set the bill on the table. "You can pay me whenever you're ready. No hurry."

"Thank you."

After the server walked away, Egypt glanced inside the

21

black bill folder, thinking she hadn't done too much damage. She made it a habit of having enough money to cover her meal even if she was going on a date. Now she was glad she did.

She put her ereader back into her bag and pulled out her wallet.

"Hello, Egypt."

She stiffened at the raspy, baritone voice that could only belong to one person. Her heart rate kicked into overdrive and unease spread through her body as she tried to keep her hands from shaking.

She slowly lifted her head only to make eye contact with the one person she had hoped to never see again.

Ross Hoakley.

Bastard. That was the only word that came to mind that best described him. Egypt tried to keep down the bile that rose up her throat. She didn't hate many people, but seeing him again made her skin crawl. Over four years since the last time they'd been in each other's presence, and she wished it was longer.

Her gaze took him in. Impeccably dressed, like usual, he wore a dark blue suit that cost more than some people made in a week. His rich amber skin gleamed under the lighting. By the look of his precisely cut, wavy hair and nicely trimmed mustache, he still maintained his rigid grooming schedule.

But when Eygpt's gaze met his dark, penetrating eyes again, all the reasons why she couldn't stand the man came rushing back.

"May I join you?"

"*Hell* no you can't join me," she snapped, hoping he would magically disappear, but he took the seat across from her.

"It's good seeing you again."

"Too bad I can't say the same." The words flew from her mouth, disgust dripping from each one. "I had hoped that you would've gotten swallowed up by a black hole by now. I guess some wishes just don't come true."

He laughed, the sound grating on her nerves like fingernails scraping across a chalkboard. Of all the people she could have run into, why him? She could deal with seeing anyone else, but not Ross. Not now. Not ever.

"I see you still have that same dry sense of humor. Just one of the many things I loved about you."

"And I see you still can't catch a hint when someone wants you gone. You didn't *love* me. You piece of shit. Now get the hell away from me," she said in a harsh whisper and pulled out enough cash to cover the check and a tip before placing the money into the bill folder.

"Don't be like that, Egypt. Besides, I've never known you to use that type of language. It's not very ladylike." Ross ran his finger across the back of her hand. Egypt cringed, gritting her teeth to keep from screaming. His touch felt like an invasion of ants racing down her spine, and she snatched her hand away.

"Don't you *ever* touch me again," she said in a low, threatening voice, anger consuming everything within her. It was because of Ross she had stopped dating. It was also because of him that she'd become afraid of men. Afraid for her safety.

Never again.

Months ago, Dakota, who was a black belt in karate and owned a dojo, had insisted on Egypt enrolling. Between her karate classes and the self-defense techniques Kenton had taught her, Egypt felt confident that she would never be a victim again. She would never again be afraid of the man sitting across from her.

Grabbing her handbag and jacket, she stood abruptly, needing to put as much distance between them as possible. Stepping around a few people as she rushed through the dining room and to the exit, Egypt could feel Ross's presence behind her.

She needed air.

She pushed through the double doors, almost hitting a woman, but didn't stop until she was down the stairs. It didn't matter that the October night had dropped in temperature. The fresh air felt good against her heated skin.

Egypt glanced at the parking lot. *Crap.* She had forgotten that she had ubered to the restaurant.

"Egypt."

Dammit. She spun around, almost losing her balance on four-inch heels.

"Go away, Ross! You and I have nothing to discuss."

"Excuse us," a man said, and Egypt stepped aside, realizing she was standing right in the walkway. There weren't as many people coming and going as it had been when she first arrived, but she still didn't want to be standing in the front of the entrance.

She also needed to arrange for a pickup, but with the way she had stormed out of the restaurant, no way was she going back in.

"Come on, Egypt. Let's go somewhere so we can catch up. It's been a long time," Ross continued, though she tried ignoring him.

As she stuffed her arms through the sleeves of her short jacket, she hurried down the sidewalk and didn't stop until she arrived at the end of the brick building.

"All I want to do is talk." He had followed her and stood too close for comfort. Now she could smell the alcohol on his breath.

"Ross, get it into your head. I don't want to talk to you. Hell, I don't even want to look at you. So step off. *Leave. Me. Alone!*"

Pulse pounding loudly in her ear, Egypt pulled the cell phone from her purse to arrange a pickup. Her hands shook so bad she could barely push the buttons. She hated how his presence affected her.

"What the hell is your problem?" Ross grabbed her arm, jarring it enough to make her drop her phone on the pavement. Her head snapped up, and memories of their last encounter flashed through her mind.

Panic swept through her body, and her heart rate

quickened. "Take your hands off of me."

He pulled her against his body. "All I want to do is talk to you, see how you've been."

Egypt twisted, trying to break free of his hold as his nose and mouth brushed the side of her neck sending fear rocketing through her. She jerked and bucked against him.

"Let go of me," she ground out. There was no one around, but either way, she didn't want this to turn into a scene. Maybe if she just...

"God. You smell as good as I remember," he murmured close to her ear, and something inside of her snapped.

"Get off of me!" She jabbed her elbow into his gut. He cursed under his breath and slumped forward but held onto her. When she slammed her foot down hard, her high heel connected with his shin, and he yelped, loosening his hold.

Egypt wanted to hit or kick him again, but instead, she pulled free, snatched up her phone and bag that had fallen, but she wasn't fast enough. Ross grabbed her forearm.

"I don't know who you think you are, but you will never fight me again."

Before Egypt could react, the back of Ross's hand came quickly across her cheek. Her head snapped to the right. The momentum of the slap sent her crashing into the corner of the building. She caught herself before her head made contact, but Egypt had to blink several times. Stars danced in front of her eyes. Her cheek felt as if it were on fire as she slid down the wall.

Breathing hard, Ross stared down at her. "See you make me crazy, and I don't want to hurt you. But you need to be taught a lesson."

Chapter Four

Tapping his fingers against the steering wheel, Kenton merged into traffic, humming along to the latest song by Drake. Some of the stress of the day drifted away as he headed to his favorite restaurant for his take-out order. Now, if only he could do something about Atlanta's traffic. Eight-thirty in the evening and the streets looked like morning rush hour.

His cell phone rang, and he pressed the button on the earpiece.

"Hello."

"What the heck, man? You don't know how to call folks back?" Angelo Gonzalez's voice came through loud and clear. "I left you two messages today."

"I know, and I meant to call you after my assignment, but by the time I made it to Supreme, I was dog-tired and ended up passing out in one of the crash rooms."

He didn't bother telling his friend that after his nap, Egypt had mentally consumed him. First in her office, and then she occupied his every thought after he tried convincing her not to go on the date. Apparently, the kiss that rocked him had no impact on her. She went anyway.

Maybe it's time to stop pursuing her.

Kenton shook the thought free immediately. Nope. He

26

couldn't give up. He wanted her.

"Oh, yeah, I heard about your new assignment. You've been catering to the diva from hell for the last couple of days." Angelo's words cut into his thoughts. "Did she have you party hopping all night and then shopping with her all day today?"

Kenton didn't miss the humor in Angelo's voice. Diva from hell was the moniker that his team had given a hip-hop singer out of LA who often hired their services whenever she visited Atlanta. Ten years Kenton's junior, Joya made it no secret that she was interested in him. But he had made it clear—he wasn't available.

"Yep. Much of the same as usual," Kenton said.

"I'm pretty sure the way she comes onto you would fall under sexual harassment."

"Maybe, but I can handle Joya. Okay, enough about me. How's it going with orientating the new guys?"

Over the last six months, their bosses, Hamilton Crosby and Mason Bennett, had hired several new recruits to join the team at Supreme. Most of the security specialists, including Kenton, came from law enforcement backgrounds. Everything from beat cops to CIA operatives. Nearly every division was represented. They referred to themselves as Atlanta's finest, and their skill sets were second to none.

"So far, so good. I'm teaching the new guys everything I know."

Before joining Supreme years ago, Angelo worked as a DEA agent. He left the Drug Enforcement Administration after a botched drug bust ended in a heavy gunfight, leaving some of their agents dead. Angelo took the loss hard, but Kenton had a feeling there was more to the story than what his friend told him.

"But getting back to why I called you," Angelo said. "I have another date with Marisol, and she has a friend. You interested in double dating tomorrow night?"

For a moment, Kenton entertained the idea, but he wasn't giving up on Egypt yet. "I'm going to have to pass, man. It's been a couple of long days. I plan to chill all day tomorrow."

Kenton turned into the restaurant's parking lot and snagged the first spot he found on the side of the building.

"You sure? It might do you good to hang out and meet someone new. Besides, it's becoming clear that Egypt don't want you." Angelo chuckled.

"Man, shut up." Kenton cut off the engine. It was no secret that some of the guys knew he was pining over Egypt. Double dating was tempting, but…

A flash of orange around the corner of the building caught Kenton's attention when he climbed out of his vehicle. His mind immediately went to Egypt, and his body stirred, remembering how gorgeous she had looked tonight.

"Hello?" Angelo called out several times. "Ken?"

"Yeah, I'm here. Sorry about that. I need to get off this phone. I'll hit you up a little later."

"All right. Let me know if you change your mind about tomorrow night."

"Will do." Kenton disconnected the call and headed to the entrance of the restaurant.

"I said get your ass up," a distant voice barked." Kenton turned the corner, almost bumping into a lanky guy with a runner's build.

But then he looked down. Shock gripped his body, and his heart slammed against his chest.

"What the hell?" He shoved the man aside as if he were a rag doll, and then he crouched down in front of Egypt.

Holding the side of her face, she blinked several times as if trying to clear her vision. Kenton carefully moved her hand from her cheek not missing the dark red tint of her skin.

"What happened?"

He helped her stand. His anxiety grew when a tear slid down Egypt's face, and then another. Her lips trembled as her gaze darted between him and the guy standing nearby.

"Talk to me. Tell me what happened."

"He hit her." Kenton's head snapped to his right where a

woman with pale skin and bluish-gray hair hurried toward them, but stopped abruptly, suddenly looking unsure. "My daughter and I were leaving, and we saw them over here. He hit her." She pointed at the guy who had been standing over Egypt. "I don't have a cell phone. And my daughter ran back into the restaurant to get help."

"Mind your own business, lady!" the man snapped and moved closer to Kenton. "This has nothing to do with you. Get away from her."

"He *hit* you?" Kenton's breaths came hard and heavy, struggling to stay in control as he stared into Egypt's teary eyes.

"I'm okay," she said quickly in a low voice, still seeming a little dazed as she clung to him. "I...he..."

Something snapped inside of Kenton. He whipped around, propelled by anger and smashed his fist into the man's face. Then hit him again, sending him flying several feet back before crashing to the ground.

"Kenton!" Egypt screamed. He felt a weak tug on the back of his jacket. "Please...don't."

He ignored the way dude howled like a wounded animal, holding his face, blood seeping between his fingers. Kenton lifted him off the ground by his shirt collar and slammed him into the brick building, pinning him with his arm pressed against his neck.

"You *hit* her?" he asked, struggling to wrap his brain around that bit of information. "I ought to break your damn neck. You ever come near her again, I will fucking *kill* you. You hear me?" His rumbling tone was lethal as he held the guy up, refusing to loosen his hold.

"Le-let me go," the man sputtered, struggling to breathe.

"What's going on here?" a loud booming voice said from behind Kenton, and several people started talking at once.

"Kenton, please. Please let him go," Egypt begged, pulling on his arm.

"Not until the police get here."

"No. Let's just go."

29

He hesitated, fury still clawing through him like an out of controlled wildfire. What the hell was this world coming to that men thought it was okay to hit a defenseless woman? He saw it too many times, and it gutted him every time. But when that woman was Egypt—the woman who meant the world to him...

He growled under his breath and jerked the guy forward, then slammed him harder against the wall, eliciting another howl.

"Sir, let him go. We can take it from here."

"Please, Kenton." Egypt continued tugging on his arm, a little harder this time. "He's not worth it. Let him go."

Seconds ticked by before Kenton eventually released the guy, letting him fall to the ground. He watched as the man scurried back on his palms and feet out of reach.

Kenton turned to Egypt. He wiped his hand on his pant leg and then lifted her chin with the pad of his finger to get a better look at her face. It was starting to swell, and he forced down the rage threatening to break free.

"Are you hurt anywhere else?"

She shook her head, her gaze bouncing around nervously at the small crowd that had gathered. "I just want to leave." She slipped her hand into his and squeezed, trying to direct him away from the crowd, but he stood firm. What was going on with her? Instead of trying to leave, she should've been insisting on reporting the bastard to the cops.

"Excuse me." An older, big man with salt and pepper hair and tanned skin came to stand next to them. "I'm Josh Kirchen, the restaurant manager. I just heard what happened. Ma'am, are you sure you're all right? I'll call the authori—"

"No," Egypt said harshly before Kirchen could finish his sentence.

Kenton narrowed his eyes at her.

"I'm fine. We don't need to call anyone. I just want to leave."

"No. Call the cops," Kenton told the manager.

"No."

30

"Don't."

Egypt and the man who hit her said in unison. He'd been sitting on the ground but stood a couple of feet away, his attention on Egypt.

"I'm sorry. I—I had too much to drink, and our disagreement got…" His voice trailed off as he looked from one person to the other. "Everything is fine."

"Are you fucking kidding me?" Kenton lunged toward him, but the manager wedged himself between them. "Your ass hit her. There's nothing all right about that!"

"Come on. Let's go. Please," Egypt whispered, and Kenton glared down at her. Why didn't she want to report this guy?

"Before you leave, we need to do an incident report," the manager said as he ran his hand through his short hair. "I assure you nothing like this has ever happened. If you will all come back into the restaurant, we—"

"No!" Egypt snapped. Everyone turned to her, including Kenton who was still holding her hand. She huffed out a breath. "Look, I'm fine. Thank you all for everything, but this was all a misunderstanding. I need to leave."

Dumbfounded, Kenton didn't say anything but didn't miss the way she shivered against him.

"Can we go now?" she asked the manager, who looked just as perplexed as Kenton.

"I-I guess so." The manager stared at the man who's name Kenton still didn't know, but would soon find out. "Sir, do you want me to call the police or an ambulance?"

"No. I'm fine, and she won't have any more trouble out of me."

"You're damn right she won't." Kenton locked gazes with the man. This wouldn't be the last time they saw each other. Kenton had every intention of seeking him out and making sure he never contacted Egypt again.

In the meantime, she had some serious explaining to do.

Chapter Five

Egypt had to practically run to keep up with Kenton as he wordlessly headed to his black GMC Yukon truck. She couldn't ever remember seeing him angry, and the firm grip he had on her hand, left no doubt that he was pissed.

Just another reason why this evening was one of the worst nights she'd had in a long time. Because of her, Kenton had just revealed a side of himself few people have seen. Mad enough to get physically violent with someone wasn't how he operated.

Then there was that look he gave her when she begged them not to call the cops. Downright angry. He had never regarded her with nothing less than compassion and respect. Tonight was a different story.

But Egypt had her reasons for wanting to keep the cops away. It wasn't safe for her to go to a police station, and just as perilous getting questioned by law enforcement for any reason. She wouldn't risk her life that way, and she had no intention of explaining her decision.

When they arrived at his truck, he unlocked the door and helped her inside.

"Damn, I didn't know your skirt was ripped," he said in a voice that held so much angst.

"Yeah, it got snagged on the brick, but it's okay. I can fix it," Egypt said, grateful the skirt had a lining, so none of her skin showed.

Kenton looked even more ticked off when he closed the door and stood at the front of the vehicle as if trying to decide on whether to get in. Earlier, in the office, he wore only a dress shirt and suit pants. Tonight, he had added the suit jacket, making his tall, muscular frame look even more powerful and dangerous. The man was downright drool-worthy and panty-dropping hot on any given day, but right now Egypt saw something else on his face. Standing under one of the parking lot lights revealed his pinched expression, making her feel even more guilty about tonight.

What had she been thinking, letting Ross follow her outside? Experience had taught her never to be alone with him, but overconfidence got in the way. Knowing she could defend herself had given her a false sense of bravado.

Never again.

Never would she put herself in that position again.

And God, what would this do to her relationship with Kenton? He was one of her best friends. To be honest, he was much more than a friend. He was special. She hated he had to find her in a weakened state, and then had to defend her.

Egypt's heart had nearly burst when he came around the corner. At first, she thought her eyes were playing tricks on her after that jarring slap, but then she heard his voice. The gentleness of his touch had been her undoing, and she hadn't been able to hold back the tears at that point.

Kenton finally climbed into the driver's seat but didn't start the vehicle. Instead, he dropped his head back against the headrest and closed his eyes. Anxiousness swirled inside of Egypt's chest. She didn't know what to say. *Thank you* and *sorry* didn't seem to be enough.

"Do you have any idea what could've happened to you tonight? That whole situation back there could've been so much worse." His voice, low and sensual was full of pain. "No more online dating."

33

Wait. He thought Ross had been her date? Of course, he did. Why would he think anything different? She battled with herself on whether or not to tell him the truth. It would only cause more questions, but she owed him that much.

Kenton turned his head. Dark, intense eyes bore into her like a gimlet through a slab of wood, and she fidgeted under his stare.

"Finding out he had hit you…I wanted to kill him. I wanted to pull out my pistol and blow him the fuck away! That's how bad that situation back there could've gotten. I wanted to end his worthless life for hurting you, and that scares the hell out of me, Egypt."

Yeah, it scared her too.

"I am so sorry. I never meant to put myself in danger, and I didn't mean for you to end up in that position."

"It's not your fault. He shouldn't have ever touched you. God, if you only knew how often the guys and I deal with domestic violence, or ex's who can't get a clue."

"I do know, which makes me feel even worse." Suddenly cold, Egypt ran her hands up and down her arms. The lightweight jacket she had on was cute, but not very functional when it came to battling the October chill.

Kenton started the engine and turned the heat on full blast. "Tell me that guy's name, and what happened tonight. I also want you to make me understand why you didn't want to file a police report."

"Kenton—"

"But not right now." He gently cupped her face, turning it slightly. "Right now, I need to get you home so you can put some ice on your cheek. It's starting to swell." The sharp bite in his tone made it clear he was still angry, but his gentle touch on her cheek was a tender contrast. When he put a little pressure on the spot, Egypt winced, only making him curse under his breath.

"Does it hurt when you open your mouth or talk? Any loose teeth? A headache?"

"My head hurts a little, and my cheek aches when I open

my mouth or talk."

No doubt the pounding in her head was a tension headache, and not one brought on by the slap. But mostly, she was embarrassed. Both Kenton and Dakota, when teaching women self-defense, harp on running away from an attacker. Egypt had been able to inflict a little pain on Ross, but her main goal should've been to run. She just hadn't been quick enough.

"Are you sure you don't want to go to the hospital and get your cheek x-rayed?"

"Positive, but thank you." She rung her hands, fidgeting under his penetrating stare. "Let's just forget tonight ever happened, okay?" Egypt hoped that would convince him to start the truck and head to her house.

"I will *never* forget tonight. It's taking everything within me not to hunt that bastard down and beat his ass. And though I didn't fight your decision, I think you're making a huge mistake not filing a report."

"Kenton, I know you don't understand, but I don't want to have to deal with cops or answer a ton of questions. Besides, it's not like they'd do anything. At most Ross might get a slap on the wrist, and then they'd let him go. I'd be the one looking crazy in front of a bunch of people because I allowed a man to hit me."

Hurt and embarrassment warred within her and Egypt turned her attention to the window. Kenton was right about one thing. No more online dating or dating period. So what if she lived the rest of her life alone. It might just be safer with less drama.

"His name is Ross, huh?"

Shoot. Of course, he had pick up on the name.

"Yes, and he wasn't my date."

Kenton's hand froze, hovering over the gear shift before he could put the vehicle into drive. His brows pinched together. "Then who the hell was he, and where was your date?" He held up his large hand before she could respond. "You know what? Let's table this conversation until we get to

35

your house. Because right now I'm tired, hungry, and—"

"Angry as hell. Not a good combination," Egypt added.

"Exactly. I have a feeling I need to be in a better frame of mind before I hear about your evening and this guy." Kenton headed toward her house but pounded his hand on the steering wheel. "Dammit. I forgot my food."

"Where is it?"

"I had ordered takeout, which was why I was at the restaurant."

Egypt's mouth dropped open. "I thought you were there checking up on me again."

He released a long drawn out sigh and split his attention between her and the road. "That was a one-time thing, Egypt. Remember, you threatened to give me the worse assignments if I ever spied on another one of your dates."

"Yeah, but I didn't know you would actually listen. When you showed up, I assumed Dakota told you where I was going and who I'd be with."

"I'm not going to lie. I thought about working her for the information, but I respect your privacy…and your decision."

Her decision to date others, but not him.

Egypt already knew they'd be good together, and the kiss they shared earlier brought that fact home even more. They had a connection like nothing she had ever experienced with a man, and she doubted she ever would. Unfortunately, there were pressing reasons keeping her from saying yes to him.

"I'm sorry for everything that happened tonight, Kenton, and I appreciate you coming to my defense."

He reached over and squeezed her hand. "Always, sweetheart. You can always count on me to be there for you no matter what."

Yeah, he could say that now. He didn't know about her past. A past that made her a danger to his life. A past that she had no intention of sharing with anyone. Not even him.

*

Kenton pulled up to the small bungalow, slowly starting

to feel a little more like himself. The night definitely hadn't gone the way he'd planned. By now he should've been at home, full from his food, and camped out in front of his fifty-five-inch flat screen. Instead, he was with the woman he adored and trying to figure out her angle. She was hiding something. He already knew getting answers from her would be like trying to pick up leaves during a wind storm.

Egypt sighed and grabbed the door handle, but Kenton put his hand on her arm.

"I'll get that for you." He started to climb out, but stopped and glanced over his shoulder when she made a sound. "You say something?"

"I know I already said thank you, but…it's been a long time since someone came to my rescue like that."

Kenton studied her, more curious than ever about this woman he once thought he knew so well.

"A long time, huh? Does that mean something like this has happened before?"

The *oh shit* look on her attractive but now swollen face would've been adorable had it not sent his protective instincts into overdrive. Irritation gnawed at his nerves. The woman was becoming more and more of a mystery to him. What else didn't he know about her?

"Look like it's going to be a long night of you telling me more about yourself."

Kenton went around to open the passenger side door and helped her out of the vehicle. As Egypt headed toward the narrow walkway that led to her house, he went to the back of the SUV. Grabbing the bag that held a six pack of beer, he also pulled out a duffel bag.

"What's the bag for?" she asked when he caught up to her.

He lifted the black canvas. "A change of clothes."

She slowed and narrowed her eyes. "Listen, I appreciate what you did for me tonight, and I plan to feed you and answer a few questions, but you're not staying."

"Think again, sweetheart. I'm too tired and wound up to

37

drive home. You might as well get your spare bedroom ready. I'm staying the night."

"I only have one bedroom. The other is my office."

Kenton shrugged. "Well, I guess we'll be sharing a bed because after the last two days I've had, I'm sure as hell not sleeping on the sofa. Oh, and I'll take the side of the bed that's closest to the door."

He almost laughed at her shocked expression. *That'll give her something to think about.*

Kenton survey the quiet, family-friendly neighborhood as Egypt unlocked the front door and disarmed the alarm.

"I would say make yourself at home, but I'm afraid you might take me seriously."

Kenton chuckled and slipped out of his jacket. Egypt reached for the garment and hung it up in the coat closet near the front door.

"Come on in. I'm going to go and change clothes. Then I'll fix you something to eat."

"Sounds good."

Kenton glanced around her small, tidy house that he had only been inside of a couple of times. From where he stood near the front door, the small dining area that flowed into the kitchen was to his left, but he walked to the right

He stepped into the living room and strolled around the space that was sparsely decorated. Considering Egypt had lived in the house for a couple of years, there wasn't much by way of furniture. The simple, tan color sofa was fairly new. Purchased a few months ago, she had recruited him and Angelo to pick it up from the furniture store and deliver it to her house. Except for the flat screen television across from the sofa, the TV stand, tattered chair, and coffee table looked to be second-hand pieces.

Kenton admired the painting above the fireplace mantle. The African artwork of women dancing, their clothing in bold colors, was truly a reflection of her style. The piece was a nice contrast to the plain beige walls. Nothing else in the room reflected her personality.

Typically, when he stopped by, it was to pick her up or drop her off. This was the first time he'd taken the liberty of roaming around. Kenton hoped that something would jump out and give him more insight into the woman he had grown to care about.

One last look before he left the room made him realize that there were no pictures of her and no family photos. None. Nowhere. At least none that he could see.

Going back to the tiny dining area, he pulled the tail of his shirt out of his pants and started unbuttoning it as he strolled into the kitchen. Considering Egypt enjoyed cooking, he was surprised that the space was just as small as the rest of the house, and the white oven and refrigerator looked as if they were nearing their end.

Kenton opened the freezer that wasn't full but had enough meat and frozen vegetables for one person. He grabbed the ice pack and turned just as Egypt walked into the room, her long dreadlocks hanging free over her shoulders. His gaze traveled down her body, stalling at perky breasts that were on full display in the white, V-neck T-shirt. Why'd she have to look so damn tempting?

His pulse ramped up, and his shaft leaped to attention at the way her nipples pressed against the garment. It didn't help matters that the blue, skinny jeans she had on molded around her curvaceous hips and thighs like a second skin.

"Damn, you look good even when dressed down." Though it was a little chilly in the house, her pretty feet, with bright orange nail polish, were bare.

She didn't say anything, only twisted her bottom lip between her teeth, barely able to hide a smile.

He held up the ice pack. "Do you have a towel handy to wrap this in?"

"Yeah, but let me get you something to eat first. You're probably starving by now. I can deal with the ice aft—"

"I can get myself something to eat. You need to put this on the side of your face before the swelling gets any worse."

"Kenton, that can wait a few minutes. Let me—"

"Damn, Egypt. Stop giving me a hard time and have a seat." He opened a couple of drawers until he found one that held dishtowels. "Here, this'll do."

She huffed out a breath. "Dakota was right. You are bossy," she grumbled as he guided her to the dining table with a hand on her shoulder.

"I wouldn't have to be if you two weren't so damn stubborn." He and Dakota verbally sparred constantly because she always tried roping him into some of her hair-brain ideas. Egypt wasn't as bad, but tonight, he'd had about as much push-back from her that he could stand.

"How do you feel about leftovers?" she asked, finally holding the ice pack against her cheek.

He rinsed his hands in the sink. "As long as it's food, I'll love it. Why? What do you have?"

"There's baked ziti that I made last night, and I believe there might still be a couple of pieces of roast chicken and collard greens in there."

Kenton pulled out every covered dish he found, as well as the loaf of wheat bread. It had been a while since he'd had a home-cooked meal, but as hungry as he was, he didn't know if it would be enough. At least it was a start.

"Are you hungry? Want me to fix you a plate?" he asked as he put the plate of food in the microwave.

"No, I'm good."

While Kenton waited for his meal to heat up, he found a sandwich bag and made another ice pack. Then put it back in the freezer. He didn't miss the way Egypt regarded him as he moved around the tiny kitchen. Female appreciation showed in those glorious brown eyes. If she thought looking at him like she wanted to have him for a snack was going to let her off the hook from answering some questions, she had another thing coming. He hadn't dived right in yet because he wanted to make sure he was ready for the answers.

When he finally sat next to her at the small round table, she watched as he ate, shaking her head each time he moaned his appreciation. The woman could throw down in the

40

kitchen.

She stood and placed the ice pack in the freezer before pulling a beer from the refrigerator and handing it to him. "So, how is it?"

"You have to ask? My plate is practically empty. It's excellent."

She leaned back against the counter and nodded, seeming deep in thought. When she folded her arms across her chest, the move snagged Kenton's attention. He was definitely a breasts man and tried not to stare, but it was hard not to. Her Coke bottle figure would attract any man's attention.

From the moment he met her, she reminded him of the singer, Lauryn Hill. Not today's Lauryn with the short afro. More like 1990's Lauryn. More like Miseducation Lauryn. The dreadlocks, those intriguing eyes, full, kissable lips, and nice curves that a man could appreciate. Like the singer, Egypt was a looker.

"Feel free to cook for me anytime."

She smirked. "I would, but I don't think I can afford to. You eat enough for three people."

"Hey, I'm a big guy. I need a lot of fuel."

Kenton shoveled another fork full of the ziti into his mouth, trying not to moan. She often brought home-cooked dishes to Supreme, especially when they had companywide meetings. Each time, the guys raved about her culinary skills.

He had often wondered why she wasn't married or in a serious relationship. Did that asshole, Ross, have anything to do with Egypt keeping herself closed off from men? It had only been recently that she'd started dating.

Kenton snatched one of the napkins from the napkin holder and wiped his mouth. Now that she seemed more relaxed, it was time to get some answers.

"All right, Egypt. Let's talk about Ross."

Chapter Six

Let's not. Egypt sighed heavily, knowing Kenton would bring up Ross at some point, but she had hoped that it would be later, much later.

Instead of responding, she watched him move around her kitchen, looking right at home. Well over six feet tall and as wide as a doorway, the sexy man filled the tight space and seemed to suck the oxygen right out of the air.

Egypt liked looking at him, soaking up every aspect of his low-cut hair, smooth dark skin, and a body she would love to be wrapped up with. He was always well groomed, and that included his thin mustache that flowed into a perfectly trimmed goatee. And damn if he didn't smell divine. The scent of sandalwood with a hint of amber had her pulse thumping loudly in her ears.

"Any day now, Egypt. Heck, I'll even get the conversation started. Where was your date, and who the hell is Ross?" Kenton asked as he shrugged out of his dress shirt, revealing a white T-shirt underneath.

Egypt swallowed hard. Warmth soared through her body. His broad shoulders and wide chest might have been covered, but the tight-weaved fabric did nothing to hide the way his muscular arms contracted with each move.

Good, Lord. The man was perfection. Pure perfection.

"Sweetheart, if you keep looking at me like that, I'll have

no other choice but to kiss you again."

Egypt's brows shot up, and her mouth dropped open. "Uh...what?"

Kenton chuckled and hung the shirt on one of the dining chairs. "You've been watching my every move for the last ten minutes. Clearly, you like what you see. After we talk, I'll be happy to let you have your way with my body."

"Yo—you wish," she sputtered, embarrassed that he'd caught her staring. He didn't need to see her drooling over him. He already knew the effect his presence had on her since she wasn't good at hiding her attraction.

He snapped his fingers. "I know what I was planning to ask you when I stopped by your office earlier. Am I the only person who didn't know that Nelson *isn't* your real brother?"

"I didn't know you didn't know. Nelson is..."

Not only was Nelson Harmon one of Atlanta's finest, he was also a very important person in her life. How could she explain to Kenton just how important he was to her without revealing too much of her past? Nelson had claimed her as a little sister, but he was actually the man who had saved her life.

Instead of saying all of that, she said, "He's just like a brother to me, and it's because of him I have my job."

"What do you mean?"

"I was out of work for a while and had no prospects. Nelson put in a good word for me with Mason and Hamilton, and they hired me shortly after."

Kenton nodded, still studying her as if he was waiting for her to say more. The man had a way of looking at people as if he could tell they were lying, or in this case, withholding the full story.

Without another word on the subject, he grabbed his beer from the table and reached for her hand. "Come on. Let's have a seat."

Once they were seated on the sofa, Egypt noticed he had removed his shoes and was walking around in dark socks. A warm, fuzzy feeling flowed through her at the sight.

Admittedly, she liked him in her space, and he looked like he belonged.

Kenton turned slightly, and draped his arm on the back of the sofa behind her. "I want to know who this Ross guy is, but first, what happened to your date tonight?"

"He canceled." She stared down at her folded hands. The night had been one disappointment after another.

"Was this before or after you left the office?"

"He sent me a text after I had already been seated at the restaurant. I ended up treating myself to dinner."

Kenton didn't respond, but he toyed with one of her dreadlocks. It felt so intimate, Egypt sighed and laid her head back, relishing the moment.

"Why didn't you call me?" he finally asked. "I would've met you there. At least then you wouldn't have had to eat alone."

"I'm used to eating alone."

"But, sweetheart, you don't have to."

What could she say to that? He made it no secret that he wanted to be more than friends. Yet, she couldn't date him. Even worse, she couldn't give him the real reasons why. Well, she could tell him about her relationship with Ross. Then he'd understand why she didn't want to risk dating a coworker again.

"Who is Ross to you?"

"My ex."

Kenton's hand stilled in her hair and seconds ticked by as the silence grew. He probably thought that she'd been in an abusive relationship when that wasn't the case at all. At least not exactly.

Kenton moved his arm from around her and sat forward. He lifted the beer bottle from the table and took several gulps before setting it back on the coaster.

"I want to know everything about the guy. Let's start with his full name." When Egypt didn't respond, he said, "Tell me. You know I'll find out one way or another."

"His name is Ross Hoakley."

"Why does that name sound familiar? What does he do?"

"He's the CFO of Hoakley Manufacturing. Ross and his brother started the company, but I heard a few years ago, his brother sold his shares to Ross. While I was with the organization, I was an administrative assistant."

"Okay, so you were dating the boss. Why did you guys break up?"

She gave a slight shrug even though Kenton was still leaning forward and not looking at her.

"We just didn't work out." He looked at her with those serious, dark eyes and Egypt huffed out a breath. "I don't want to talk about this. It's over. Just drop it."

"The hell it's over. That asshole hit you. In the face. In public."

Egypt winced then started to speak, but Kenton stopped her by lifting his hand.

"I don't care if he was drunk, high, or whatever. That still doesn't make it okay. I'm a little surprised that you wouldn't want to make sure he didn't have a repeat of tonight with someone else."

"Of course, I don't want him doing anything like that to anyone else!" she snapped and lunged from her seat. "Do you have any idea how embarrassing tonight was? He caught me off guard. Yes, he was a jerk when we were together, but he never hit me."

"Are you sure?"

"What type of question is that? Of course, I'm sure. We dated years ago. It didn't work out, and shortly after, I started working at Supreme." Standing near the fireplace, Egypt stared at her favorite painting. "I had hoped when I left Hoakley Manufacturing that I would never see Ross again. He wasn't..." She stopped and rubbed the side of her still aching cheek. "He's not a nice guy."

"No shit," Kenton mumbled and strolled out of the living room. Within seconds he was back, carrying the icepack that he had made earlier, along with the towel Egypt had been using. "Come and sit back down."

Not bothering to argue, she reclaimed her seat and put the ice on her cheek. Hopefully, the swelling would be gone by morning.

With his arm around her shoulder, Kenton pulled her close and placed a kiss on her temple. Such a simple gesture, but Egypt felt as if he'd given her a lifeline. The guys at Supreme and their spouses were her only friends, her family. She didn't have anyone else and having Kenton come to her rescue tonight, and now hanging out with her, meant so much.

No, she didn't want to talk about Ross, but it felt good not to be alone. The events of the evening, and her interaction with Ross had shaken her more than she cared to admit.

"The last thing I want is for you to relive something that hurt you, but I think it will do us both good if you tell me about your relationship with Ross."

Egypt leaned away and studied him. "Why? What are you going to do to him? Because I'm sure you're not asking just to be asking."

"The only thing I'm going to do to Ross is make sure he stays away from you."

Egypt didn't want Kenton anywhere near her ex-boyfriend, but saying that to him would be a waste of time. Like the other men at Supreme, he was fiercely overprotective and did whatever he wanted to do.

Instead, she reflected on her past relationship with Ross. Thinking about him, she couldn't help remembering her own bad choices. Maybe she could blame her terrible decisions on being young and inexperienced, but she'd been twenty-eight. Naïve yes, but not that young.

"We dated for about five months if you can call it that. At first, it was meeting for coffee or breakfast before work. Then it was a walk occasionally through Piedmont Park at lunchtime. I was okay with how slowly our relationship progressed. I wasn't very experienced at dating."

Actually, that was an understatement. Egypt could count on one hand how many men she'd been with and still have three fingers left over. Her lack of experience was also a reminder that Kenton was out of her league.

"Dating someone I worked for made me a little uneasy," Egypt continued. "And part of me was always a little unsure about him."

"Why?"

She gave a slight shrug and lowered the icepack. Kenton moved her hand back up to her cheek, Egypt rolled her eyes, which only made him flash that sexy grin. He really was handsome, and more than that, he was the nicest man she'd ever met.

"Getting back to Ross. What made you unsure about him initially?"

"For the most part, he was all right to work for, but if he was having a bad day, everyone felt his wrath. Ross wasn't beyond yelling if someone screwed up an order, or he would fire people for no apparent reason. Once, he was so pissed at an intern that he swiped everything from her desk onto the floor."

"Did he ever do anything like that to you?"

"No, actually he was always nice to me, at first."

Tension crept through Egypt's chest as flashes of memories invaded her mind. Ross had been good at making her feel special. The occasional bouquet of flowers delivered to the office, the compliments on how nice she looked and the constant praise about her work went a long way. Until they didn't.

How could she have been so wrong about him and his intentions?

"What exactly happened between you two, Egypt?" Kenton, usually a patient person, had an edge in his voice that proved her hesitation was wearing on him.

He blew out a breath and brought the beer bottle to his lips, taking a long drag of the dark liquid.

"He almost raped me."

Chapter Seven

Beer spewed from Kenton's mouth, spraying them both and landing on the table in front of the sofa. "Wh-what?" he croaked, pounding on his chest while coughing. He'd heard her loud and clear, but the question popped out anyway.

He wiped his forearm across his mouth. Instead of cleaning up the mess on the table, he turned to Egypt, who looked both embarrassed and horrified.

"But he didn't," she said in a rush. "Things got out of control one day in his office, and—"

"And now I know why the bastard didn't want the cops involved tonight, but what I *don't* understand is why you didn't. Clearly, this asshole has a problem."

"He might have a problem, but it's not what you thi—"

"If he manhandled you, trust me, he has done the same to someone else. You keeping quiet is only giving him the power to go after others, Egypt! What the hell does he have on you? It's like you're condoning his behav—"

"Stop!" She threw the ice pack across the room and shot up from her seat. "Just stop. I'm done talking. I didn't tell you any of that so you can judge me. You don't know..." Frustrated, she ran a hand through her locks. "You...you don't know me like that!"

Now Kenton was out of his seat, standing in front of

48

her. "I *do* know you. I know enough to know that you don't usually take crap from anyone. You're quick to set someone straight if they step out of line. You're also the one who has gone beyond the call of duty to help and defend others, but I'm confused as hell. Why are you protecting this guy?"

"I'm not protecting him. I'm protecting myself!" Egypt screamed, shaking uncontrollably.

A tight fist squeezed Kenton's heart as he looked at her, shaking in front of him. She folded her arms around herself, and her teary-eyed gaze darted around.

She was scared, but of what?

Instead of saying anything, he pulled her roughly against his chest, holding on tight as if that would make her fears go away. What the hell had happened to her? How was not reporting this guy protecting her? Normally, a fierce advocate, she wasn't the type to run scared or allow someone to mistreat others. But this...

Kenton had witnessed her raise over ten thousand dollars, within a few days, for a homeless shelter. Then she helped find jobs for their clients. So many examples of her efforts to help those who were less fortunate came to mind.

Considering all she did for others, including Atlanta's finest, it was easy to forget she probably had her own life issues. She was a woman with a big heart. Apparently, one with secrets and maybe scars too. Internal or external, Kenton didn't know, but something had happened to her. He just had to find out what.

Egypt lifted her hands and pushed against his chest, forcing Kenton to loosen his hold. "Excuse me. I need to um...I need a moment." She hurried out of the room.

He huffed out a breath and leaned against the wall, the night's event starting to wear him out. It was safe to say he'd handled this conversation completely wrong. There had always been a mysterious air around her, and now some of it was coming to light. She'd said Ross had never hit her before, but that he had tried to rape her.

Anger, like a noose, tightened around Kenton's neck as

he picked up the ice pack and returned it to the kitchen. Snatching several napkins from the holder on the dining table, he cleaned up the mess he'd made with the beer. His mind galloped with one question after another. Why was she protecting Ross? What was she afraid of in going to the police?

More importantly, despite them being good friends, it was apparent that she didn't trust him. At least not enough to share this part of her life with him.

With the television remote in his hands, he settled back on the sofa and turned on the TV. He'd give it a few minutes before going to check on Egypt, but first, he needed to get his own frustration under control.

A short while later, when she returned to the room, Kenton sat up straight. Her cheek was still a little puffy, and her eyes were red but other than that, she looked like herself. Looking like she was back in control.

She sat on the sofa, keeping space between them. "I'm sorry. I shouldn't have snapped like that. I know you're only trying to help."

"And I'm sorry I pushed too hard." Though he knew he was taking a chance that she'd pull away, Kenton reached for her hand. "By now, you have to know how important you are to me, and not just as my friend. If someone hurts you, they hurt me. I'm not going to lie, seeing Ross standing over you and then hearing what he did to you, it was hard. Hard as hell. So of course, I want to beat his ass and make him sorry he ever stepped to you.

Staring down at their joined hands, Egypt squeezed. "You're one of my best friends, and I appreciate everything you've done for me tonight, but... Some topics are off limits."

"Is that because you don't trust me?"

The last thing he wanted was for her to shut down on him, but Kenton could almost see the walls around her going back up.

"You're one of few people I trust, but there are some

aspects of my life that I have no intention of sharing with anyone."

Kenton remained silent as he processed that bit of information. In their business, some of the first thoughts that come to mind when dealing with closed-mouthed people was to—do a background check. Supreme had run background checks on all of them. Maybe he could get access to her information, but he wanted *her* to tell him everything. Digging into her life without her knowledge would be a last resort.

"Can we keep everything that happened tonight between us?" Her troubled eyes sought out his.

Kenton hadn't planned on saying anything to anyone, even though he wanted to file a report with the cops on her behalf. The night's events were her business. He was just glad he'd been there to stop that guy from hurting her more.

Kenton brought the back of her hand to his lips. "I won't say a word, but if you insist on dating anyone *other than* me, you have to promise to be careful. You also have to agree to more self-defense training and remember what you've been taught."

"I'm done with dating. I've had enough of men."

"Wait. You're not including me in that group, are you? I'm like no other man you'll ever meet. Baby, if you give me a chance, you'll never want anyone else. After tonight, I'm more convinced than ever that we belong together. That you and I—"

"Kenton, don't start." She groaned, but he didn't miss the smile that played around her gorgeous lips.

"Don't start what?" He feigned ignorance.

"You know what. We've had this conversation a thousand times. How about we table your pursuit of me for another day?"

"Okay, I'll drop it for tonight, but since I'm staying, why don't we—"

"You don't have to stay. I'll be fine."

"Yeah, but I'm too tired to go home. Besides, I don't feel like being alone tonight. I need you." He gave her his best sad puppy face.

She laughed, the sweet sound filling him with warmth.

He released her hand and put his arm around her shoulder. Despite their heavy conversation, spending the evening at her house felt normal. Like they did this all the time. Having someone to come home to was what he was missing in his life. Deep in his heart, he felt that someone was Egypt.

Kenton inhaled deeply, loving how amazing she smelled, like vanilla with a hint of lavender. The soft scent only added to the comfort he felt in being in her presence. They might not be a couple, but she always made him feel desired, and...comfortable. He could be himself with her. It wasn't that he didn't feel comfortable with others, but there was just something different about being with Egypt. Something he couldn't really put into words.

"How about we find a movie on TV. Maybe something with suspense and action."

She picked up the remote. "Now that I know that you're into chick flicks, how about we watch one?"

Kenton dropped his head against the sofa, mentally kicking himself for mentioning *Pretty Woman*, earlier. "Please don't make me watch a girlie movie. I say we watch what I want tonight and watch something you want to watch next time."

"Fine. Ya big baby."

He laughed. "Now you're starting to sound like Dakota." She was always calling him names during one of their bantering sessions. "Do you have any popcorn?"

"God, man. Do you always have to be eating?"

"Actually, no." He leaned in close, nuzzling her ear and making her squirm against him. Normally, he kept his flirting to verbal sparring, but since kissing her earlier, touching her was like a need he couldn't fight. "We could be doing something else. Maybe hugging, kissing, which could lead to se—"

"Uhh, I'll go get that popcorn." She scurried out of his

hold. Kenton watched, appreciating how good her butt looked in the tight jeans, as she sauntered from the room.

Hot was not a strong enough word to describe the woman.

He could tell he was wearing her down. Secrets and all, Egypt Durand would one day be his.

Chapter Eight

Egypt nestled deeper into the warmth that surrounded her, unwilling to open her eyes. Her internal clock told her it was morning and time to get up, but she couldn't make herself move.

I'll lie here a few more minutes.

Just as she started to drift back to sleep, movement caused her eyes to snap open. Her heart rate amped up.

What the...

Suddenly, patchy memories of the night before leaped into her mind, and she bolted upright. At least she tried to.

"Where you goin'?" Kenton's sexy, sleep-filled voice filled her ears, his strong arm tightening around her waist.

Egypt stiffened.

Oh. My. God.

Her mind reeled as she recalled them watching a movie. *Training Day.* Though Denzel was her favorite actor, she had only made it through the first half of the movie. At some point, Kenton had talked her into stretching out on the sofa. The last thing she remembered, was that she was using his lap as a pillow.

So how'd she end up on top of him, wrapped in his strong, muscular arms, their faces closer than they should be? At least they were fully clothed. Well, mostly. Before the movie started, she had changed out of her jeans and into yoga pants, and he had been fully dressed. But now, her hand rested on his thigh. His well-built, beefy, bare thigh.

With that realization, a sweet thrill shot through her body, sending waves of desire blasting to every nerve ending as her hand felt around. When the heck had Kenton stripped down to his boxer briefs? She wanted so badly to glance down and see what this incredible, hot man was working with, but...

"Stop thinking, sweetheart. Your thoughts are keeping me from going back to sleep."

This man. He never ceased to amaze her and make her laugh.

Smiling, she lifted her head and slapped at his hard chest. His eyes were closed, but he was very much awake. "Kenton, you can't go back to sleep. You have to get out of here. You might have the day off, but I don't. I need to get ready for work."

"Not yet. It's still early." He rotated his body to the side and in turn, pressed her against the back of the sofa. Considering his size, it was a wonder they both fit on the piece of furniture, but she was pretty sure his long legs hung over the arm of the sofa.

"Kenton, get up." When he didn't budge, Egypt huffed out a breath and wiggled against him, trying to make her getaway.

Big mistake.

She froze.

"I should probably be embarrassed since you've been greeted by my morning woody," Kenton said, sounding too sexy for his own good. He turned onto his back, pulling her with him. "I can't help it. You turn me on."

"W-well, you need to turn yourself off and tell your um...your man part to relax, 'cause nothin's happening here. Now let me up." After a slight hesitation, he loosened his hold but didn't move his massive arm from around her.

Egypt knew she should make her escape, but she'd be

55

lying if she didn't admit that being on top of him felt good. *Damn* good.

Having a big, strong, sexy man, whose thick shaft pressed against her, was a little too tempting to pass up. Unable to resist, she placed her hands on either side of his shoulders, and did a slow slide down his body, intentionally brushing against his erection.

Holding back a moan was almost impossible when his rock-hard length bumped against her most sensitive spot, and liquid heat pooled between her thighs. Now she was the one who should be embarrassed. Using his body to satisfy the lustful ache growing at the center of her core. All they had to do was lose the clothes, and nothing would prevent him from sliding into her.

The thought sent a flash of heat soaring through her body. Or maybe it was the way they were now grinding against each other like high schoolers in the backseat of their parent's Buick, with out of control hormones raging.

"Damn, woman." Kenton groaned, locking her against him with a firm hand cupping her butt cheek. "You can't be doing this shit unless you're seriously tryin' to get something started," he whispered close to her ear, squeezing her butt as he nipped at her neck and continued moving beneath her.

When his lips found hers, Egypt moaned, the sound of her pleasure filling the quiet room as he hungrily devoured her mouth. She'd been wanting to kiss him again after what they had shared in her office, wondering if the connection had been a fluke.

Nope. Definitely not a fluke.

Kenton held the back of her head and deepened the potent lip-lock, sending fireworks shooting off inside her brain. She savored the sweetness of his experienced lips, but common sense told her to put a stop to the kissing and the grinding. They were friends. They shouldn't be doing this. Yet, her sex-starved body craved him...and only him. Kenton was probably the only man who could get her juices flowing without getting her naked. If only they...

We can't.

I can't.

The words ricocheted through her mind, but how could she stop? The sensual ache between her thighs was growing more intense. Their bodies moved as one, kissing and simulating the act of lovemaking. How many times had she fantasized about getting busy with him, feeling him buried deep inside of her? All it would take was for them to get rid of their clothes.

No. No, we have to stop. But...

As if reading her mind, Kenton pulled his mouth from hers and stopped moving, but held onto her. His chest heaving, he closed his eyes tightly, as if willing his body under control. "We can't do this," he muttered, the words spoken so quietly, Egypt wasn't sure if he was talking to her or himself.

"What?" she croaked, surprise, relief, and a bit of disappointment waging war within her.

"I mean we can, but not like this. I want you. *God*, I want you so bad, but I don't want you regretting our first time together. If we would've kept going, that's exactly what would've happened. I know you're not ready for what I'm offering. I want all of you. Not just your body, and I'm not settling for less than that."

The adrenaline pumping through her body moments ago waned, and Egypt dropped her forehead to his shoulder, knowing he was right. What the hell had she'd been thinking? It didn't matter how much she wanted to have sex with him, and only a tease would start something she couldn't finish.

"I'm sorry. I am so sorry. I shouldn't have let it get that out..."

"Don't. Don't apologize. This was on me," he said, his large hand still cradling her rear end. "This is more proof of how much we want each other. When we finally do make love, and *we will*, there won't be any regrets."

Egypt shook her head, her forehead rubbing back and forth against his shoulder while her locks swished side to side.

It would be fruitless to argue. She wanted Kenton in more ways than one. Wanted him more than any man she had ever met. If only circumstances weren't keeping her from making that a reality.

He moved his hand and rested it against the small of her back as their bodies settled down.

"I don't know what's holding you back, but I know it's something. Just so you know, I'll be here when you're ready."

"I can't ask you to wait for me," she said, her voice muffled against the crook of his neck. Even the next day, his natural masculine scent was still intoxicating. She slowly lifted her head. "You are the sweetest, kindest man I've ever met, but we're friends...and coworkers. We can never be more than that."

Catching her off guard, Kenton raised up into a sitting position, still holding her close and showing off how strong his ab muscles were. Now she straddled his lap.

"Why?" he asked, studying her eyes as if trying to gather some hidden answer.

"Kenton, we've already been through this. You're one of my best friends. I never want anything to come between us. I never want anything to hinder our relationship, and I never want to lose you. Besides, office romances don't work."

"I disagree," he said immediately. "Just because your relationship with Ross went nowhere, doesn't mean that ours will fail."

"But what if it doesn't work?"

"It will."

"What if the physical attraction we share fades away?"

"It won't."

"Kenton," she ground out in frustration.

"Egypt," he said in his usual patient tone. "We will never know how good we can be together if we don't at least give us a chance. If we take our friendship to the next level, we might end up with a relationship that exceeds anything we could have dreamed up. And if we find out that we're incompatible," he shrugged, "then we go back to being just friends."

"It wouldn't be that simple. You don't know if we could still maintain our friendship."

"Yeah, I do."

"No, you don't!"

"Babe, we will *always* be friends. Nothing will *ever* change that."

Egypt swallowed the emotion inching up her throat. He seemed so sure, but he didn't know everything. He didn't know her as well as he thought he did.

She cupped his cheek, running the pad of her thumb over the light scruff on his face as she imagined what it would be like to wake up to him every morning. As a little girl, she dreamed of getting married right out of high school and then having babies. Life didn't always go according to plans, and dreams didn't always come true. The world as she knew it had been ripped apart, and she was still suffering the effects.

She wrapped her arms around Kenton's neck and placed her chin on his shoulder. They'd had this conversation more times than she could count. Always ending up at the same place. They both wanted something that neither of them could have.

Egypt couldn't deny their chemistry. Maybe in another life, they would've been able to pursue whatever this was brewing between them. Unfortunately, this was the life she'd been dealt, and it didn't include Kenton as more than a friend. She just had to figure out how to stay in control and not succumb to the lust rushing through her.

When Kenton's arms folded around her, holding her tightly against his body, it felt like all was right in her world.

But it wasn't, and it never would be. That constant reminder of why they could never be more than friends kept invading her mind.

He was former FBI.

*

Egypt caught herself staring off into space, something she'd been doing off and on since arriving at work. One night. Kenton had stayed with her one night, and from the moment he walked out the door that morning, her house hadn't felt the same. She hadn't felt the same. It didn't help that he had planted a searing kiss on her before leaving, saying he wanted her to think about him all day.

She leaned forward with her elbows propped on the desk. Closing her eyes, Egypt rubbed her forehead as if that would help clear her mind.

Their relationship had shifted, making her imagine what it would be like to...

Her eyes snapped open. *Enough already.* "Just *stop* thinking about him," she grumbled into the quietness of her office. She scanned over her to-do list, ranking the tasks in the order of importance, then got to work.

The rest of the day went by in a blur, and Egypt hadn't realized how late it was getting until Hamilton walked in.

"Got a minute?"

"For you? Always."

Like his team of security specialists, Hamilton usually dressed up for work. Today was no different. He wore a dark blue suit with faint pinstripes, tan dress shirt, and a paisley tie. He looked sharp and authoritative like an owner of a Fortune 500 company.

"I need a favor," he said holding up a green folder that Supreme usually used for potential clients. He claimed the seat in front of her desk.

"What's the favor?"

"I need you to do some research for me. I know you're swamped, and I started to give this project to Rebecca, but I need your expertise and thoroughness. You're great at getting answers to questions I haven't thought to ask."

"Wow, flattery. Should I be nervous about this assignment?"

It wasn't unusual for him to ask for background checks, and sometimes credit reports on their potential clients. However, this sounded like it would be more involved.

"No need to be nervous. You've earned that praise. I

can't imagine running Supreme without you," he said seriously, then held up the folder in his hand. "Today I met with this potential client. She thinks her soon-to-be ex-husband has been doing business with some questionable people and may be involved in something illegal."

"Have they threatened her?"

"No, but her husband stopped by her apartment the other day. When he left, some guys she'd never seen before, were waiting outside for him. According to her, they exchanged words, then roughed him up before leaving. He claimed it was just a misunderstanding—"

"But she doesn't believe him," Egypt finished for him.

Hamilton nodded. "Not only that. Yesterday, when she stopped by their house to pick up the last of her belongings, she found $10,000 hidden in their guestroom closet. According to her, he never kept that much money in the house, and if he's in any trouble, she doesn't want to get caught in the middle."

"I can see why she's seeking our help."

That was the one thing she didn't like about the services Supreme offered. Often times, they didn't know how dangerous a situation could be until it was too late. At least that's how Egypt saw it. Their people were more than qualified to handle themselves. All had extensive experience in some form of law enforcement and or the military. She didn't like knowing that her family, which is how she saw them, were putting themselves in harm's way.

"I assume she questioned him about the money," she said.

"He hasn't returned her calls."

Egypt accepted the file folder. Hamilton was a sucker for women in this type of situation, but whatever else mentioned during the meeting must've set off his—*what don't we know*—meter. Otherwise, he would've just accepted the job.

"Do you want me to dig for anything in particular?" Egypt asked as she opened the folder, curious about this potential client.

Her hand stilled when she saw the woman's name.

Meesha...Hoakley.

There was no way she could be related to Ross...could she? What were the chances of running into him one day and two days later, hearing that he might be in some type of trouble? Egypt had known that he'd gotten married a year after she left the company, but...

Ross Hoakley.

Her chest tightened as she quickly skimmed the information in the file. *Crap.* Ross's name was in the space that asked for *any additional information.* Would she ever be rid of the guy? Now she had to dig into his background. Egypt had hoped seeing him the other day would be the last time she'd ever have to deal with him.

"Egypt?"

Her head snapped up, and Hamilton's concerned expression bore into her.

"What's wrong? Do you know Meesha?"

"Uh...no, but I know her husband."

Chapter Nine

Kenton pulled up to the gated community, glad there was no one at the guard stand. Instead, he used the keypad on the call box to get onto the property.

Earlier, he had called in a favor. Which was something he didn't make a habit of doing, but this was important. He needed to take care of this issue once and for all.

After punching in the entry code, he waited as the oversize security gate slowly opened. He drove through the community, passing one huge home after another, looking for the street that would take him to Ross Hoakley's home.

Deep down, he knew paying Ross a visit wasn't a good idea, but all day, he couldn't shake what Egypt had admitted to him. The thought of anyone trying to force himself on her made Kenton crazy. Which was why he had contacted Lazarus Dimas, a former Atlanta police detective. Now Laz worked with him at Supreme, but still had connections in high and low places. Without needing details on why Kenton wanted Ross's information, Laz had delivered.

Kenton slowed in front of a large, Tudor style brick home with dormer windows and a three-car attached garage. He double checked the information on his cell phone against the address on the mailbox before parking and shutting off the engine.

According to his intel, Ross should be pulling up in the next few minutes.

Just don't do anything stupid.

The warning vibrated in Kenton's mind. He didn't want Egypt, or any other woman, to endure pain at the hands of Ross again. Since leaving her that morning, Kenton hadn't been able to think of much else. It didn't matter that she wasn't officially his. He felt a fierce protectiveness toward her that he couldn't explain, and there was no way in hell he could sit back without doing something. He had to ensure Ross stayed away from her.

All I'm going to do is talk to him.

Kenton glanced at his watch. At almost seven-thirty in the evening, the sun had just set, and the October night offered a cool breeze through his partially lowered window. The air did nothing to tap down the anxiousness surging through his body, but memories of waking up with Egypt that morning brought a smile to his face. Despite sleeping on her sofa, it had been the best sleep he'd gotten in a long time. Probably because she had been curled up against him. Which was something he could get used to.

When a car turned the corner, Kenton straightened at the headlights coming into view. The vehicle slowed and parked in Ross's driveway.

"Welcome home," Kenton said to himself, glad the guy didn't pull into the garage. After confirming that the BMW's license plate number matched the information that he had, Kenton exited his truck.

"Mr. Hoakley?" he called out the moment Ross climbed out of his car, a briefcase in his hand. Looking as pristine and arrogant as he had the day before, he squinted at Kenton.

"Yeah, who are you?"

"A friend of Egypt's," Kenton said as he closed the distance, noticing the moment recognition dawned in Ross's eyes. To the man's credit, he didn't shrink back despite being several inches shorter, and at least thirty pounds lighter than Kenton.

"What are you doing here?" Ross glanced around, finding none of his neighbors outside. "How did you find me?"

Kenton stopped a foot away from the guy. "It doesn't matter. I thought we needed to talk."

Ross huffed out a breath. "I said all I had to say last night. I don't want any trouble, and I'll stay away from Egypt."

"Yeah, about that. Now that I've learned that you tried to force yourself on her, I—"

"Is that what that little tease said?" His face twisted into a snarl. "What other lies did she tell you?"

"Are you saying you didn't try to rape her?"

"Of course I didn't!" he ground out, irritation dripping from his words. "We were dating. The slut wa—"

"Be careful," Kenton warned, fists balled at his side as anger crawled through his body. All he planned to do was ensure Ross stayed away. But if the man started talking crazy, he couldn't guarantee that he would leave him unscathed.

"I didn't do anything that she didn't want. One minute the woman is all over me. Then all of a sudden, she changes her mind. You know how it is, man," Ross said with a shrug, acting as if he and Kenton were friends.

The arrogant ass.

"Hell, it's not like men can just shut it down after things start getting hot and heavy. She might've been a little shy about getting busy in my office, but I didn't do anything that she wasn't begging for. She…"

Kenton didn't even feel himself move. Suddenly, his hand was gripping the man's neck. He shoved him against the luxury vehicle.

Ross's eyes grew wide, and his briefcase fell to the ground. "Get…off me."

Kenton squeezed the man's neck, ignoring the way he gasped for air. "Did Egypt say no?" he asked through gritted teeth. "Did she try pushing you off her? Did she tell you to stop?"

65

"Didn't...rape her."

"You *tried* forcing yourself on a defenseless woman. Similar to what you did yesterday, right?"

"I—I stopped. Di—didn't...rape her." He panted, pulling down on Kenton's wrist, trying to free himself. "Can't...breathe."

Kenton tightened his hold. He should let go. But he couldn't. He hated men who took advantage of women. Making them afraid of every other male that came into their life. He had seen it too many times during his career and had no tolerance for assholes who couldn't take no for an answer.

"Now you know how it feels when a woman says stop, but the perpetrator, *you*, don't heed the request. Are you panicking? Are you afraid for your life? Scared that you're going to die, and no one will come to your rescue? That's how they feel. That's how *Egypt* felt. And I'm sure she hasn't been your only victim."

Fury soared through Kenton, making him angrier by the minute. He'd bet money that Egypt hadn't been the first or the last woman that Ross had mistreated. Kenton hadn't intended to put his hands on the guy. All he'd planned to do was talk. Now he wanted to scare the shit out of the man. Make him think twice about touching Egypt or any other woman inappropriately again.

"Go near Egypt again...." Kenton's face was inches from Ross. "And I will hunt your ass down and make you sorry you ever met me. Assault another woman, and I will *destroy* you," he growled, before jerking him away.

Ross bent over coughing, struggling to catch his breath as he rubbed his neck. Kenton slowly backed away, moving toward his truck. When he first arrived, he knew it was a bad idea to pay Ross a visit, but now he was glad they'd had a conversation and an understanding.

With one last look at Ross, who glared back, Kenton climbed into his Yukon. After pulling away from the curb, he checked his rearview mirror, seeing that Ross was still standing next to his vehicle.

It wasn't his nature to threaten people, but when it came to Egypt, Kenton would do a lot more than just threaten.

*

The next morning, Kenton climbed out of his SUV and grabbed the muffins, and coffee, that he had picked up on the way to his friend's house. He jogged up the five concrete stairs and rang the doorbell of Caleb Zander, a good friend and former therapist for the FBI.

"Well, hi there," Dora, Caleb's wife, greeted. She opened the door wider and stood on tiptoe to place a kiss on Kenton's cheek. "Come on in."

"It's awfully quiet in here."

"That's because our rug rats are at my parents' house," she said of their two-year-old son and four-year-old daughter. "It felt good to get ready for work without the usual drama."

He gave her one of the coffees and muffins that he'd picked up, and they chatted a few minutes before he asked, "Is the old man up yet?"

"Oh yeah, he's up. He's camped out in his office like usual, probably watching CNN or MSNBC since he has the morning off. Go on back."

Kenton strolled pass the staircase that led to the upstairs and turned down a short hallway. The soles of his shoes against the hardwood floors were the only sounds until he reached the last door on the right.

"So, this is what you do when no one's watching," he said from the doorway. Caleb, leaning back in his chair, had his feet propped on the desk. Dora had been right. His attention was on the flat screen television. Don Lemon plastered across the screen making a rare a.m. appearance.

"What's up, man?" he asked, lowering his feet to the floor and meeting Kenton in the middle of the room. "I would shake your hands, but they seem a little full. I hope some of that is for me."

"You know it. I wouldn't come over empty-handed."

"I take it you had the nightmare again. Otherwise, I doubt you would've graced me with your presence this early

67

in the morning. And the fact that you brought my favorite muffins and strong coffee means you're shaken up pretty good."

Kenton chuckled. "Well, damn." He handed his friend a cup of coffee and the bag of muffins, then made himself comfortable on the leather sofa. He took a sip of the dark liquid. "Am I that predictable?"

"Yeah, but I will never turn down an excellent cup of Joe or a sweet morning treat. So what's up?"

"Had the dream again."

"I figured as much."

"I keep seeing Quaid's lifeless eyes staring up at the sky, and Santana's outstretched hand trying to reach me. I feel…"

Kenton's chest tightened. Helplessness had a choke hold around his neck, as flashes of the dream invaded his mind. He leaned forward and set the coffee cup on top of a magazine, huffing out a breath hoping to remove the heavy weight settling around him. At least yesterday he hadn't woken in a cold sweat, which sometimes happened after the dream. Spending the other night with Egypt had taken his mind off of his own issues.

But last night, everything rushed back to him. The ambush. Seeing Quaid and Santana go down. Then there were the bullet wounds he had sustained. According to the doctor who had operated on him, it had been a miracle that he had survived his injuries. He had, for the most part, recovered physically with an ache here and there. Mentally and emotionally, would he ever be able to *really* put that time in his life behind him?

"It's been awhile. You haven't mentioned having nightmares in well over a year. What do you think triggered the dream again?"

Kenton didn't bother telling him that it had been the second nightmare within days. During his recovery, he'd been required to meet with a therapist, which he did for a few months. When he decided to leave the FBI, he still wanted to talk to someone. He just didn't want it to be in a formal setting, and he didn't want it to be considered a therapy session. Caleb seemed to be the obvious choice. They talked often, but with him, it felt more like two friends discussing their day.

"The anniversary of their death is coming up. That's the only thing I can think of that might've triggered the dreams to start again."

Caleb took a careful sip of his coffee and stared at Kenton over the rim before setting the cup down. "That could be it, or is there something else going on in your life, something that might be causing stress?"

"Nothing I can think of. I've had some long work days, but I'm still lovin' my job."

"Are you still blaming yourself for Santana and Quaid's death?"

Sometimes he hated having friends, or a therapist in this case, who knew him so well. "How was the poker game last week?" Kenton asked instead of answering.

Caleb smirked and shook his head. "Alrighty then. You don't have to answer, but the dreams are probably connected to the anniversary and the fact that you're still blaming yourself for their deaths. Kenton, you—"

"I already know the speech. It wasn't my fault." He said the words, and he wanted to believe them, but… "Let's go back to discussing the poker game."

"What else have you been up to?" Caleb asked.

Kenton chuckled, and reached for the bag of muffins, pulling one out for himself. "Now who's the one avoiding questions? I take it poker night didn't go well."

Caleb gave a noncommittal shrug. "It was okay. It's nice to get together with the fellas."

"Does that mean your pockets were lighter once the game was over?"

"You're such a wise ass. If you start back playing with us, then I'd have a better chance of walking out with some money."

"Ha, ha, ha. Nah, man, I can't afford to play with you

guys. The stakes are too high."

"Yeah, you're right. Soon I might not be able to afford to hang with the group either. Unlike you, I don't make the big bucks. How's life at Supreme?"

"Life is great. No complaints. I work with a bunch of cool guys...well, people."

"And in people, I assume you mean the *gorgeous* Ms. Egypt."

"If that's your way of asking how my pursuit is going, I'm making progress. I think."

"Man, you've been saying that for months." Caleb laughed. "From what you've told me of Egypt, she sounds like a helluva woman, but maybe you should cut your losses and move on. You know wifey has been wanting to fix you up with one of her friends. It might be time to take her up on her offer. Her matchmaking track record is good."

"I'll keep that in mind."

But Kenton couldn't see himself with anyone else. At least not until he knew for sure there was no chance with Egypt. If their kisses and the way their bodies responded to each other were any indication, she'd be coming around to his way of thinking soon.

But first, he needed to figure out what deep secret held her back. He knew it wasn't her fear of fraternizing. Something else was keeping Egypt Durand from him, and he had every intention of finding out who or what.

Chapter Ten

Before reaching the kitchen at Supreme Security, Kenton could hear Angelo singing about ordinary people taking it slow. If he hadn't known better, he would've thought John Legend, the R & B artist, was in the building.

"You really should find an agent and start making some money off of that voice," he said strolling into the state-of-the-art kitchen.

Angelo stood in front of the refrigerator with the door open and barely glanced over his shoulder. "Good morning to you too. And I think about finding an agent each time I have to deal with a client who doesn't want to do what I say to keep them safe."

"Yeah, and some make me want to strangle them my own damn self," Lazarus Dimas said strolling into the kitchen.

"That's what I'm talking about." Angelo closed the refrigerator, a small bottle of apple juice in his hand. "Well, some of us have work to do. I'm outta here. Catch y'all later." He fist bumped them and slipped out the door.

Kenton carried a cup of coffee to the table while Laz filled his travel mug with the strong brew. "You ready for our assignment?"

"Yup, Egypt sent me the information last night." Laz

stood next to the table. At over six feet tall, he was a little shorter than Kenton and not as wide, but the man exuded power and danger. Part Greek, part Irish, his fiery personality matched his genetic background.

Despite the rumors of Laz being a dirty cop, Kenton new better. His friend was a strong-willed man ready to do whatever necessary to get bad guys off the streets. Making him all right in his book. He couldn't think of anyone, with maybe the exception of Angelo, who he'd want to have his back. Loyal to a fault, Laz would give his life for his family and friends.

"So how did it go with the info you asked for yesterday? Did you take care of your *situation*?"

"It's done," Kenton said, giving a noncommittal shrug. Saying more to Laz, a person who was a master interrogator would lead to more questions. Egypt didn't want the other night at the restaurant mentioned to their friends, and Kenton planned to respect her wishes.

He and Laz discussed logistics of their upcoming assignment. The one they were scheduled to begin in just over an hour.

"Excuse me, guys."

Kenton glanced at the new front desk receptionist standing in the kitchen doorway. Her blue-eyed gaze bounced from him to Laz and then back to him. He wasn't surprised to see that her long hair, which was blonde last week, was now red. She changed hair color as often as she changed clothes.

"Kenton, there are a couple of detectives here to see you."

He frowned and lowered his mug to the table. "All right. I'll be right there." She nodded before leaving them alone.

"What's that all about?" Laz asked, eyeing him warily.

"I have no idea." But in the back of his mind, Kenton couldn't help wondering if Egypt's ex had filed a complaint.

"Need some backup?"

Kenton chuckled. "With your reputation at Atlanta PD?

72

I don't think so. They might hall my ass to jail just by association."

"Ha, ha, whatever."

They strolled down the long hallway toward the front of the building. Kenton slowed, surprised to see Ashton Chambers, Laz's old partner, and another guy.

"What's up, Ash?" Laz said, shaking the big man's hand, and Kenton followed suit.

They'd met a few times at events that Journey and Laz hosted. Kenton also heard that Ashton was thinking about joining Supreme's team for a few short-term assignments.

"What's going on fellas?" he asked, his question mostly directed at Ashton.

"This is my partner, detective Milton Adams." Ashton introduced the tall, lanky man and Kenton shook the guy's hand. Laz kept his distance. Considering the way the two men glared at each other, it was safe to say there was bad blood between them.

"Mr. Bailey, we need to ask you a few questions," Adams said.

Kenton directed them a short distance away from the receptionist desk to the waiting area. The spot held a couple of leather sofas, a table and offered enough privacy to where conversation couldn't easily be overheard.

"What's this about?" He split his attention between the two men.

"Do you know a Ross Hoakley?" Ashton asked.

Kenton narrowed his eyes. "Why?"

Ashton let out a long breath. For the first time since finding out they were in the building, alarm swept through Kenton. Had the guy gone to the cops after all?

"I'll take that as a yes," Adams said, his smug tone grating on Kenton's nerve. "How well do you know Mr. Hoakley?"

"I don't *really* know him at all," Kenton said truthfully.

"That's interesting. We heard that you and Mr. Hoakley had a run in at a restaurant, as well as exchanged heated words last night. Are you telling me that you beat up a guy you didn't know?"

Kenton could feel Laz's gaze on him. They both knew that there were only one or two reasons why detectives would show up asking questions.

Kenton rubbed the back of his neck, hoping to ease some of the tension building. "Exactly why are you here?"

"We need to ask you a few questions. How about coming down to the station with us," Ashton said only loud enough for them to hear. Kenton appreciated the fact that he was trying to keep the visit as calm as possible. He was conscious of the receptionist looking at them from across the room.

"You can't ask your questions now?" Laz asked.

"We'd rather talk to Mr. Bailey *privately*." Adams gave Laz a sideways glance. This guy had to have serious balls to be looking at Laz as if ready to get something jumping off. Clearly, he didn't know who he was dealing with. "We can either talk here *privately*, or you can come down to the station. We'll also want to speak with the woman who was with you the other night," Adams said.

Ashton made eye contact with Kenton and then nodded toward the door. "Why don't we take a ride."

There was no way they'd know that Kenton had been at the restaurant that night unless there were surveillance cameras in the parking lot. If that was the case, and if Ashton had seen the video, he had to know Egypt was the woman who'd been with him. And until Kenton figured her real reason for not wanting to go to the cops about Ross, he didn't want to reveal her name just yet.

"You know what? I don't th—"

"Let me see your hands, Mr. Bailey." Detective Adams smug expression grew harder, and he eased the front of his suit jacket back, revealing his holster and gun.

Kenton almost laughed. Was that move supposed to intimidate him? Besides roughing up Ross a little, he hadn't done anything wrong, and this guy had the audacity to try and flex.

"Let me see your hands," Adams repeated, his voice rising and impatience showing. "Palms down. Now!"

Kenton huffed out a breath and did as he was told. His chest tightened when he had to reveal his slightly bruised knuckles on his right hand. The only way someone would notice the fading bruises is if they were looking down hard at his hands the way the detective was doing now. It didn't prove anything, but the restaurant's surveillance video would confirm the altercation. It would also show what happened to Egypt.

"This is bullshit. What's *really* going on here?" Laz asked Ashton.

"What's going on is that this doesn't concern you!" Adams snapped.

Laz got in his face. "Look here, asshole. I don't know what your beef is, but don't come here trying to flex. If you have a problem with me, then let's take this shit outside."

Kenton got between the two men and faced Laz. "Chill, man. I got this. In the meantime, can you take care of getting someone to fill in for me?"

Laz glanced at his watch and cursed under his breath. They needed to be at their client's house soon. "Yeah, I'll handle it, and Ashton, I'll catch you later." He didn't bother saying anything to Adams, only glared at him before walking off and mumbling something about calling Journey.

Journey Ramsey-Dimas, his seven-month pregnant wife, was an Atlanta assistant district attorney. More than that, she was a good friend with connections. Kenton would answer a few of their questions, and if the situation warranted a lawyer, he knew Journey would only be a call away. Or he could contact Supreme's attorney.

"Okay, it's just us. Tell me what this is about." Kenton didn't bother looking at Adams, deciding he already didn't like the guy. Instead, he gave his full attention to Ashton.

"We're investigating an incident that happened at a restaurant the other night, as well as…" Ashton's voice trailed off.

"As well as what?" Kenton prompted.

"The murder of Ross Hoakley."

Chapter Eleven

Yawning, Egypt typed command after command, trying to hack into Hoakley Manufacturing. She really didn't have to go to such extremes, but a few minutes ago, she had slipped through one of their systems authentications. Which was odd. Hoakley wasn't a small business and used to have a more secure system. Now the excitement of seeing how deep she could go spurred her on.

What were the chances that Ross's soon-to-be ex-wife would come to Supreme Security for protection? Hamilton had admitted to forgetting that Egypt had worked for Hoakley prior to joining Supreme's team. And after a long conversation, she told him everything she knew about Ross, except that they'd dated.

Technically, the night before, she had found more than enough useful information about Meesha, Ross and his company, including the couple's pending divorce, and financial records. She also learned that Ross's company was currently being sued. The pleadings had already been filed, and from what she could gather, Hoakley was being accused of overbilling one of their customers for the last five years.

Egypt eyed the thick file folder sitting on the corner of the desk. Out of all the data she found, what disturbed her the most were the numerous sexual assault charges against

Ross. All of the cases settled out of court but knowing he had a pattern of assault was alarming. Kenton had been right. If Ross assaulted her, he had probably done it to someone else or would do it to others.

That was partly why she dug deeper into Ross's background. Guilt haunted her for not reporting the incident from the other night, as well the one years ago. Back then, had it not been for Ross's assistant walking into his office, Egypt couldn't be sure that she would've been able to fight him off. Scared and embarrassed, she had gotten out of there in a hurry, and for the next few weeks, stayed clear of Ross. A month later, she had landed the job at Supreme Security.

Huffing out an exhausting breath Egypt got back to work. She might not be willing to report Ross's abuse, but if she found something shady going on with his company, she would report it, anonymously of course.

There was a knock on her door, and Egypt made her screen go black.

"Come in."

"What's up, your majesty?" Laz asked, his penetrating hazel-green eyes zoning in on her as he strolled into the office. Egypt could so see what her friend, Journey, his wife, saw in him. The man screamed testosterone with his powerful build and a swagger that would make any woman take a second or third look.

"I told you guys to stop calling me that, and before you say it, don't call me Queen either." Her boss, Hamilton, had once mentioned her being the queen of Supreme, and the guys had been referring to her as that ever since.

"All right, all right. I won't say it."

"Okay, then what can I do for you?" Egypt asked. "Wait." She glanced at the time. "Laz, you shouldn't be here. You and Kenton have less than an hour to get to Mrs. Brockman's house."

"That's why I'm here. We have a little problem."

A sense of foreboding settled in Egypt's chest, and she braced herself for bad news. She prayed nothing had happened to Kenton. Normally by now, he would've stopped in and wished her a good morning. So far, she hadn't seen or heard from him since the day before.

"Where is Kenton? Is he okay?" she asked, hoping Laz didn't pick up on the quiver in her voice. Considering how he was looking at her, it was safe to say she didn't hide her concern well.

"He's been held up with…something," Laz said with a slight hesitation while studying her as if she knew what that *something* was. "Can you move a couple of people around and put someone else with me this morning? I know the client wanted at least two of us with her all day."

"Are you going to tell me where Kenton is?"

"I'm sure you'll hear from him soon, but in the meantime, hook me up with someone else."

Since he didn't sound too concerned about Kenton's whereabouts, Egypt tried to tap down the anxiety swirling inside of her. She worried about all of them whenever they went on assignments, especially ones like the one they were headed to. Mrs. Brockman, a wealthy socialite who had used their services in the past, was dealing with an abusive husband who had been recently released from jail. She was comfortable with the security she had at her estate, but out in public, she wanted personal protection.

"Myles is on standby today," Egypt said of the former CIA agent, Myles Carrington. He'd been with Supreme for a few years. "I'll give him a call. Do you want to meet him at the client's house or—"

"Tell him to be ready in ten." Laz headed to the door but slowed and turned to her. "Did you happen to hang out with Kenton the other night?"

Egypt was slow to respond. She'd made Kenton promise not to mention that night to anyone. Had he told Laz? "Why do you ask?"

After a short hesitation, he gave a slight shrug. "He's been…different the last couple of days. I was wondering if the change had anything to do with you."

She couldn't tell if he was fishing for information or if he was telling the truth about Kenton. Then the left corner of his mouth lifted into a slight grin, and Egypt bit her bottom lip debating on what to say.

"Ah, I see."

"I didn't say any—"

He lifted his hand and headed for the door. "No need to say another word. As for Kenton, he'll be in touch." He left the office as quickly as he had entered.

Egypt sat back in her seat. *What was that all about?*

Whatever it was, it involved Kenton, and she hoped that he was okay.

*

"I don't care what you think you know. I didn't kill the guy," Kenton said for the umpteenth time in the last twenty minutes.

Dropping his head back, he blew out an annoyed breath and stared up at the single-bulb light fixture that hung over the metal table. He hadn't been at the police station long, but sitting in an interrogation room with Detective Adams was frustrating as hell. Especially when Kenton knew they had nothing on him, and he had a feeling Adams knew he was innocent too.

"I think that you beat the man to death as payback for striking your woman."

Kenton didn't say anything. He didn't bother correcting his assumption that Egypt was his woman, because in Kenton's heart, she was. But this was the first time Adams had mentioned how Hoakley had been killed, and probably didn't realize he had slipped up.

"So far, neither you or Ashton have given sufficient proof that I had anything to do with Hoakley's death. I sure as hell didn't *beat* him to death. Now since I haven't been formally charged, I'm assuming you don't have any evidence to suggest otherwise. I think it's time you let me get back to work."

Adams had asked him a few questions regarding the

restaurant incident but mainly kept circling back to the altercation in Ross's driveway the night before. Ross had a security camera in the front of his home, but not on the side of the house where a neighbor had found his body. He'd been killed between eight p.m. and midnight.

Adams placed his palms on the table and leaned forward, the smug smirk on his face growing.

"Did you not tell Hoakley that if he ever put his hands on your woman again that you would kill him?"

Anger stirred inside of Kenton. Adams was like a persistent, irritating gnat that wouldn't leave him alone. Kenton didn't have to answer any more questions. He already knew they didn't have enough to hold him. The only reason Kenton hadn't left yet was because he wanted to learn more about the murder. But each time he thought about how Ross had manhandled Egypt, made him want to punch something.

"Answer the damn question!"

"That asshole slapped her!" Kenton snapped, pissed that he let this guy rile him. "You saw the video, detective. Hoakley is almost twice her size, and he backhanded her. What the hell wou—"

"Ross Hoakley might've been bigger than her, but he's *dead* now. So answer the question. *Did you or did you not* tell him that if he put his hands on the woman again that you would kill him?"

Kenton reined in his frustration and studied Adams. He wasn't trying to get the truth and solve a case. No, this was a man trying to intimidate, and Kenton wasn't interested in stroking his ego or helping him make a name for himself.

Instead of answering the detective's question, he said, "Usually when someone is murdered, you look at the spouse first. Have you done that? Have you even questioned other people in his life, people he worked with? Why are you in such a hurry to pin this on me?"

"Answer the damn question!" Adams yelled.

"You know what? I'm done. I didn't kill Hoakley, and I'm not saying another word without a lawyer. So how about

81

that phone call now?"

Adams banged a hand on the steel table. "Innocent people don't usually need a lawyer. If you want to call your attorney, that must mean you have—"

"You won't need that phone call, Mr. Bailey," Ashton said, his tone formal when he strolled back into the room. He had been missing in action for most of the questioning.

Kenton spotted someone behind him and smiled when he realized it was Journey. He stood when she walked in.

Over seven months pregnant, she was as stunning as ever wearing one of her jazzy, skirt suits. The woman had a way of looking professional while being stylish enough to be mistaken for a runway model, even with her large belly. Kenton had often heard people say that pregnant women had a glow, and in Journey's case, it was true. Her smooth brown skin glimmered, appearing healthier than what it had been a few weeks ago.

She had given them all a scare. Laz had been a wreck. They'd gotten a call saying that she had fainted at work and had been rushed to the hospital. He and a few of Supreme's men had gone to be by Laz's side. Mainly to make sure he didn't go postal while waiting for news on Journey's condition. Finally, after a few hours, it had been determined that she'd been dehydrated, and in need of rest. She had been released the same day.

Kenton was glad to see her at the station. He didn't know if Laz had called her, or if she happened to be in the building, which wouldn't have been unusual.

"This is no longer our case," Ashton said to Adams. "It's a federal case now."

Hmm...interesting. What the hell had Hoakley been involved in? A few possible scenarios came to mind.

Money laundering.

Drug trafficking.

Sex crimes.

Whatever the situation, Kenton was sure the murder hadn't been random.

82

Ashton stayed near the door with his hand on the handle. "You're free to leave, man."

"Thanks." Kenton glared at Adams and then walked out of the room with Journey. "Good morning, ADA Ramsey," he finally greeted.

"That's *Mrs.* Journey Ramsey-Dimas to you."

Kenton laughed and pulled her in for a hug. They had become good friends while she and Laz were dating. Once they married, Journey had officially become part of Supreme Security's family.

"How you doin' this morning?"

"I'm fine. However, there was a time when I wouldn't have been surprised to see Laz...and maybe even Angelo in an interrogation room, but you? Never would've imagined."

"I know. There are some places I try never to end up. How much do you know?" Kenton asked as they walked side by side through the squad room and headed to the hallway. They passed several desks where detectives were either on the phone or chatting animatedly to each other. The sight brought back memories of Kenton's time with the FBI and the fact that he didn't miss the agency.

"So, you and Egypt, huh?" Journey said, grinning.

Kenton chuckled but gave nothing away. He remembered Laz saying something similar months ago.

"What's happening with this case? Why are the feds involved?" Kenton asked.

"Oh no you don't," Journey whispered, getting in his face and stabbing him in the chest with her pointy finger. At only 5'6", she was a force to be reckoned with, making her a fierce prosecutor. "I'm not giving you any information until you give me answers. What the hell was Egypt doing with Hoakley? And why didn't she file a report against him the other night? I saw the video."

"Don't get me started about that," Kenton mumbled.

"Considering how hard that man hit her, I'm glad you punched him."

Kenton sighed. The detectives had shown him the

83

surveillance video, only making him wish he had punched Hoakley harder. "Let's talk over there." He nodded toward a quiet corner away from prying ears. "First of all, any information about Egypt, you'll have to get from her. As far as Hoakley, he was very much alive when I left him yesterday."

"I'm sure, but that doesn't mean the feds won't pay you a visit."

"Yeah, I know. What's up with that anyway? Why is it their case now?"

Journey shook her head and gave a slight shrug, letting Kenton know that whatever she knew, she probably couldn't go into details. "All I can say is that Ross Hoakley was under investigation. The feds are being tight-lipped. So good luck in getting any info out of them."

Kenton still had friends in the agency and could make a few calls. He only wanted to make sure whatever Hoakley was involved in didn't touch Egypt. More importantly, whatever she was hiding, because he knew she was hiding something, he hoped it didn't involve Ross Hoakley or Hoakley Manufacturing.

Chapter Twelve

"I'm sorry, sir. Mr. Crosby still hasn't made it in," Egypt said to a caller, who had been trying to reach Hamilton for most of the morning. Hamilton had called and left a voice message while Egypt had been away from her desk, saying that something had come up and that he would be in touch.

"Do you know when he'll be in?"

"Unfortunately, as I mentioned before, I don't know. I can transfer you to Mr. Crosby's voicemail if you like."

"I already left a message. Thanks."

Egypt stared at the phone when she realized the man had hung up without saying bye. She could understand his frustration, but how hard was it to say goodbye before hanging up? It wasn't her fault that Hamilton was unavailable, which was a little odd. She hadn't talked to him all day, but he'd left a couple of messages, and one was to reschedule two of his morning appointments. He usually kept her abreast of his whereabouts. Now that she thought about it, both he and Kenton were acting out of character. Maybe they were somewhere together.

"I need to stop being such a worry-wart," she mumbled and set the phone back into the cradle. The guys could take care of themselves. They didn't need her worrying about them like some mother hen.

She went back to the task at hand, knowing that she was close to getting into Hoakley's computer network despite all of the interruptions. Moments later, excitement scurried through her body and a smile spread across her face.

Yes. I'm in!

At least at first glance, she thought she was in. Egypt started scrolling but jumped when a bull-horn sound blared through the computer speakers.

"What the heck?" She stared at the screen for a second, and then it went black.

Panic roared through her body.

"Oh, no. No. No. No." Her heart raced as she jiggled the mouse around and then pressed on the keyboard keys, trying to bring the screen back up. "Come on. Come on. What the heck is going on?"

This was a first. Not that she had hacked into many systems, but during Egypt's senior year of high school and the first couple of years in college, hacking had been her guilty pleasure. Not something she was proud of, but she loved the challenge. And when she got into a system, she never did anything to sabotage anyone's data. It was mostly a game to see if she could get in. That was enough reward.

"What have I done." She kept pressing the keys, her nerves twisting inside of her as the minutes of darkness ticked by. "This is not good."

She dropped down onto her knees to double check the computer cables. They were all plugged in. Reclaiming her seat, Egypt continued to press keys and move the mouse hoping for a different outcome. She had no idea what caused the horrid bull-horn blast and was even more baffled by the suddenly black screen.

"Egypt?"

Egypt screamed, and leaped from her seat. Her heart lodged in her throat. "Kenton. Oh my God, you scared me." Her hand rested over her heaving chest as if that could slow her pounding heart.

"Sorry. I guess you didn't hear me knock." He walked in,

closed the door and approached the desk, staring at her with narrowed eyes. "What's wrong?"

She glanced at the blank screen. "Uh, I...um...I was having a computer problem. Where have you been? I've been calling you all morning."

She moved from around her desk, her heart rate slowly going back to normal. That is until she got closer to the man she hadn't been able to stop thinking about. Just the sight of him sent a wave of heat soaring through her body. The attraction was getting more intense by the day, and Egypt had no idea how to rein it in.

But now was not to time to gawk at the man. She needed to get back to her computer issue. First, she needed to find out why he'd been missing in action.

"Is everything okay?" What she really wanted to ask was if they were okay. He had texted her in the afternoon the day before, but she hadn't heard from him since.

"Yeah, sorry I didn't get back to you. I got your message. By the time I was able to call, I figured we could talk when I came into the office."

He studied her. His dark, penetrating gaze bore into her with such intensity, Egypt frowned. "What?" She touched her face, wondering if she had something on it. "Why are you looking at me like that?"

He moved closer. "You don't know, do you?"

Egypt tensed, realizing for the first time since Kenton walked in how solemn he seemed. Which was so not like him. Normally, whenever he stopped by her office, he flirted shamelessly or cracked jokes. Not today. Today he wasn't smiling. Now that she really took a good look at him, he looked a little haggard. Sure, he was still incredibly handsome in his dark suit and white dress shirt, but his black, white, and gray tie was loose and askew. Not like him.

"Did something happen? Are you hurt?" Egypt didn't know why she'd asked the last question since he seemed okay physically. But before she could stop herself, her hands trailed over his broad shoulders, and down his thick arms, before resting on his broad chest as her mind raced. It was as if she had to determine for herself that he was physically all right.

She gazed up into his troubled eyes, and he covered her hand with his, securing it to his chest.

"Sweetheart, I'm fine." His words were spoken softly as he brought her hand up to his lips and kissed it, sending a sweet trimmer through her body.

They might not be a couple, but he meant more to Egypt than she was willing to admit. "If that's the case, then what's wrong? You're freaking me out a little."

"It's Ross."

Egypt's pulse thumped loudly in her ear. She leaned back, slipping her hand from his. "Ross? Didn't we agree that we weren't going to discuss him again?" The moment the question was out of her mouth, she thought about her computer and how it had gone haywire after getting through their firewall. "What does he have to—"

"He's dead."

Egypt gasped. Bile rose to her throat. "Wh-what?" She shook her head, trying to process what he was saying until it became clear. Fear replaced the shock that had just rocked her body. "Oh. My. God. I thought you said that you wouldn't do anything—"

"I didn't," he said simply and turned away, running his large hand over the top of his head and let it slide to the back of his neck. When his gaze met hers, she knew there was more, and she wasn't going to like whatever he had to say. "Ashton and another detective took me down to the station for questioning."

"I don't understand. If you didn't do anything to Ross, why would they think you had anything to do with his death?"

"Mainly because I went to see Ross last night."

"What? *Why?*" The quiver in her voice matched the irregular beat of her heart. "Why couldn't you leave it alone? What happened at the restaurant was settled there. You didn't have to go to him."

"Did you hear what I said?" He moved forward, stopping within a breath from her. "I *didn't* kill him. When I left Ross, he was alive."

"I heard you." Egypt swallowed, her mind racing too fast to put coherent thoughts together. On shaky legs, she moved to one of the chairs in front of her desk and dropped down in it. "I—I can't believe this. We just saw him. What happened?"

Kenton sat next to her, and his arm stretched across the back of the seat as he told her about his and Ross's conversation the night before. A panicked anxiousness swept through Egypt and settled into her body. She listened as he recapped how the detectives showed up and escorted him to the police station, accusing him of murder.

Egypt jumped up suddenly and paced back and forth across the carpeted floor. "This is all my fault. I knew Ross was bad news. If I hadn't left the restaurant...if I would've just gone back in when he followed me out, this wouldn't have happened. You wouldn't have gotten involved."

Kenton stood, reached out and touched her arm, effectively stopping her from moving. "This is not your fault."

"Yeah, it is. It's because of me you hit him, and things just went downhill from there."

Kenton grunted without saying anything and pulled her close. Egypt sighed and rested her head on his chest, loving how good it felt being in his solid arms. Still, his strong embrace did nothing to calm her ragged nerves. But then something else dawned on her.

"Oh no." She pushed against his chest, and her hand went to her mouth. "Now they know I was there. They're going to want to talk to me." All these years she had managed to keep a low profile and build a life that she could be proud of. Now, this.

"Stop. Before you freak out, right now only Ashton knows you were the woman in the restaurant's video and he didn't mention your name...yet."

89

Her hands shook, and heart pounded against her rib cage. All these years she'd been able to stay clear of law enforcement, been able to protect herself. One run-in with Ross and it's like casting a spotlight on her and her life.

Egypt slid her sweaty palms down the sides of her slim skirt as her mind raced. "What happens now? What did you say to get them to let you go?"

"Well, actually, I don't know what Ross was involved in, but he and his company have been under investigation. The FBI is taking over the case."

"Oh no," Egypt whispered. Panic stampeded through her body as hysteria built within her and her vision narrowed. She stumbled, grasping for something to hold onto until Kenton wrapped his arm around her waist.

"What? What is it?"

"I—I...I messed up. Kenton...I—I ha—hacked into his company's network and now they might—"

"You did what?" he roared, holding onto her shoulders, forcing Egypt to look at him. "Have you lost your mind?"

Before Egypt could respond, her office door burst open. Hamilton stood a few feet away, with a cell phone plastered to his ear and his brows bunched together, looking as if he could commit murder.

"Wiz is on the phone. You care to tell us why you were trying to hack into Hoakley's Manufacturing company?"

Chapter Thirteen

Kenton had his hand at the small of Egypt's back and could feel her shiver against him. To say he was shocked to learn that she tried hacking into Hoakley's computer network would be an understatement. He had already determined that there were things about her he didn't know, but this...

"I—I was trying to get more information for you," Egypt said to Hamilton.

She would've been more convincing if she hadn't been wringing her hands and looking terrified. Kenton would do everything he could to protect and stand by her, but Egypt made it hard by keeping secrets.

"Wiz, hold on a second. Better yet, I'll call you in a few." Hamilton moved farther into the room. "Do you have *any* idea how much trouble you'd be in if Wiz didn't have a safety feature on our computers?"

Cameron "Wiz" Miller, part-owner of Supreme Security and computer guru, worked out of the Chicago office. The former Navy SEAL was a master hacker and used his many skills to develop numerous apps and software, some he'd sold to the government.

Egypt stepped forward. "I know, and I'm sorry. I have the info you requested, and I wanted to see what else I could find on Ross and his company."

"And you," Hamilton said to Kenton, "What have you gotten yourself into?"

Kenton held up his hands. "Are you accusing me of something?"

"I heard about you beating up Ross Hoakley. Is it true you got hauled in for questioning regarding his murder?"

"How do you know—"

"I've spent the last two hours with Mrs. Hoakley. Then on my way here, I get a call from an FBI friend. He mentioned needing to question one of my guys—you."

Kenton shook his head. "Okay, I'm confused. There's a Mrs. Hoakley? And how do you know her?" he asked Hamilton. Had Egypt told him about her encounter with Ross the other night?

Kenton diverted his attention to Egypt, and the pleading in her dark eyes answered his unspoken question.

"This is turning into a long story. A story that you two seem to be deeply involved in." Hamilton divided his attention between Kenton and Egypt. "Both of you, in my office. I want answers." He walked out without a backward glance.

Kenton rounded on Egypt. "What the hell was that all about? Why were you researching Hoakley? And hacking? And did you tell Hamilton about the other night?"

Egypt dropped down in the nearest chair. "No. I didn't tell him anything. He has no idea that Ross and I have a history."

"And the hacking?" Kenton pressed.

Egypt scowled before explaining the project Hamilton assigned her to and what little she knew about Mrs. Hoakley. Kenton didn't believe in coincidences. The fact that Ross's wife had sought out Supreme for protection, had to be intentional.

"So why hack into the company's mainframe? You already had enough to determine whether or not to take on Mrs. Hoakley as a client."

"Like I told Hamilton, I wanted to get more information

for him."

"I want the truth, Egypt."

She glared at him. "You're calling me a liar?"

Technically he might've been, but that wasn't his intention. Yet, he knew she wasn't being totally honest.

"If the FBI is going to question me, I want to know as much as possible about you and your ex."

Egypt closed her eyes and sighed as she rubbed her forehead. "If the FBI questions you, that means they're going to want to question me too. I can't talk to them," she mumbled the last comment as if talking to herself. "My life was destroyed because of the FBI. I will *never* trust them."

"The FBI destroyed your life?" Kenton asked, his voice a combination of exasperation and disbelief.

Egypt's head shot up. The wide-eyed, startled look on her face made it clear she hadn't meant to say that much.

"I...nothing. We should probably head to Hamilton's office."

Kenton crouched in front of her. "You have to know by now that you can trust me."

"I know. Kenton, I trust you more than anyone, especially right now," she said, her voice just above a whisper. "One day I'll tell you everything. I—I just can't right now."

Kenton studied her troubled eyes before nodding. That was good enough for him at the moment. He stood and extended his hand. "Come on. Let's get this over with."

He tugged on Egypt's hand and pulled her up. Once she was standing, she tried to smooth the wrinkles out of her black skirt.

Kenton's gaze followed her moves, admiring the way the garment hugged her luscious curves as if it was painted on. Typically, when he stopped by the office, he looked forward to seeing what she was wearing. Today he'd been so focused on asking about Ross, that he hadn't taken in her attire. The sexy, bright pink blouse highlighted her dark skin and dipped low enough in the front to show a little cleavage without being inappropriate for work.

His eyes traveled lower, to the straight black skirt that stopped above her knees, and then lower. He was more of a breast man, but no one could deny she had a gorgeous set of legs. And the thick four-inch, black heels with fuchsia accents enhanced her toned calves.

"Do you have another date tonight?" he asked before he could stop himself. Granted, she wasn't officially his, but a wave of possessiveness flowed through his body. The thought of her with someone else made him crazy.

Egypt's brows dipped into a frown. "No. I told you I'm done dating. Why do you ask?"

"'Cause you're looking hella good." He grinned at the way she lowered her eyes demurely, a shy smile playing around her kissable lips. Then a thought popped into his mind. "Did you dress like this for me?"

Her mouth dropped open. "Wow. You really think highly of yourself, don't you? I dress for me, and for your information, I always look like this."

Kenton chuckled and shook his head. "No, you don't. You always look amazing, but you never wear your blouses that tight or your skirts that short to work. And you're showing quite a bit of cleavage there," he said moving closer to whisper in her ear, his hand on her hip. "But I don't mind, baby. I love that you're trying to look good for me."

Egypt swatted him away. "Whatever, and keep your hands to yourself. Let's go and get this meeting over with, and pray I still have a job."

Egypt grabbed a folder and flash drive from her desk, and Kenton followed her out of the office. No way was she losing her job, he thought. Hamilton worshiped her. Her skills and ability to take care of the security specialists and the company were second to none. Egypt had come through too many times for one mistake—albeit a huge mistake—to cause her to lose her job. And Kenton already knew that if this stunt got her into any legal trouble, Supreme would have her back.

At least he hoped.

94

*

Hamilton was on a video conference call when they walked into the office. Egypt heard Wiz and Mason's voice, and her heart dropped. She had worked so hard to be a model employee, someone the higher ups counted on, and more importantly, trusted. Now her job was at risk.

It was her fault. Trying to hack into Ross's company was a dumb move.

"All right guys, our troublemakers just walked in," Hamilton cracked, not looking as pissed as he had moments ago. He turned the computer screen around a little, giving Egypt and Kenton a better view of Wiz. Mason was on Hamilton's speakerphone. "Where should we start?"

"I'll start," Egypt volunteered. She stood in front of Hamilton's desk and set down the items in her hands. As promised, Kenton was by her side. He hadn't said anything, but his strength and support of her was palpable. "First, let me apologize for going too far in looking for information on Ross."

Egypt explained what she had uncovered about Ross, his marriage, and the company. The trio listened, stopping her occasionally to ask a few questions. Seconds ticked by before anyone said anything, and Egypt tried not fidgeting under Hamilton's powerful stare. Her pulse raced as she waited for someone to say something. Anything. It might've been too premature to think that she wasn't getting fired.

"I appreciate the work you did on this project. It sounds like you were as thorough as usual," Hamilton finally said. "But—"

"How the *hell* did we not know that you had hacking abilities?" Wiz asked. A slight grin tilted the corners of Hamilton's lips, and Mason's chuckle filtered through the cell phone.

Egypt's knees went weak, and she dropped down in the nearest chair, relief flooding her body. She might've put on a brave front, but it would have killed her to lose the job she absolutely loved.

"Make no mistake, we're not condoning this behavior, and the fact that you did this at Supreme pisses me the hell off," Mason said. "But we value you, Egypt. You always show up. You never complain, and you have always gone beyond the call of duty for us. However, we can't have a situation like this again."

"In the future, I trust that you'll use better judgment," Hamilton added.

"And no more hacking...or trying to hack," Wiz said.

Egypt nodded, emotion tightening inside her throat. These guys were her family. Knowing that she had disappointed them, and put the company at risk, was almost too much to bear. Hamilton and Mason were fiercely protective of Supreme, and Egypt had crossed the line.

Never again. She would never again do anything to betray their trust.

"All right, so that we are all clear, Egypt didn't hack into Hoakley's Manufacturing, but she came damn close. I have a few security measures in place to keep hackers out, as well as protect our systems internally. The alarm that I'm sure you heard through your computer, alerted us of a few things. You had typed in a command that hackers often use, and you stumbled upon a site that was being monitored," Wiz explained.

Egypt frowned. "What do you mean monitored?"

"There are...eyes, for lack of a better description, that has that network under surveillance. My initial research didn't reveal who was watching until Hamilton mentioned Hoakley's death, and the call from the FBI."

Egypt's heart thumped wildly in her chest. Thank God Wiz had been able to shut her down. Hacking was a federal offense and guaranteed jail time if caught. She didn't even want to think about what would've happened if she'd gotten into the network that the feds were monitoring.

"I knew you had a computer science degree. Where'd you pick up the hacking abilities?" Wiz asked.

"It's not something I really do...often. My uncle taught

me the basics when I was a sophomore."

No way could she tell them that her Uncle Billy had taught her how to hack into the high school's server to change her biology grade. After that, she tested her computer abilities in other areas. When her parents found out all that Shady Uncle Billy, as her mother referred to him, had taught Egypt, they stopped him from coming by the house.

"I—I didn't even know for sure if I could get into Hoakley's because they had some serious firewalls. I just needed..." her voice trailed off when she noticed Hamilton's brows rising toward the sky. "Nevermind."

Hamilton glanced at his watch. "Though I'd love to know more about this particular ability of yours, we have another pressing matter. Tell us what happened at that restaurant?"

Egypt gasped.

"Don't look so surprised. You already know. Between me, Mason, Wiz, and Malik," Hamilton said of the founder of Supreme, "we have a lot of friends, especially in law enforcement. It's not hard to get information, whether we want it or not. Which is why we constantly remind our team to watch what they say and do outside of these doors. You two represent us whether at work or on the streets."

Mason cleared his throat. He'd been out of the office and on vacation for the past week and wasn't scheduled to return for another two weeks. "A friend from Atlanta PD, who recognized Kenton, sent me a video of the incident at the restaurant. Though a little fuzzy, and after watching it twice, I could make out Egypt. Now we want the story behind the incident."

At some point, Kenton had moved closer to her chair, and Egypt met his unwavering gaze. It was safe to say he was waiting to see how much she wanted to tell.

"Any day now," Hamilton said, rocking in his desk chair, his attention bouncing between them.

"I used to date Ross."

Egypt recounted the story, starting with her date

canceling. The more she shared, the more disappointment knotted in her gut. After the way things ended between her and Ross, she shouldn't have been anywhere alone with him. Telling the guys about why he had backhanded her, was the hardest part. No man had ever hit her before, and she vowed never to let it happen again.

Kenton squeezed her shoulder. "I showed up shortly after. I happened to be picking up a takeout order and ran into them. When I found out what Hoakley had done, I..."

"Handled him," Hamilton finished. He leaned forward, his forearms folded on the desk. "Anyone of us would have done the same thing. What I don't understand is why you didn't report the incident to the cops."

"I-I didn't want the co-cops involved," Egypt stammered. "Ross agreed to stay away, and that was enough for me."

The tension bouncing off of Kenton was almost as nerve-racking as the suffocating silence that filled the room. Hamilton stared at her in that way that always made Egypt a bit uncomfortable, as if knowing there was more she wasn't saying. All the guys had mastered the *look*.

Hamilton finally diverted his gaze to Kenton, but instead of him saying anything, Mason spoke. "Kenton, since you had already taken care of Ross, what made you pay him a visit last night?"

Egypt's heart thudded against her chest. Kenton hadn't told her exactly why he'd gone to Ross's house, but she already knew. She shouldn't have ever put him in this position. She should've kept her mouth shut about the incident in Ross's office all those years ago.

"I wanted to ensure that he stayed away from Egypt, and by the time I left, we had an understanding...and he was alive."

"Well, so that you understand, the FBI will be here later today. I'm sure they're going to ask you two more questions than we asked. So be ready to cut the bullshit. Whatever else Hoakley did to you," he looked at Egypt, "be ready to come clean."

Egypt swallowed hard, trying to push down the anxiety exploding inside her chest. How could she confess that Ross tried to force himself on her, and she hadn't reported it? Besides Kenton, the only other person Egypt told was Nelson, her long-time friend, and confidant. If only she could call him. He was the only person who knew everything about her, and Hamilton had him on a long-distance assignment for Supreme.

"Egypt, we're a family, and that includes you too," Mason said. Egypt had temporarily forgotten he was on the phone. "We have your back."

On that, Egypt bit her bottom lip, trying not to get emotional. All she had was them. At the moment, she couldn't express how much she appreciated and needed these people in her life.

She quickly swiped at rogue tear and made sure no others would follow. No way would she fall apart in front of them.

"Listen, I have a meeting to get to, but Ham, you or Mase hit me up later regarding the meeting with the FBI," Wiz said. "Egypt, I'll be in touch. I'm curious to learn what other computer skills you have. Kenton, thanks for looking out for our girl." With that, he signed off, and Mason followed suit.

"Why don't you two get out of here and get some air. I'll have the front desk monitor calls for the rest of the day. Just be back here by five."

"Come on. Let's go," Kenton said and escorted her to the hall with a hand at the small of her back. "Get your jacket and purse and meet me in the parking lot."

"Kenton."

"Just do it Egypt."

She nodded, too emotionally spent to argue, and headed to her office. It was tough enough meeting with the guys who cared about her. How would she get through a grilling by FBI agents?

Chapter Fourteen

"You're awfully quiet," Kenton said to Egypt as he steered his truck toward Chamblee, a suburb of Atlanta, where his favorite burger joint was located. He hadn't eaten since that morning, and even then, the muffins and coffee hadn't been much. Now that it was late afternoon, he was hungry enough to eat a whole cow. "What are you thinking about?"

"Do you solve all problems with food?" she asked solemnly, but Kenton laughed.

"It's either food or sex, baby. Since I didn't think you'd go along with the latter, I figured a big, fat juicy hamburger would fill my stomach and take your mind off our meeting."

Egypt graced him with a smile, but it didn't reach her troubled eyes. Since Kenton didn't know what she was hiding, he had no clue how to help.

He reached over and covered her hand, gripping it within his. "Listen, I know you're worried about being questioned by the feds, but I promise, it's going to be okay. Trust me. If they were concerned about you or me being involved in anything shady regarding Ross, we would've heard from them already. My guess is that they have a solid lead into what happened to the guy, or they have a possible suspect. Questioning us is just formality."

Egypt didn't look convinced but squeezed his hand. The fact that she hadn't pulled away from him was encouraging.

"I don't know, Kenton. I want to believe you, but…"

"But you don't trust the FBI," he said with resignation, though he found that realization troubling. "Does that mean you don't trust me either? I'm a former agent. Deep down I'm still one of them."

Now that Kenton had put the question of trust out there, he wondered if that was why she'd been keeping her distance. Because he was former FBI. She blamed the agency for destroying her life, but he still had no clue into how or even why.

Egypt eased her hand from his hold. "You already know I trust you, but experience has taught me to be careful." Then she snorted. "Says the woman who tried, failed, and got caught attempting to hack into an organization." Disgust rolled off her words before she turned to stare out the passenger window.

Yeah, Kenton was still a little thrown by that bit of knowledge. Her trying to hack into someone's company and continuing to keep secrets should make him want to run in the opposite direction. Instead, it made him more curious about the woman sitting next to him.

"You know what?" he said. "Why don't we, for the next two hours, forget about Supreme, the FBI, and anything else surrounding work. Besides eating, I also considered finding a place to shoot pool."

"I didn't know you shot pool. Are you any good?"

"Sweetheart, I'm good at everything I do."

Egypt rolled her eyes. "Arrogant much?"

Kenton shrugged, unable to keep the grin from spreading across his face. "What can I say? When you're good, you're good."

"Anyway, so why aren't we playing pool instead of heading to the burger joint?"

"One: because I'm starving. And two: because I wouldn't

have been able to focus on the game with you there."

Her arched brows bunched together. She really was a beautiful woman, and even more so since she didn't seem to know it.

"Why wouldn't you be able to focus? You're the one telling me not to worry about the interrogation that's coming."

"My distraction has nothing to do with the FBI," he mused. "It's all you."

"Oh, please. I haven't shot pool since college. I'm not that good, and it sounds like you're the best."

"Well, the last part is true," he said smugly. "But right now, I can barely focus on driving with you sitting over there looking all sexy. Just thinking about you bent over a pool table, in that tight skirt hugging your fine ass, has me—"

"Oh, knock it off. You're acting like I never wear skirts. I wear them all the time."

That was true. Besides the tight outfit and looking a little sexier, something was different about her today. She seemed the same, yet something had changed. Kenton couldn't quite put his finger on it. Or maybe it was him.

He glanced at Egypt to find her still looking at him puzzled, and his heart did a little giddy-up. Their connection had always been powerful, but since their encounter with Ross and then spending the night together, their bond was stronger. That protectiveness, and maybe even a little possessiveness that he always felt toward her was more profound than ever.

"Yeah, you wear skirts often, but today you look smoking *hot*."

She grinned shaking her head but didn't say anything. He was almost positive she had him on her mind when she dressed that morning.

"Since our work day is technically not over, maybe I should take you home so you can change clothes. Wouldn't want you tempting one of the agents during questioning. He might try to get with you, and then I'll have to kick his ass for looking."

Egypt laughed. "Okay, just stop with the nonsense. I'm suddenly hungry. Hurry up and get us to this burger place. I've wanted to try one of their sandwiches since it's all Dakota talks about," she said of Hamilton's wife. "You have her hooked on these burgers. Poor Ham has to make a trip there at least twice a week to battle her cravings."

"Poor, *Ham*? You should be saying poor me. *I'm* the one she called yesterday afternoon. Mind you, it was my day off, and I was at home. Which is at least twenty, twenty-five miles from the burger joint. She gave me this sob story about needing lunch because my future godson was starving, and she couldn't leave the dojo."

"That's what big brothers and future godfathers are for."

"Yeah, right. So far I'm getting the short end of this pretend brother crap."

Egypt laughed. Dakota, an only child, often said Kenton was the brother she always wanted. "Don't act like you don't love it. That woman dotes on you all the time. Like the homemade cinnamon rolls, and that four layered chocolate cake she made you the other week. It's a good thing Hamilton isn't the jealous type. You would be looking for another job and maybe in a different city."

"True, but Ham knows he has nothing to worry about. Dee is crazy in love with the man, and you're the only woman for me."

"Man, you're really pouring it on thick today." She grinned, and if her skin wasn't so dark, he would see a blush tinting her cheeks.

Interesting how when she smiled at him, warmth spread through his body, making him want to keep her happy. Gone was the worry and sadness in her eyes from earlier. In its place was the sparkle that he'd grown to look forward to seeing each day.

Caleb had once asked him what was it about Egypt that had him vying for her attention even though she kept shooting him down. The more time Kenton spent with her, the easier it was to answer the question. He loved the way she made him feel.

The other day, he'd been able to be her hero, coming to Egypt's rescue when she needed him most. That night at her place, he was her comforter, wiping tears away and keeping bad memories at bay. He felt needed and desired when it came to her, and this was the first time in his life that he wanted to be all of that to a woman.

He pulled into the restaurant's crowded parking lot. Clearly, he hadn't been the only one craving a Bad Daddy's Burger. No surprise since their burgers were hands down the best in town.

Kenton finally found a parking spot at the back of the building. "Sit tight, and I'll get the door for you."

"I guess you weren't the only one with this idea. That parking lot is packed. Hopefully, we'll get a seat," she said, holding Kenton's hand as she climbed from the Yukon.

"It's fairly big inside. I'm sure we'll be fine."

Kenton closed the door and engaged the locks without releasing Egypt's hand. Instead of heading into the building, he backed her up against the truck and claimed her lips.

Despite the drama of the morning, Kenton had thought about this moment more than once, and now he was taking what he wanted. Instead of pushing him away, like he half expected, Egypt slipped her hands inside his suit jacket and wrapped her arms around his waist. Kissing her with everything he had in him, he needed her to feel how much he cared about her.

As their tongues tangled, feverishly exploring each other's mouth, Kenton tuned out the sounds around them. He cradled the back of Egypt's head, pulling her even closer, deepening their connection as the intoxicating kiss grew more intense. It anchored him in place and confirmed what he already knew. Egypt was his.

*

Egypt's heart thumped wildly as Kenton's demanding tongue thrust deeper, and his hands moved to her hips. She allowed herself to get lost in the moment, feeling his thick shaft pressed firmly against her stomach, proving he was just as turned on.

He would never understand how much she needed this. Needed this closeness. Needed to be transported to a happier, more peaceful place. That's what she felt whenever they were together. At peace.

A calmness surrounded her, and she held on tight as he made it easy to forget about the horrors of the outside world and forced her to be present in that moment. His deep, sensual moan filled her, and his experienced lips were insistent, yet tender. Egypt didn't want to stop kissing him. She didn't ever want to let him go. And that should scare her, but instead, it gave her hope that she could have the type of romance she always wanted.

A car horn blared, and Egypt jumped. She broke off the kiss, but Kenton didn't release her. After glancing over his shoulder, he moved in closer, effectively shielding her with his large body from the car pulling into the parking spot next to them.

"I guess that's our cue to go on inside," he said.

"Why the kiss?" Egypt asked as they walked around the building. He held onto her hand, and she didn't pull away, enjoying the comfort of the gesture.

"I wanted to help you relax."

She laughed. "*That* was supposed to make me relax? I'm pretty sure my pulse is off the charts, and my blood pressure has doubled."

Kenton flashed that sexy grin that made her all tingly inside. It was such a cliché, but his smile truly did light up her world. The last hour at work might've been crappy, but spending time with this man was quickly making up for it.

"I just thought of something. This will officially be our first date."

Egypt rolled her eyes and shook her head. "This is not a date. This is two people getting something to eat in the middle of the day."

"So what, you think we can't have a *lunch* date?"

She didn't say anything. What could she say? Did it really matter what they called this outing?

Once inside the restaurant, Egypt inhaled, taking in the enticing smells of succulent spices, onions, and something zesty filling the air. Suddenly hungrier than she'd been moments ago, she was glad they hadn't had to wait long to be seated. They dodged servers carrying plates loaded with food as the hostess showed them to their table. Egypt took in her surroundings. The place wasn't a diner or greasy spoon establishment. It was larger with a long bar, and the mounted televisions, photos, and paraphernalia covering the walls gave it a sports bar vibe.

At the table, she perused the menu, and her mouth watered just reading the lengthy descriptions of the burgers. Everything sounded good, but she eventually settled on the smokehouse burger and tater tots.

She noticed Kenton hadn't reviewed the options. "What are you getting?"

"My usual, a *bad ass burger.*"

"*That's* the name of it?" she asked, scanning the menu again before reading, *ten-ounce patty, buttermilk fried bacon*, and the list went on and on. "That thing sounds like a heart attack waiting to happen."

"Best burger in town."

"I'll take your word for it."

Once they place their order, it didn't take long to get their food. The first bite into her sandwich had Egypt closing her eyes. *Oh, my goodness. This is good.* It was no wonder Kenton and Dakota loved the place. They were right, best burger in town.

"Told you," Kenton said, and Egypt frowned at him.

"Told me what?"

"Told you it was the best. The look on your face and the erotic sounds you're making over there says it all."

She laughed. "Whatever. I didn't make any sounds." She took another bite of her sandwich while eyeing his dishes. "It amazes me how much you eat." Besides the sandwich, he had ordered a large salad, fries, and onion rings. Kenton was a big guy, but from what she could tell, he didn't have a lick of fat on him.

"I've always had a healthy appetite, but I don't eat like this all the time. Maybe once a week. I usually try to stick with fish, chicken and lots of vegetables. This isn't the norm. I missed lunch, and I'm starving. So I suggest you get to eating. Otherwise, I'll be eating your food, too." With his fork, he speared one of her tater tots.

"Hey!" she said with mock indignation, narrowing her eyes at him. "Stay out of my plate unless you want me eating some of your food."

"Sweetheart, you're welcome to anything I have, and I'm not talking about just food." He wiggled his brows, and Egypt couldn't help laughing.

"You don't stop do you?"

"Nope. Not when there's something I want. Or someone." When she started to speak, he lifted his hands out in front of him as if surrendering. "I know. I know. You *can't* date me, and this is not a date, and blah, blah, blah. As of right now, we're dating. So if some of those chumps you've gone out with lately decide to call you, tell them to lose your damn number. You're taken, and I'm definitely the jealous type. I'm just sayin'."

Egypt leaned back in her seat laughing and wiped her mouth. "You are too much. How you gon' tell me that we're dating? Shouldn't that be something we agree on?"

They bantered back and forth, and Egypt did more laughing than eating. She had a feeling dating Kenton would provide more fun than she'd had in a long time. Still, she was hesitant, but maybe it was time to trust her feelings for this incredible man. Maybe it was time to trust him with her life.

Chapter Fifteen

The next day, Egypt paced the length of her office. The interrogation had gone fine after she and Kenton returned from lunch. But when the FBI got to the last question, asking if she went by any other names, flashbacks from sixteen years ago bombarded her. It had been a struggle to keep herself together, especially when she lied and said she had no other names. All night, memories of the past invaded her mind. Memories she thought she would never have to revisit.

Egypt squeezed her eyes shut to keep from going back to that dark place. She wasn't in Chicago. She wasn't in South Carolina. And she was no longer in Los Angeles.

I'm in Atlanta.

No one knows my real name.

I'm safe here.

Now all she had to do was get through the next couple of hours. When she arrived to work, Hamilton had informed her that the FBI wanted Supreme to work with them on Ross's case, and he agreed. Saying that one day Supreme might need to call in a favor, and the more allies they had, the better.

In Egypt's heart, she knew that all FBI agents weren't bad, but her experience had taught her to be wary of them anyway. Well, not all of them.

108

The two dozen pink roses sitting on the desk in a crystal vase brought a smile to her face. They arrived an hour ago and were the highlight of her morning. Lowering her head, Egypt inhaled the sweet scent, and then picked up the small card that had been delivered with them.

Now that we're dating...

She couldn't fight the grin that spread across her face. No matter what she told Kenton the day before at lunch, he insisted they were dating. Not that she put up much fight. The idea of being his woman made her giddy inside.

The intercom on her desk buzzed.

"Yes."

"Hey, Egypt. Agent Griffith and two other agents are here. Do you want me to send them up?"

"Yes, please. I'll meet them at the elevator." Egypt straightened, a slight tremor gripping her body.

Just be cool. They're not here for you.

When she arrived at the elevator, the doors opened. "Hi, I'm Egypt. Welcome to Supreme Security."

"Thanks, I'm Agent Damien Griffith," the taller of the three men said. He looked to be in his late fifties early sixties, with smile lines around his deep, blue eyes and dark brown hair that was thinning on top. He turned to the other two men. "And this is Agent Jay Franklin, and you've already met Agent Lamar Jones."

Egypt nodded, feeling a little uncomfortable with the way Agent Franklin's dark gaze traveled the length of her body. In his early forties, with skin the color of milk chocolate and a short military haircut, he had a swagger about him. Maybe even a cockiness if his confident smirk was any indication.

She'd been around enough guys to recognize a man's appreciative inspection and was glad she had opted for a pants suit, feeling more professional than sexy. But his leer held a bit of hunger she didn't like.

"Follow me," Egypt said and started walking down the hallway, her high heels clicking against the travertine tiles. "I'll show you to the conference room. There's a whiteboard, plenty of pens and notepads, oh and a projector as requested. You can let me know if anything else is needed. Right in here." She stepped into their largest conference room. "May I get either of you something to drink? Coffee? Soda? Water?"

"Coffee would be great," Agent Griffith said, and Agent Jones agreed.

"Can you point me in the direction of the men's room?" the creepy Agent Franklin asked. He wasn't a scary looking guy, but in addition to the way he'd checked her out moments ago, his presence made her uneasy.

"Sure. Follow me."

"Have we met before?" the agent asked. "You look familiar."

Egypt shook her head robotically. "N—no, I don't think we have. Here's the restroom." She pointed to the closed door and maintained a comfortable distance between them until he moved closer.

"I rarely forget a pretty face, maybe we—"

"You must be one of the feds," Kenton said, stepping out of the restroom, his gaze meeting Egypt's before turning to the Agent.

"Uh, yeah, I'm Agent Franklin, and you are?"

"Kenton, a security specialist here. Myself and a few others will be sitting in on the meeting." The men shook hands and Egypt didn't miss the fact that Kenton hadn't given his full name. Was that intentional or an oversight?

"I was just saying to Egypt that she looked familiar." Franklin returned his attention to her. "I think we should talk, get to know each other before I leave, figure out where I know you from."

"Is that right?" Kenton said dryly, staring at the man who was around six feet tall with a lean build, and that same smug smile as earlier.

Instead of sticking around, Egypt used that opportunity to make her exit. "I'll have coffee in the conference room shortly." She hurried away before either of them could respond. Normally, drinks would've been set up already, but it had slipped her mind.

In the kitchen, Egypt quickly prepared the coffee and poured it into one of the oversize thermal dispensers they used for meetings. Then she placed a few bottles of cold water, juice and soda in a bronze bucket.

"Hey. How's it coming?" Kenton strolled into the kitchen, looking dangerously delicious in a black suit, and a black shirt and tie.

"Hi," she said, breathier than intended, but who could blame her? The man was big, sexy and as tempting as a package of double-stuffed Oreo cookies. "The coffee is done."

"All right, I'll carry it for you, then come back for the other drinks."

"Thanks, I appreciate that since I forgot to bring the rolling cart back after using it to transport some materials upstairs. I'll grab everything else." Egypt gathered cups, napkins, and condiments, placing them on a tray. She turned from the counter and almost dropped everything when she slammed into Kenton's hard body.

"Whoa." He steadied her and took the tray from her hands, setting it on the table while keeping a hold of her arm. "Sorry about that. I guess I got a little too close."

He was close all right. Close enough for Egypt to inhale the woodsy scent of his cologne and feel his warm breath brush across her face. She had to fight the overwhelming desire to reach up on tiptoe and touch her lips to his for one of his scorching kisses.

"God, I want to kiss you so bad," he whispered next to her ear as if reading her mind, and placed a feathery kiss behind her earlobe. Then another on her cheek.

Each kiss felt like an enticing caress, sending a flutter of excitement rushing through her body with a promise of much more. But they couldn't. They were at work. Even if she wanted to feel his mouth on hers, they had to remain profess...

111

The thought flew from her mind when Kenton captured her mouth with his. Within a heartbeat, need spun through Egypt like tumbleweed during a tornado. She couldn't get enough of him, especially when his tongue explored the inner recesses of her mouth the way it was doing now. Each time they came together like this, she craved more.

The strong arms around her waist loosened, and his large hands glided up her body and then cupped her face as he deepened the kiss. This man, this incredibly sweet man made her feel so wanted, so desired. Egypt marveled at how his big, strong body was such a contrast to his gentleness. She knew they should stop and get back to work, but she didn't want him to stop. Ever.

"Don't start nothing in here that you can't finish," Angelo said, and Egypt leaped away from Kenton. "Sorry to interrupt, but Ham sent me for the coffee."

"O—Okay, we were just getting ready to take it up," Egypt said, wiping a shaky hand over her mouth.

"Riiight. Tell it to someone who didn't just catch you two making out. All I can say is—it's about damn time. Y'all been skirting around each other for months, trying to pretend there's been nothing between you."

"Whatever, man. Just grab the damn coffee and get out." Kenton handed Angelo the large coffee dispenser.

Egypt noticed that he and Angelo were both dressed in all black. They were close in height and build, but Angelo was more of a pretty boy with diamond stud earrings in each ear, and wavy hair pulled back into a long ponytail that hung down his back.

"What happened to white shirts with black suits?" she asked of their usual formal uniform.

"That was changed yesterday to black on black."

Egypt nodded, remembering Hamilton talking about the security team making the small change to their business attire. "Cool. It's a nice look."

"*Nice?*" Angelo said in mock disgust and headed to the door. "Woman, you better recognize. We look like total bad asses."

Egypt laughed as he walked out of the room, saying that he'd meet them upstairs.

"How about another kiss?" Kenton pulled her to his side, placing a kiss against her temple.

Egypt eased out of his hold. "Not here. No kissing at work, and no more until after our second date."

Kenton grinned and handed her the tray while he carried the drinks. "So, we really are dating, huh? Good. I'll pick you up tonight at seven."

"Wait. I didn't say..." Egypt started, but his long strides carried him out of the kitchen, forcing her to jog to catch up. "The least you could do is ask me, and not just assume I'll go out with you."

"Oh, sorry. Tonight, at seven all right with you?"

"Yeah, but next time—"

"I'll ask." He winked, then pursed his lips and blew her a kiss. "Oh, and stay away from Agent Franklin. I saw the way he looked at you."

"Surely you're not jealous."

"Damn straight I am. You're a sexy, desirable woman. I'm not going to stand by and let some chump like him try to push up on you."

"You know him?"

"No, and I doubt he knows you either. I'm not buying that line about you looking familiar. The asshole wants to get to *know* you."

Egypt didn't say anything else, just nodded, hoping that was all there was with Franklin.

They took the stairs instead of the elevator, and when they arrived in the conference room, everyone was there. Besides Hamilton and Angelo, Myles and Laz were in attendance.

Egypt quickly organized the coffee and condiments on the long table in the back of the room, and let everyone know that they could help themselves. She was halfway down the hall before Hamilton called out her name.

She turned and started back. "Yes?"

"I'd like for you to join us. I want your take on everything since we might have to do some juggling with the schedules. And before you protest, you can hang out in the back."

"Okay. Let me run to my office, and I'll be right back," she said calmly, though inside she cringed. She understood playing nice with the feds, but she didn't want to work with them.

By the time Egypt returned, Agent Griffith had started the meeting. She went to the coffee dispenser and poured herself a cup of the dark brew. Then she found a spot at the back wall near Kenton and Angelo.

Egypt surveyed the room that now seemed small with so many tall and wide men taking up the space. For whatever reason, everyone, except Hamilton and two guys Egypt didn't recognize, were standing around the perimeter of the room, their arms folded across their chest.

She slowly sipped the steaming coffee, listening as Agent Griffith shared intel regarding Ross and his company. He couldn't disclose everything, but he did provide them with information surrounding their reason for soliciting Supreme's help.

"What made you put Hoakley and his company under surveillance?" Hamilton asked.

"We had reason to believe they were trafficking drugs through the company, and as of late, money laundering. Hoakley has been under investigation for a few months as we're building a case against him. The guy was good. *Sneaky bastard.* He evaded all of our traps as if he had inside help."

Kenton straightened, his body noticeably going rigid at that comment. Maybe he was wondering the same thing that she was thinking. Was that inside help within Hoakley Manufacturing...or the FBI? Egypt wouldn't be surprised by the latter which made her even more uncomfortable about Supreme getting involved.

"It's a perfect set up that Mrs. Hoakley is now a client of

yours," Griffith said.

He stood at the front of the room near the oversize screen. Every so often, he'd press the presentation clicker, and photos popped up on the screen. He showed three consecutive pictures of Mrs. Hoakley with her looking around before climbing into a two-door Mercedes Benz.

"As of right now, we don't know for sure if she's as innocent as she claims. Her responses to our questions are inconsistent, but her fear that her husband's enemies will come after her seemed believable. Like Mr. Hoakley, if she is doing anything illegal, she's good at covering her tracks."

"Are you saying that while we're providing protection for her, you want us to also spy on her?" Myles asked.

Griffith nodded. "Yes, we'd like for you guys to report back anything you see that might be suspicious. Who she talks to, who she visits or those who visit her. We have agents watching Mrs. Hoakley, but we can only get so close without probable cause."

Hamilton cleared his throat. "Wait. We've worked with various law enforcement divisions, and participated on numerous task forces over the years. But what we will never do, is risk the integrity of our company. My guys will not be spying on our client and then reporting back to you. If Mrs. Hoakley does something illegal while on our watch, then we will inform you."

And that was why Egypt loved her boss. Outside of Dakota and his son Dominic, Supreme Security and the Atlanta's finest team were his top priority. He was also relentless in offering the best, most dependable service to their clients. Egypt had the utmost respect for Hamilton and how he conducted business.

"I understand," Griffith said. "But we still want your guys involved in other aspects of this case."

Egypt remembered Laz once saying that Supreme's guys could do things that law enforcement couldn't get away with. She never asked for details but now wondered just how involved Supreme would get in the case.

"We already froze Ross Hoakley's accounts, but there were two that included his wife's name on them, and we'll be monitoring them. Also, in scouring through Hoakley's personal computer, we found new intel," Griffith continued. "Years ago, the FBI took down a ruthless crime family out of Chicago. Shortly after, the patriarch of that family died, and it was all quiet from those left behind.

"Recently, we determined that the eldest son of this family has rebuilt their empire here in Atlanta. Unfortunately, he's moved into the LinKenzoy family's territory, and we don't want a turf war. So far, we haven't been able to get this guy on anything. He's savvier and a helluva lot more ruthless than his father."

Two photos appeared on the screen, and Egypt's heart stopped.

No. No. No. It can't be.

"Marco Pisano is now the head of the family, and he is one dangerous son of a bitch. We believe Ross Hoakley was working with Marco and the relationship went bad. We just haven't been able to prove that Marco Pisano is responsible for Ross Hoakley's murder."

Egypt didn't hear anything else. Chills seared a path down her spine, and her body trembled with a vengeance. Panic like nothing she had ever experienced gripped her, and the coffee mug slipped from her hands, crashing to the floor. Hot liquid splattered over her hands, and she yelped.

Kenton and Angelo moved in unison, blocking her from view.

"What's wrong?" Kenton whispered, his hand cupping her cheek, his worried eyes searching hers.

Someone wiped coffee off her hands, but Egypt couldn't speak. She couldn't stop shaking. Her chest heaved. The suffocating sensation, like someone holding a pillow firmly over her face, was too much. She couldn't breathe.

Before she could process what was happening, Kenton rushed her out of the room.

"What happened?"

116

"What's going on?"

Several people talked at once, and Egypt couldn't process who the voices belonged too. But when strong arms wrapped around her, lifting her off her feet, she knew who was carrying her.

Kenton.

"I—I ca—can't brea…" she wheezed. The heaviness in her chest was so overwhelming. She was going to die.

Chapter Sixteen

With Egypt in his arms, Kenton hurried into Hamilton's office with Angelo hot on his heels. "Come on, sweetheart. I need you to calm down." Kenton sat on the sofa with Egypt by his side, and she slumped against him her chest still heaving as she struggled to get air. It was killing him to see the tears streaming down her face.

"I'll grab Kleenex and water. Need anything else?" Angelo asked.

"No." With a gentle hand on Egypt's back, Kenton nudged her forward. "Put your head down, and try to take some deep breaths." With her head between her knees, her shoulder-length dreadlocks framed her face as he rubbed her back. "That's it. Just breathe. You're okay." The calm in his voice didn't match the hammering inside his chest, but he kept telling her that she was fine, that she was safe.

What the heck had triggered a panic attack? One minute everything was normal, and she was sipping her coffee, the next minute...

Kenton had to steady his own breathing. His pulse was racing like an out of control train heading downhill. Egypt had scared the hell out of him. The fear in her eyes, the shaking, and her inability to speak threw him off balance.

He thought back on the last bit of information that

Griffith shared, and tried to recall what she might've seen or heard. Photos. There had been photos on the screen.

The Pisano family. Marco Pisano.

What the hell did she know about them? The thought of her anywhere near Marco had Kenton's chest tightening. While with the FBI, he'd heard of the Pisano family. They made the famous Gambino family out of New York look like choir boys.

But there had also been a moment in Griffith's speech that had given Kenton pause. It was disturbing to think that someone within the FBI could have been feeding Hoakley and the Pisano family information. That thought only reminded him of how he, Santana, and Quaid had been ambushed because of a traitor within the agency.

Kenton looked up when Angelo returned with the box of tissue and a bottle of water.

"I'll leave these. I'm heading back to the meeting, but holler if anything else is needed."

"Thanks, man."

Angelo left the office, closing the door behind him. Kenton released a long, drawn-out sigh and laid his head against the sofa while continuing to rub Egypt's back. Several minutes ticked by before her breathing sounded normal.

"You okay?" he asked, stuffing a few sheets of tissue into her hand. While she wiped her face, he opened the water bottle for her, and then swapped it for the used Kleenex.

After a few sips, Egypt tried handing him the bottle.

"Drink a little more."

She did as told without arguing and for Kenton, that was a sign that she wasn't herself yet. Normally, Egypt challenged him at every turn.

"I have to go," she rasped, still not looking at him. This time he did take the bottle when she handed it to him.

Kenton leaned forward and wrapped his arm around her. "Where do you need to go?"

She finally glanced at him, her eyes brimmed with tears. "Away from here. I can't stay." She tried to stand, but he held her firm.

"No. Not this time. I'm not letting you off the hook. We're not leaving until you tell me what the hell happened back there. What's going on?"

He noticed the moment her sadness turned to anger, and she pushed against him. "I can't stay here!" she yelled, her voice thick with emotion. He loosened his hold, and she shot up but wobbled on her heels before he stood, steadying her.

"You can't stay here? Where? The office? The building? Where can't you stay, Egypt?"

Kenton had a bad feeling the "here" was Atlanta, but she didn't answer. He blocked her path to the door and didn't care that he was crowding her. "Does whatever you're running from have to do with the Pisano family?"

Egypt swallowed hard and the fear he spotted in her eyes moments ago returned.

Okay, now we're getting somewhere.

"Talk to me. You have my word. I won't let anything happen to you."

"You can't promise that, Kenton. No one can."

"Well, if you can't talk to me. Stay and talk to Hamilton."

She shook her head, tears slipping down her cheeks. "I can't," she whispered.

He gently wiped her tears. "You've said more than once that you trust me. If that's true, I need you to prove it. Tell me why you have to leave?"

"Because…Marco Pisano wants me dead."

Chapter Seventeen

"What?" Kenton choked out, shock dangled from the word, and his mouth hung open. He stared at Egypt as if seeing her for the first time. "How the hell did you get involve with the Pisano family?"

Egypt released a shaky breath and ran her hands down her face, still reeling from the terror of seeing Marco's photo on the screen. Still remembering the evilness in his eyes when he made her a promise years ago.

You're going to pay for ripping my family apart.

And Egypt believed him.

Still shivering, she rubbed her hands up and down her arms. It didn't matter that she wore a suit jacket. She couldn't seem to get warm.

"Kenton, I know you want answers, but I have to go. I'm not safe here," she said, her voice shaking despite trying to keep herself together, which she was failing at miserably. Standing in that meeting, seeing Marco's face, her nightmare had become too real. "Once I'm settled somewhere, I promise I'll call."

She made a move to go around Kenton, but he blocked her path and gripped her shoulders, forcing Egypt to look at him.

"Really? You tell me some shit like that about Pisano,

121

and you think I'm going to let you walk out of here? Clearly, you don't know me."

"Kenton, please. I ca-can't stay. Marco will find me, and he *will* kill me. He accused me of ripping his family apart. He told me I was going to pay." She bit back a sob, unable to look at Kenton as a tear slipped down her cheek. He wiped it away.

"Sweetheart, I know you're scared, but I *can't* let you go. If Pisano *is* after you, being with all of us is the safest place for you."

In her heart, Egypt knew he was right, but in her head, all she could think of was—run. It was only a matter of time before Marco found her. More importantly, she didn't want any of her friends to get hurt because of her.

"And there's another reason you can't leave me. We have a date tonight, and I'm holding you to it."

Egypt tried to laugh, but sobbed instead, sounding like a wounded puppy. She knew he was trying to lighten the moment, which only made her care for him that much more. Her heart ached knowing that she'd never get a chance to explore a relationship with him.

"Aw, baby. Come here." Kenton pulled her to his hard body and his strong arms encircled her.

Egypt leaned into him, absorbing his strength and wishing that the last fifteen minutes had only been a dream. She tried to calm down, but even the sweet kiss Kenton placed against the side of her head didn't help the fear raging through her body.

She didn't want to leave town. Atlanta felt like home, and for the first time in her adult life, she had friends. But running and taking care of herself was all she knew. Marco was ruthless. He wouldn't think twice about putting a bullet in her head.

A sense of foreboding, like an ominous cloud, weighed her down, siphoning what little energy she had left. Marco's face kept replaying in her mind, and her heart rate soared as fear continued to build.

How could he be in Atlanta? Did he know she was there? There was no way Pisano just happened to move his family's operation to Atlanta.

He was closing in.

"Come and have a seat. It's time you tell me everything."

Egypt sat on the sofa and wiped her face, watching as Kenton shook out of his suit jacket and draped it on the back of a chair, his thick biceps flexing with each move. When he sat next to her, he loosened his black tie and undid the top button on his dress shirt. "Now, talk to me. How do you know Marco Pisano?"

"When I was seventeen, his father had my uncle killed...and I witnessed the murder."

*

Kenton just stared at Egypt. To witness a murder at any age was a traumatic experience but as a kid?

He shook his head and tried to brace himself for whatever else she'd share. So far, the last few minutes had been one shock after another. He'd known that Egypt had secrets, but he wouldn't have guessed they involved murder and a notorious crime family.

Never ask a question unless you're prepared for the answer.

Kenton watched her carefully. It was clear she wasn't as unaffected as she was trying to let on. The fidgeting, rubbing her hands up and down her thighs, and the fact that she hadn't looked at him in the last few minutes proved just how uncomfortable she was.

She leaned forward, resting her elbows on her thighs and closed her eyes. "It's a long story. I had hoped by moving to Atlanta, I could finally put that time in my life behind me, but somehow it seems to keep popping up. It's like I'm never going to be able to move on from my past. My nightmare."

"Why don't you give me the short version. Like, where did this happen?"

"Southside of Chicago where I grew up."

Chicago? Hell, all this time he thought she was from L.A. At least that's what she'd told him years ago. What other lies had she spewed…and why?

"I had just graduated from high school a few days earlier, and me and one of my friends were trying to hurry home because we both were supposed to be in the house before the street lights came on. But we were late, as usual."

A slight smile tilted the left corner of her lips as if remembering happier times, but it disappeared just as fast.

"We cut through the backyard of this abandoned house, and just before we reached the front, we heard tires screeching, car doors slamming, and then people arguing."

Egypt finally made eye contact, and Kenton couldn't take his gaze from hers. Each time she looked at him, those gorgeous doe-like eyes pulled on his heartstrings. It didn't matter what she was involved in. He would do anything to protect her.

"In our neighborhood, when you hear people arguing, you automatically go the other way knowing a fight or gunshots would be next. It was *that* dangerous. We started to go back the way we came, but then I heard my uncle's booming voice, arguing, and I froze. My friend tried to get me to leave, but *I didn't.*"

Egypt pressed her fingers against her temple, then closed her eyes again.

"No matter how many times I play that night in my head, I don't know why I stayed."

"Were you and your uncle close?" Kenton asked, needing to keep her talking.

"At one time. He was the one who taught me everything there was to know about computers. He was my father's younger brother and super smart. My mother hated him, said trouble followed him around. That night…"

"Tell me," Kenton said gently when it seemed she wouldn't continue.

"There were five men: my Uncle Billy, his best friend, and three others, one was Marcelo Pisano, Marco's father. He stood out. The man looked like money. Fancy suit, shiny shoes, bling on his fingers, and a big, expensive looking car that only high-end drug dealers rolled in.

"My uncle and one of the other men argued about some deal that went bad, and the guy blamed my uncle. But Uncle Billy didn't back down, told the guy he was full of shit and that one of these days he wouldn't be able to hide behind his badge."

Hide behind his badge...

The words rattled in Kenton's head, but he forced himself to pay attention as Egypt continued.

"My uncle just kept talking and said, '*Your ass is going to get got.*' I didn't know what that meant at the time, but the guy pulled out a gun."

The tension bouncing off of Egypt was palpable, and Kenton reached for her hand, rubbing his thumb over the back of it. She looked depleted, which was understandable considering what she was telling him.

"Pisano said something in Italian to the guy with the gun, and then he climbed into the back seat of the car. I think Uncle Billy and his friend understood Italian because they started backing up. Then I heard something like a faint pop, but wasn't sure what it was until my uncle's friend dropped to the ground."

"The gunman had a silencer?"

Egypt nodded. "The gunman turned the pistol on my uncle. He said..." Egypt swallowed, tears filling her eyes as she bit her bottom lip. "*I'll keep hiding behind my badge because your ass won't be around to say a damn thing.* He shot my uncle in the head."

Damn.

"I-I let out a little scream and then covered my mouth. I was so scared that they had heard me."

"Had they?"

"Yes. I couldn't get my feet to move. I just stood there shaking in the shadows. But the shooter headed in that direction until Pisano said something through the window. After another glance my way, he hurried away. Too afraid to run or do anything, I just stood there while my uncle and his friend bled to death."

I'll keep hiding behind my badge.

Unease swept through Kenton as those words played inside his head. No wonder she didn't trust law enforcement.

Tears trailed down Egypt's face, but she quickly swiped them away. "Everything was a blur after that. Cops came from every direction, and I had to tell them what I saw. Then one day the FBI showed up at our door."

An icy trail of dread slithered through Kenton's body.

I'll keep hiding behind my badge.

Now the words taunted him. "Egypt, who shot your uncle?"

Her sad eyes met his. "A dirty FBI agent."

Ah hell.

Chapter Eighteen

Egypt stared down at her hands as Kenton released a string of curses. She knew he didn't want to hear that one of his own had been dirty. Though she didn't know the whole story about why Kenton left the FBI, she'd heard that he had lost a witness under questionable circumstances.

Kenton shot out of his seat and paced around the room aimlessly while rubbing the back of his neck. "Tell me the rest."

Egypt hesitated, not wanting to say anything that would drum up bad memories from his time with the FBI. But she had promised to tell him her truth, the good and the bad, and the way he was looking at her left no room for debate.

She continued, explaining how the FBI agent that had shot her uncle had been working for the Pisano family. Once the men were in custody, the feds built their case and wanted her to testify, but initially, Egypt's parents had been against the idea, fearing her safety. Her father had just returned from burying his only brother. The thought of putting Egypt at risk hadn't sat well with him. He hadn't agreed until the feds told them that without Egypt's testimony, her uncle's killer might walk.

"I testified."

"Hold up." Kenton stopped in the middle of the floor.

127

"Are you telling me you testified against a *crooked* FBI agent and Pisano, in a *federal* case? Did the feds offer you and your family witness protection?"

"They did. My mother fought the idea, not wanting to leave her family and friends, but my father insisted that we get protection. I agreed to testify against the FBI agent and Marcelo Pisano, Marco's father."

"How did Marco get to you?"

Egypt's pulse amped up at the mention of his name. "After the trial, my parents, my little brother, and I went into WITSEC with new identities, and they moved us to South Carolina. We were there two years, and I was in my second year of college. Marco confronted me."

Egypt's chest tightened as she recalled one of the scariest days of her life. She knew who he was immediately since she had researched him and his family prior to the trial.

Kenton walked back over and sat next to her, and just having him nearby helped.

"I was heading across campus to get to my next class, and Marco came out of nowhere. Scared me to death. He said *I thought it was time we met. It's because of you the FBI destroyed my family and caused my father's heart attack. You're going to pay for ripping my family apart.* Then I saw the knife. Before I could react, he jammed it into my side and pulled it out. I don't recall much after that. I remember the pain and falling to the ground. I also recall someone...or people screaming, but supposedly no one saw Marco."

Kenton didn't say anything. He leaned forward and ran his hands down his face. Egypt was tired of talking, but he insisted that she finish.

"WITSEC moved us immediately. With new identities, they relocated us to Seattle and my life was awful. My mother hated me, saying it was because of me their lives had been ruined. If I had been at home that night in Chicago, I wouldn't have witnessed anything."

Kenton looked at her but didn't speak.

"I lived with that guilt for years and totally shut down. It wasn't until I decided to leave WITSEC—"

"Wait. You're not under their protection?"

Egypt shook her head. "They couldn't protect me. Otherwise, I wouldn't have gotten stabbed. As far as I was concerned, I was better off on my own, especially since my relationship with my family was strained. With some help—"

"Nelson," Kenton interrupted, piecing together what she'd told him, with what he already knew about her. "Was he your handler while you were with WITSEC?"

"No, I wasn't introduced to him until I was getting ready to leave the program. The U.S. Marshal who assisted my family told me about Nelson. He had recently left the agency and was living in California at the time. Long story short, Nelson helped me change my identity again. I lived in L.A. for several years, and a year or two after graduating from college, I moved to Atlanta. And you know the rest."

"No, actually, I don't. From what I knew about you since being here, is that you were from LA, had a computer science background, no family, and you worked in corporate America for fifteen years. Right now, I don't know what's true and what isn't. I have no idea what your real name is, your age, nothing," he said bitterly before standing again. Egypt stood too, but kept her distance.

"Kenton, Nelson is the *only* person who knows my story, and now you. When I entered WITSEC, I was told that my best chance of staying alive was to forget my past. They insisted I not tell anyone, not even if I ever decided to get married. I had to pretend that life I left behind never existed. It was for my safety. You know how secrets are. If you tell one person, it's no longer a secret. Anyone could slip up and give away my identity and whereabouts to the wrong person."

Kenton leaned against the wall that held a landscape picture and stared down at his dress shoes. He was quiet for so long, Egypt wasn't sure if he would say anything else.

She understood. Her life and what she'd been through was a lot to take in. Besides, as long as Marco Pisano was out there, she would never be free to live the type of life she'd dreamed of having. And based on a conversation she and Kenton had years ago, Egypt knew he wanted marriage and kids one day.

Kenton finally looked at her. The solemnness on his face let her know that whatever had been growing between them was over. "I know better than anyone the importance of keeping information like that quiet. It could be a matter of life or death. It's just—"

"It's just that I didn't tell you the truth about me long before now. Well, at least you know why."

Egypt maintained the distance between them while she looked him up and down, wanting to memorize every inch of him. He was a fantastic man, a real sweetheart, and she knew in her heart that they would've been great together.

Now, she would never know since she needed to move on. At least talking to him made her feel better, stronger. She was a survivor. For so many years she had taken care of herself, kept herself alive and she would continue to.

"Is your family still in Seattle?" Kenton asked, and Egypt was a little surprised by the question.

"No. They're dead."

His mouth fell open. "Shit...Egypt...I'm sorry."

She shrugged. Numbness spread through her body as she reminded herself why she would never trust her life to law enforcement. "I blame the FBI and the U.S. Marshals who were supposed to be protecting them."

The office door swung open. Egypt startled, heart slamming against her chest. Hamilton walked in. He glanced between her and Kenton before his gaze zoned in on her.

"You okay?" he asked, moving further into the office and setting his Ipad on the desk.

Egypt nodded, hoping he wouldn't ask what happened to her in the meeting. She loved Hamilton like a big brother, but at the moment, she didn't have it in her to share the details of her past with anyone else.

"Kenton, I need you in the war room in five minutes," Hamilton said without looking at him, his attention still on her. He'd given one of the meeting rooms that name a few months ago. No doubt they would discuss their new roles with the FBI.

Egypt didn't care. She had no intention of sticking around.

Chapter Nineteen

Kenton sat in the back of the small meeting room dazed and unable to concentrate as Hamilton briefed three additional security specialists, who hadn't been at the meeting with the feds.

Kenton rubbed his forehead, still reeling from what Egypt had told him. Memories of his past resurfaced, the parts that had been gnawing on his conscious for the last few days. As an FBI agent and friend, he had failed Santana the same way the agency and the Marshals had failed Egypt.

How was that possible? Keeping people safe was their job. And they had all fucked it up.

And what the hell was he going to do about Egypt? He could barely look at her after she'd shared her disturbing past, knowing that people she should've been able to count on had botched up her protection. Kenton also couldn't help worrying that there were more dirty agents and Marshals in the system. Some who had probably been bought by the Pisano family.

If he could, he would hunt down every rogue agent that existed, but that wouldn't help Egypt. He wasn't sure what to do about her. Right now, Hamilton had her waiting in his office to find out next steps.

Kenton tuned back into the briefing.

"Yes, we are tightening up our security measures in every aspect of what we do here at Supreme," Hamilton explained. He had mentioned earlier that some of the new procedures that were being implemented were things they should've been doing from the beginning.

The meeting lasted a few more minutes before Hamilton dismissed everyone. "Kenton, I need you, Laz, Angelo, and Myles to stick around," he said as everyone else exited the room. They all gathered at the front. "Since you guys are the closest to Egypt, I'm going to need you to keep an eye on her."

"Why? What's going on?" Laz asked.

"I can't give much detail, but she's had a run in with Marco Pisano in the past."

"Shit, no wonder she freaked when his name was mentioned in the meeting," Angelo said.

"Myles, I'm making you lead over Mrs. Hoakley's protection. Identify three other guys, and set up a schedule. When you're not working her detail, I'd like you to assist with guarding Egypt if necessary," Hamilton instructed, and Myles nodded.

Early in his career at Supreme, Myles tried to make everyone believe he'd been a case officer with the CIA, someone who managed agents. Kenton didn't believe that at all. Myles processed information, acted, and responded to situations more like an operative than someone who sat at a desk. Kenton wouldn't be surprised to find out that the guy had spent most of his career undercover. His investigative and reaction skills, as well as his ability to blend into an environment was second to none, except for maybe Laz. Both men were relentless in getting answers, and wouldn't hesitate to remove anyone who got in their way.

Hamilton gave a few more instructions before letting the guys leave. All except Kenton.

"You okay?" Hamilton asked, looking at Kenton critically.

"Yeah. Just worried about Egypt."

"I'm not talking about Egypt. I'm talking about you. I know it couldn't have been easy to hear about a crooked FBI agent or the possibility of there being others helping this family."

"So you knew about Egypt's past?" Kenton shouldn't have been surprised since Hamilton seemed to know everything. He had only spent a couple of minutes with Egypt after Kenton left his office. So there was no way she could've told him much of anything at the time.

"Yeah, Mason and I know. When Nelson came to us on her behalf regarding a job, he filled us in. She doesn't know, but at some point, soon, one of us will tell her."

Kenton nodded, wondering how Hamilton would determine a good time to let her know. No doubt she'd figure it out when she found out her boss was assigning part of the team to shadow her.

"Until we know what we're dealing with, I want someone on Egypt at all times. She might not be in any danger, but I'm not willing to take that chance."

"She's not going to go for that."

"Maybe not, but I'm sure you can make her see reason. This is no time for her to be Miss Independent. We're not giving her a choice. One of us will be on her whether she likes it or not. I'm hoping you'll be willing to take lead. We'll move people around on some of the assignments to make sure your schedule is flexible."

Kenton stared at his boss. Though he had tried being discrete in his pursuit of Egypt, most of them knew how he felt about her. But no one, except for Laz and Angelo had actually called him out on it. Laz took every opportunity to rag him about his *crush*, as his friend liked to call it.

"I'll take care of getting her to see reason, but I can't be a part of the team to guard her," Kenton finally said.

Hamilton leaned against the edge of a long table and folded his arms and crossed his legs at the ankle. Minutes ticked by before he spoke. "No one will protect her the way you will."

Kenton ran his hand over his low haircut. "I beg to differ. Our guys are the best. I would trust her life in any of their hands." He said the words, though he knew it wouldn't be easy to see someone else spending twenty-four/seven with her.

"Why not you?"

Kenton stopped moving and slowly turned to his boss. "This...all of this is bringing up too many memories. If anything happened to Egypt on my watch, it would kill me. Too many people have failed her and I..." he shook his head. "I can't risk failing her too. Besides, she'd be too much of a distraction."

Hamilton chuckled and pushed away from the table. "Remember my distraction last year? No one is more distracting than my woman."

"Okay, good point." He would never forget the first time he'd met Dakota. Hamilton had assigned himself to protect her from an unknown enemy. And during their stay at a safe house, Dakota made it clear that she was interested in more than just a bodyguard. Dakota was like a tornado, gathering up everything in her path. For Kenton, she had become an important part of his life too, like having another sister. There wasn't anything he wouldn't do for her.

"So, I know all about distractions," Hamilton continued. "And normally I wouldn't recommend guarding someone you're attracted to. It's not the best practice, but I trust that you'll take care of Egypt."

"This is different, Ham. I can't shake the fear of—"

"You're one of the best security specialists we have. Don't start doubting your abilities now. You won't fail her. I know that, and deep down I think you know it too."

Kenton didn't usually lack self-confidence, but this was Egypt they were talking about. If anything happened to her under his care, it would destroy him.

I can't fail her.

＊

Egypt quickly changed into an Atlanta Falcons

135

sweatshirt, skinny black jeans, and running shoes before pulling the rolling suitcase, that she kept packed, from under the bed. She hated leaving Supreme without saying goodbye, especially since Hamilton had mentioned them talking after his meeting. Egypt already knew that he'd want to know what happened earlier, and she was done sharing. It had wiped her out emotionally after talking with Kenton, and she'd had to leave before she lost her nerve.

Right now, her only regret was not seeing Kenton before she left town. The withdrawn expression on his face when he walked out of the office broke her heart. She wanted so badly for him to understand why she hadn't told him about her past. He claimed to understand, but the coldness she felt from him said otherwise.

Egypt grabbed a duffel bag from off the top shelf in the closet and a few more clothes. There'd been a time when she didn't have much to fill up a suitcase, preferring to live with as little as possible. Now that she'd been in Atlanta for so many years, she had accumulated not only clothes, but material items as well.

She went to the far corner of her bedroom and moved the upholstered chair aside. Lifting the corner of the carpet, she removed a loose floorboard where she stashed cash. Supreme paid very well, and she had saved the majority of her paychecks. Living in a bubble for so many years, afraid Marco would make good on his promise, had scared her that way.

Her pulse amped up just thinking about the man. She hurried, grabbing the envelope with cash, and shoving it into the side pocket of the duffel bag. Lastly, she went back to the closet for her gun case. That was another thing about getting too comfortable. She had stopped carrying her Smith & Wesson 9mm. Opening the case, she loaded the chamber and put the weapon in her oversized handbag.

Egypt's heart broke with each stepped she took carrying the bags to the front of the house. Within twenty-four hours, the life she had built had fallen apart.

Keep it together, girl.

Instead of ordering a car the way she normally would, Egypt searched for the number of a taxi company to keep from leaving a paper trail. She knew Kenton, Hamilton or one of the other guys would search for her once they realized she was gone, but she planned to cover her tracks.

"Okay, I think..."

Her hand flew to her chest when a loud banging on the front door scared her. Instead of grabbing what she could carry and heading for the back door, Egypt grabbed her gun. Now that she knew Pisano was in Atlanta, she was taking every precaution, like she used to do.

Tiptoeing to the front door, her pistol at her side, Egypt looked through the peephole.

Agent Franklin? Why is he here?

Egypt stepped back debating on whether to open the door. He had no business at her home. Had he followed her? She shook the thought free. It wasn't like he couldn't find out where she lived.

"Just be cool," she told herself, and pulled opened the wood door, but left the screen door latched. Instead of saying anything, she just looked at him, waiting for him to speak.

"You're probably surprised to see me."

"You could say that."

"Can we talk?"

"Go ahead," she said with more bravado than she felt, and held the gun behind her back.

"I mean inside. May I come in?"

"Agent Franklin, as far as I'm concerned, we have nothing to discuss."

"I could insist you let me in."

"Not without a warrant." Kenton's deep voice startled her as he climbed the stairs that were off to the left. Where had he come from? His truck was nowhere in sight.

"What are you doing here, Franklin?" Kenton asked, his steely gaze lethal.

"Not that it's any of your business, but I wanted to make sure Ms. Durand didn't have any more information on

Hoakley. I understand they were an item a few years back. I wouldn't be doing my due diligence if I didn't at least follow up."

Kenton glared at him but spoke to her. "Egypt, do you have anything to add to whatever you've already told the FBI?"

"No, I told them everything."

"In that case, have a good evening, Agent Franklin. If you need to question Egypt further, you'll need to do so through her lawyer. The contact information was given to the agent who interviewed her."

She didn't have a lawyer, but Hamilton had insisted that if she or Kenton needed one, they should use Supreme's attorney.

They watched as Franklin marched back to his dark sedan and pulled away.

"Okay, unlock the door," Kenton said, his hand on the handle.

Butterflies fluttered inside Egypt's stomach as she studied him through the screen door. It was a chilly October afternoon, but all he wore was his dress shirt and pants, without a jacket or the tie he'd been fumbling with earlier. He was one sexy man. Just looking at him had heat filtering to areas of her body that hadn't been touched in years.

Egypt shook herself. Only moments ago, she was wishing that she'd had a chance to see him one last time. But Kenton was one of the reasons she hadn't stuck around at the office. It would've been too hard to say goodbye.

"What do you want, Kenton?"

"I want you, but you already know that."

I want you, too. Egypt wanted to say, but it seemed like too much to hope for that they could ever pursue a relationship. She had too much baggage. Knowing it would be futile to tell him to go away, she let him in.

"What's with the gun? Do you even know how to use it?"

Egypt glanced at the firearm before slipping it into her

handbag. "Yes, I do."

Instead of commenting more on the gun, like she expected, he stood next to the bags. "Going somewhere?"

"We already talked about this. You know why I have to leave."

"Where are you going?" His voice went low and deep, lacking the humor that she was accustomed to with him. He folded his arms across his chest, bringing attention to his thick arms, arms she wanted to be wrapped up in.

Egypt walked over to the African painting hanging over the fireplace, unsure if she could take it with her. The abstract piece was one of the first splurges when she moved into the rental. "It's probably best you not know," she finally said to Kenton before turning to face him again.

"You really don't get this whole dating thing, do you? We're supposed to be spending time getting to know each other. How are we going to do that if you don't tell me where you're going?"

"Really, Kenton? I'm terrified that a gangster, who wants me dead, is closing in, and you're talking about dating?"

He shrugged and decreased the distance between them. "What can I say. I always thought of you as a fighter, not someone who would allow a man to run her away from the life she's built. What I don't understand is how you can leave me, the guys, and Dakota and Journey without saying goodbye?"

A stab of guilt lodged in her chest. "You think this is easy for me? You guys are the only family I have. Of course, I don't want to leave, but I'm not going to sit around and wait for Marco to make his move."

"Good, because I wouldn't expect you to. You're a fighter, Egypt, and a survivor. Most people would've given up and crawled under a rock after being confronted by the asshole. But you didn't. You got knocked down and got back up, stronger than ever."

Egypt gave an unladylike snort. "You make me sound way braver than I am."

Kenton pulled on the front of her sweatshirt until they were inches apart. Staring into his eyes, Egypt didn't miss the heart-tingling tenderness of his gaze. Luscious heat swarmed her body to the point of being unbearable, and all she wanted to do was fall into his embrace.

"I *can't* let you go. I need you here with me. Besides, Pisano might not even know you're in town."

"But he might know that I am."

"Then we'll deal with him together." Kenton brushed his soft lips over hers and hope blossomed in her chest. "I need you to trust me when I say that I have your back. I'm not letting anything happen to you. So, if you leave home, I'm going with you. If you head to a hotel, I'm going with you. And sweetheart, if you're thinking about leaving town, I'm leaving town with you. All day, every day, I'm yours."

"What about work?"

"That's all been taken care of."

"Uh, no. I already assigned you a job that starts tomorrow. Remember?"

Kenton grinned, pushed her dreadlocks away from her face before gliding the back of his fingers down her cheek. "I know, but the boss has given me a new assignment."

"What assignment? I didn't see anything on my desk."

"Meet your own personal security specialist. Kenton Bailey at your service, ma'am." He leaned forward, giving a dramatic bow. "I go wherever you go. Whatever you want or need—I'm your man, and I mean that literally." He wiggled his brows and Egypt couldn't hold back the laugh.

"I don't know what I'd do without you, and the rest of my Supreme family."

Kenton pulled her into his arms and kissed the top of her head. "You might feel differently when you find out what I have planned as part of your security detail."

Egypt leaned back and glared at him. "Exactly what do you have planned?"

"Let's just say that I'm glad you're already packed because you're moving in with me."

Chapter Twenty

Kenton drove away from Egypt's house, expecting more resistance against his spur-of-the-moment idea of moving in together. Hamilton had suggested they hold up in a safe house until they knew more about Pisano. Kenton knew Egypt wouldn't go for that. Or maybe he really hadn't wanted to go that route. A safe house would constantly remind her of the looming danger. Staying with him could still give her the protection she needed, and give him a chance to take her mind off Pisano and the gravity of her situation.

"Does everyone know?" Egypt asked.

Kenton anticipated this question, especially after he initiated the around-the-clock protection.

"No. Only Hamilton and Mason know your story." Kenton gauged her reaction. He had no intention of keeping anything from her. If they were going to build a relationship, the way he planned, they needed to be upfront. Honest. "Nelson told them before you were hired."

She hesitated, slightly. "I never knew. I guess I shouldn't be surprised he told them."

"My guess is that Nelson wanted as many people watching your back as possible. That way if something were to jump off, and he wasn't around, he would know that you were protected."

"Like now," she said quietly. Kenton's heart swelled at the appreciation he heard in her voice.

"All Hamilton told the guys, and by guys I mean Laz, Angelo, and Myles, is that you had a run-in with Pisano in the past. As far as I know, no one at Supreme knows anything else. Ham made it clear that he wanted all of us to keep an eye on you for the foreseeable future. The only way anyone will ever know about what you've been through is if you tell them. Your secret is safe, Egypt."

His arm was resting on the center console, and Egypt covered his hand with hers. "Thank you for everything. When you walked out of the office, I honestly thought you were upset with me."

"Not at you. I hate that you've gone through hell, and I'm pissed that the FBI and U.S. Marshals failed you. I definitely wasn't mad at *you*. I guess after you shared your story, my own shit from the past started messing with my head. I'll tell you about that one day...soon."

Egypt nodded. "Okay, and I'm going to hold you to that. And just so you know, I trust you more than anyone. I hope you understand why—"

"I get it, but I'm not sure I understand why you wouldn't go out with me, especially if you say you trusted me."

"I knew if we dated, I would fall for you."

Kenton still didn't understand, and she must have read the confusion on his face.

"If anything had ever gotten serious between us, I would've wanted to be totally honest with you. Tell you everything about my past. And since I was told that I should pretend my past never existed and never speak of it..."

It was slowly starting to make sense. "So if you didn't date me, then you wouldn't have to tell me you're not who you say you are."

Egypt removed her hand and sighed deeply. "When you put it like that, it sounds awful."

"I didn't mean for it to, but think about it Egypt. You have said more than once that you trust me. Why couldn't you trust me with that information?"

She didn't respond, and he was uncomfortable with the answer stabbing his gut. "Because I was former FBI?"

Egypt turned to look out the window, and he knew the truth.

"You thought I'd never believe that there were bad agents out there."

She remained quiet, and Kenton tried to distance his personal feelings from the security issue at hand. He had to be subjective and clear-eyed. He couldn't imagine how awful her life had been during the past sixteen years. She'd been just a kid when everything went down. Which brought up a ton of other questions he wanted to ask, but not tonight. And probably not tomorrow either. They'd both been through a hell of a day. If he was tired, he knew she had to be mentally and emotionally exhausted.

"How about we not discuss this for the rest of the evening and only think about our date?"

A slow smile spread across Egypt's face. "You are relentless. Can't we postpone our date? It's been such a long day. I just want to eat a little, take a long bath, and go to sleep."

Kenton brought her hand to his mouth and touched his lips to her soft skin. "I know, sweetheart, but I don't want you wallowing in everything that happened today. I have a nice evening planned, and I guarantee it'll be relaxing."

Despite the darkness in the truck, shadows of light crossed her face as they sped down the highway. She studied him for the longest time before saying, "You're right. If we're going to try this *dating thing*, I shouldn't be canceling on you already."

Kenton chuckled and maintained the hold on her hand. It had been a while since he dated anyone exclusively, and he looked forward to spending more time with Egypt.

Except for Maxwell's song, *Whenever, Wherever, Whatever,* flowing through the speakers, they rode the rest of the way to his home in comfortable silence. A short while later they pulled into his Lawrenceville neighborhood.

"God, it's dark out here. This is why I like living in the city. There aren't enough streetlights or sidewalks, for that matter, out here."

"Yeah, I agree. It definitely feels a little country, but in this area, you can get more house for the money." He pulled onto his street, passing one large home after another. "A three thousand square foot house in the city would cost twice as much as I paid for this one."

"*This* is your house?" Egypt said with surprise when he pulled into the driveway and the overhead garage door lifted.

"Yep, this is home." He had purchased the house almost four months ago after selling his condo in the city. Not only was this place bigger, but it was closer to where his father lived. Traveling to and from work was a little tiring thanks to traffic, but overall, he liked the quiet expanse of the new place.

They climbed out of the Yukon, and Kenton grabbed Egypt's bags and reached for the painting that had been over her fireplace.

"Why'd you insist on me bringing that painting?" Egypt asked, carrying her purse and duffel bag.

"Because I've seen you stare at it often and know how important it is to you. Am I right?"

She twisted her mouth. "I think it's the colors. I love how vibrant it is and how at peace I feel when I look at it. Don't ask me why. I'm not sure, but maybe it also has something to do with the painting being the first purchase I splurged on when settling in Georgia. For the most part, after leaving South Carolina, I traveled light, not really getting attached to anything or anybody."

Before Kenton could respond, the door to the house swung open.

"It's about time you guys got here." Dakota stood in the doorway, her hand on her hips.

"I thought I told you to be gone by the time we arrived," Kenton said with exasperation.

Dakota rolled her eyes. "You know I don't listen to you. Besides, I haven't talked to my girl in days. So move."

Egypt laughed, and Dakota gave Kenton a little shove.

"You would think pregnancy would soften her manners," Egypt joked, and the women embraced, holding onto each other for a long time before Egypt pulled back. "Girl, you do not look like you're seven months pregnant."

"Most of the time I don't feel like I am either, but I have to admit, I'm so ready for this little guy to be born. But enough about me." All humor was gone and replaced with concern on Dakota's face. "Ham said you're under protective watch and moving in with Kenton for a while. What's going on? He wouldn't give me any details."

"Hopefully, it's nothing, but someone from my past, a guy I'd like to forget, is in Atlanta and the guys are…um…just being overprotective."

The look Egypt gave Kenton made it clear that she wasn't ready to share more.

"Okay, what aren't you guys telling me?"

"Dee, don't you have someplace you need to be? Like anywhere but here?"

"Yeah, yeah, yeah, I know. You want her to yourself. But I'm going to find out what's going on."

"Nosey ass woman," Kenton mumbled, rearing back when Dakota playfully swatted at him. "I don't know how Hamilton puts up with you."

"Oh, please. That man would be lost without me."

She was right. Hamilton worshiped the ground she walked on.

Kenton walked into the house, assuming they'd follow. He half expected to see Journey, since she and Dakota were both supposed to be there to help with his surprise. As he strolled into the kitchen, he was greeted by the scent of garlic, onions, and tomatoes, but no Journey.

The moment the thought filled his mind, Journey came from down the hall where the half bath was located.

"You all right?" he asked, noticing she looked a little

tired as she rubbed her growing belly.

She waved him off. "I'm fine, but *Laz's* daughter keeps kicking me, and now she's laying against my bladder. I have a bad feeling that when she makes her appearance in this world, she's going to give me hell just like her father."

Kenton chuckled. He found it funny that whenever the baby was giving her trouble, she called it Laz's daughter or Laz's baby. More ironic than that though was the fact that his friends were expecting at the same time. Gatherings were going to be more boisterous.

He set Egypt's bags down near the stairs and carried the painting to the family room. Removing the landscape portrait from over the fireplace, he replaced it with Egypt's and then stepped back to admire it. If the picture was important to her, it was important to him.

Kenton turned to find Journey smiling at him from the dining area. "Egypt loves that painting. The fact that you brought it with you guys," she placed her hand over her heart, "you are truly a sweetheart, Kenton Bailey."

He winked. "Yeah, but don't tell the guys. I don't want them to think I'm soft."

"Your secret is safe with me. Where's Egypt?" Journey lit the tapered candles adorning the table and countertops.

"She was right behind me until Dakota showed up. I thought the deal was that you two were going to be gone by the time we got here."

"That was the plan, but Dee insisted on seeing Egypt. Who am I to argue?" Journey said in mock defeat.

"Yeah, right." Kenton appreciated their concern for Egypt, even though neither of them knew what was really going on. He grabbed a beer out of the refrigerator, preferring something stronger.

"Don't open that." Journey nodded toward his beer bottle and lifted a silver bucket. "I bought wine. So, how is Egypt?"

Kenton glanced toward the garage door. What was taking so long for them to come in? "She was packed and planning to leave town."

"Well, I'm glad you caught her. Otherwise, you and Laz would've had to hunt her down. I'm not totally sure what's going on, *yet*, but Laz seemed really concerned about her safety. And when *he's* concerned, that means it's serious. This is no time for her to be alone."

Kenton nodded. "I agree. Hopefully, I calmed some of her fears." Before the night was over, he wanted to take her mind off of the last couple of days.

"This place is huge." Kenton heard Egypt say before she and Dakota came into view."

"Hey, girl." Journey moved across the room and hugged her.

Egypt smiled and regarded the women. "Hey, yourself. You and Dee are looking too cute with these growing baby bumps. Just think, in two months we're going to have little ones to dote on."

"I know, right? Actually, it's more like a month and a half for me, but who's counting?" Journey draped an arm around Egypt's shoulders. "I'm glad you're here."

Egypt's gaze met Kenton's. His heart lurched in his chest. When she looked at him like that, with love and admiration, he wanted to be her everything.

She broke eye contact and glanced around, zoning in on the bouquet of flowers and candles on the breakfast bar and the nearby dining table. "Kenton, your home is lovely, but what's all of this?"

"This is us helping with you guys first date," Dakota said before Kenton could respond.

"It's our second date," he corrected. He had to admit that they'd done a good job creating the romantic vibe he was going for. "Egypt, make yourself at home while I take your bags upstairs. And you two," he said to Dakota and Journey. "Be gone before I get back."

"We can't leave yet. We're waiting for Angelo to pick us up," Dakota explained.

Kenton got to the third step and stopped. "He's in the

driveway."

"What? I didn't know he was here." Journey glanced out the family room window.

"Yeah, he sent me a text. So you guys can leave. Thanks for everything. Now get out."

*

"Your ungrateful ass needs to learn how to be more gracious," Dakota said, but Kenton kept going up the stairs like he didn't hear her. Once he was out of earshot, Dakota swung around to Egypt. "Second date? You've been holding out on us."

Egypt held up her hands. "No, I haven't. He's counting our lunch yesterday as our first date, and I haven't talked to you guys in days."

Dakota glanced back at the stairs. "Either way, you need to keep us informed. I have a ton of questions."

Journey grabbed two canvas bags that were on the barstool. "Well, she's going to have to answer questions later. Angelo's waiting, and if I don't get home soon, you know Laz will send out a search party."

Journey was telling the truth. Laz was crazy protective of his wife, especially after a drug dealer had threatened her life months ago.

"Besides, Kenton wants Egypt to himself." Journey grinned and wiggled her eyebrows. Egypt's cheeks heated. Finally agreeing to date Kenton was one thing, but knowing that others knew was going to take some getting used to.

"Okay, but before we go, I know there's more going on than you and the fellas are letting on. So, what's up?" Dakota asked.

"Long story short, a guy I had a bad experience with in the past is now in Atlanta," Egypt said quietly. She planned to stick with Hamilton's story and leave as much of her past in the past. "And I love you guys for doing all of this, but please tell me that neither of you cooked the dinner," she cracked.

Her friends were the best in their respective careers, Dakota a business owner and former stuntwoman, and

Journey, an assistant district attorney. But neither of them could boil water without burning it.

"I see you have jokes." Journey nudged Egypt with her hip, moving her out of the way as she placed an additional candle on the table.

"No, we didn't cook, but we picked up some of your favorites, including all the fixing for strawberry shortcake. Just open the fridge." Dakota unwrapped the covered dishes, revealing Beef Brasato and pappardelle, fettuccine alfredo, a small container of spaghetti and meatballs, bread and a large tossed salad. Egypt didn't bother commenting on the massive amount of food knowing Kenton could devour the feast himself.

While they finished up, Egypt glanced around the first floor. She took in the entire space from her spot near the dining table, and her attention landed on the fireplace. Her breath caught.

He hung my picture?

The realization hit her like an arrow to the heart, sending goose bumps racing over her skin. That had to be the most thoughtful thing anyone had ever done for her. If Kenton hadn't already had a special spot in her heart, this kind gesture would have sealed it.

Tearing her eyes from the picture, she headed to what she knew would be her favorite room in the house—the chef's kitchen. She gawked around in awe, marveling at the quartz countertops, white cabinets, and top of the line stainless steel appliances. *My dream kitchen.* She ran a hand along the sleek handles of the double ovens. This had to be for show. Kenton wasn't much of a cook.

"Okay, I think that's it." Dakota put her hands on her hips and nodded to Journey. The pair stood back and admired their handiwork for a moment. Then Dakota turned to Egypt. "Now, let's discuss Kenton."

"Dee, don't start. This—"

"If you want him, you're going to have to make it clear and go for it," she said, ignoring Egypt's protest.

Dakota always spoke her mind. She and Journey knew how much Egypt cared about Kenton and had always wondered why she shot down his advances. Now that he knew about her past, and still seemed interested, Egypt would love to pursue a relationship with him. But in light of Pisano being in Atlanta and Egypt being unsure of what to do next, the last thing she needed was to get any more serious with Kenton.

"Now is probably not a good time," she said to her friends. "I have too much—"

"I'm not trying to hear excuses. I want you to finally have what Journey and I have found—the love of a good man." Dakota shrugged into a short denim jacket that matched her distress jeans. The gray, long-sleeved T-shirt she wore looked as if she had a ball—bigger than a basketball, but smaller than a beach ball—tucked beneath it. "For months, I have watched you and Kenton together. You guys are closer than some married people. It's time you stop fighting the inevitable."

"I rarely agree with Dee, but this time she's right," Journey added. "The heat between you and Kenton is intense. And I know for a fact he'd do anything for you, and I believe that works both ways."

That was true. Egypt could count on Kenton, and there was nothing she wouldn't do for him. But did that mean they should take their relationship to the next level right now?

"Whatever is *really* going on that has put you two under the same roof, take advantage of it. Life is too short, E," Dakota said. "If you want him, go for it. You don't want to look back with regrets about what could've been between you two. And another thing, the man is *hot*. He ain't gon' chase you forever. Some of the women at the dojo have been checking him out, and those witches are aggressive."

Yeah, Egypt already knew about some of the women vying for Kenton's attention. On occasion, he taught self-defense classes at Dakota's dojo, and Egypt had witnessed a few women hitting on him. Kenton took the attention in stride, never seeming interested, but what if the harmless flirting turned into something more?

"You need to let him know without a doubt that he belongs to you," Dakota said with conviction.

"Dee, I'm not you. I—"

"You don't have to be like me. Just make sure he knows that you're interested in more than a friendship."

When Dakota met Hamilton, she hadn't been shy about her interest and had pursued him full force. Egypt wasn't shy, but her limited experience with men made her awkward around them. She didn't possess the same self-confidence and take no prisoners boldness as Dakota.

Kenton trotted down the stairs loudly. "Why are you two still here?"

"Yeah, yeah, we're going. You know how this woman is," Journey said pulling on Dakota's arm and heading to the front door.

"E, remember what I said," Dakota yelled before the door closed behind them.

Kenton had changed out of his work clothes and into a tan T-shirt and blue jeans, looking too tempting for words. "Do I even want to know what that was about?"

"Nah, just girl talk," Egypt answered a bit too quickly, aware of how he filled the room and that ache in her heart.

Dakota was right. Egypt didn't want to wake up years from now regretting that she didn't follow through on this romance with Kenton. He was everything she could ever want in a man, a partner, a husband. She had to go for what she wanted. Now.

But with her lack of experience, she just wasn't quite sure how to go about doing that.

Chapter Twenty-One

Kenton put the last forkful of fettuccine alfredo into his mouth, thinking about how Dakota and Journey had hooked him up. When he came up with the dinner idea, he knew he wanted Italian food, something Egypt loved, as well as her favorite dessert. But Kenton hadn't considered wine, music, or more importantly—candles, something he didn't own. Now the flickering flames illuminated the table and enhanced the romantic vibe he'd been going for. They also cast just enough light for him to admire the beautiful woman sitting next to him.

"Ready for dessert?" he asked, wiping his mouth with the cloth napkin, something else he wouldn't have thought to get.

"What did you have in mind?" Egypt's suggestive tone had Kenton cocking his head, looking at her through narrowed eyes to determine if again he was reading too much into her words tonight.

For the past forty-five minutes, they'd had great conversation, discussing everything from movies, music, and even sports. Egypt was one of few women he knew who followed professional football, as well as basketball. But her flirtatious comments and the seductive glint in her alluring eyes during dinner had caught him off guard.

He had intentionally stayed away from suggestive topics, not wanting to come on strong or make her uncomfortable. He had also decided that he'd take things nice and slow in the early stages of their relationship, especially while they were staying under the same roof. But now, if the signals he was picking up were accurate, she was interested in more than just a romantic dinner tonight.

Kenton moved his chair around to Egypt's side of the table, bringing them close enough to touch lips. He wrapped his arm around her and brushed his mouth over hers. Then lowered his voice. "As for dessert, I was talking about strawberry shortcake, but if you'd prefer something different, maybe something a little more decadent just say the word."

Egypt stared at him for the longest moment, a spark of interest radiating in her eyes, but then she burst out laughing. Falling against him and slapping the table with her hand as if Steve Harvey had just told her a joke.

"What the hell is so funny?"

"You," she said, barely getting the word out around her laughter. "God, you crack me up."

"I wasn't trying to be funny. I was going for sexy, charming, and maybe irresistible, but definitely not funny. It's a good thing I'm not sensitive since you're all up in here laughing in my face."

That only made her crack up more, tears brimming her eyes as she doubled over in the chair, struggling to catch her breath.

This was how Kenton wanted her—carefree and happy. He wanted to keep her laughing, hoping she'd forget about her past and be the lighthearted, cheerful woman he had fallen for.

"Are you done?" he asked in mock disgust, unable to hide the smile pushing its way through.

She giggled and brushed away a couple of tears. "Okay, okay, I'm sorry. I didn't mean to laugh at your seductive efforts, but man, you need to work on your game."

"Wait. You callin' my game lame?"

"Aaand as for dessert," she cupped his cheek, her mouth less than an inch from his, "why don't we make the strawberry shortcake and then see where that leads." Her voice had dropped an octave and the seductive smile on her face was beyond evocative.

Kenton chuckled and moved his chair back to where it was, trying to ignore the way she made his dick twitch. "See, when you say and do shit like that, tempting me with your words and sexy voice, you need to understand something. You're playin' with fire."

"Well, if you'd get your mind out of the gutter, my words and voice would be a non-issue."

Chuckling, Kenton extended his hand to Egypt and led her into the kitchen. Little did she know, it wasn't only her words that turned him on, it was the whole package. Her beauty. Her caring nature and the fact that she could throw down in the kitchen were only a few of her qualities he found endearing. She also laughed at his jokes. What man wouldn't fall for a woman who laughed at his jokes?

"I hope you know how to put this cake together because I don't have a clue." Kenton opened the refrigerator and pulled out the angel food cake, huge strawberries that had been sliced and placed in a glass dish, and whipped cream. "What else do you need? A plate? Bowl?"

Egypt thought for a moment. "If you have more of those large wine glasses, we can use those."

Kenton frowned but pulled down a glass from the top shelf of the cabinet. "You're going to put cake in a wine glass?"

"*We* are going to."

"I think I'm going to pass. Just make one for you."

She opened her mouth to say something, but closed it and got to work on her dessert. She started with the strawberries, putting a few in the glass. Next came cake and then the whipped cream. She repeated the process until the glass was full.

"You sure you don't want some?" she asked, grabbing a

spoon from the utensil drawer. Then they headed back to the table.

"Not right now, but you go ahead. Tell me how it is."

Kenton picked up his wine and drained the glass, but knew he'd need something stronger with the way Egypt was moaning.

Damn, she was killing him tonight. Surely the cake wasn't all that.

"Oh my goodness. This is sooo good. You have to try some." Egypt cut a piece of the cake with her fork and held it out to him, a twinkle sparkling in her eyes.

Yeah, she really was fucking with him, but damn if he didn't like this side of her.

"Open up," she said sweetly.

Leaning forward, Kenton stared into her eyes and did as instructed, allowing her to insert the fork into his mouth. He closed his lips around the utensil, and the sweet taste of strawberries, cake, and whipped cream melted on his tongue.

He didn't know what she was thinking, but the way her eyes zoned in on his mouth as she slowly pulled back the fork, told him all he needed to know.

She wanted him.

"You're right, that is good. You know what would make it better?"

Egypt gulped, eyeing him warily as she set the fork on the table. "No. What would make it better?"

Kenton covered her hand with his before taking her finger and dipping it into the whipped topping. Egypt gasped. Without a word, he brought her long, slender finger to his mouth and slid his lips over the first two joints, allowing his tongue to swirl around the digit.

He loved the way she squirmed in her seat as he licked, teased, and sucked the cream off her finger, as he got caught up in the taste of her sweetness. He didn't miss the pool of heat in her eyes and the way her pupils dilated, which only made him want to taste the rest of her.

He pulled back to the tip, swirling his tongue again

before removing her finger from his mouth. "Yeah, that was much better."

Egypt cleared her throat and slowly eased her hand from his. "Um…alrighty then. How 'bout um…let's um…How about that tour?"

Now Kenton was the one laughing. "See, sweetheart. You ain't ready for all of this, but when you are, I'll be right here waiting for you."

*

After showing Egypt the man cave and game room, located in the walkout basement, Kenton escorted her back to the first floor.

"Why such a big house?" Egypt asked.

"I'm a big guy. I already told you when I bought the truck, I don't like anything small."

"Oh, yeah, that's right," she said dryly, rolling her eyes.

"Come on. Let me show you the alarm system." They headed upstairs. The panel was near the door that led out to the garage. Not only did Supreme provide personal security, but they also installed and monitored home security systems.

"I didn't realize you had the maverick 2000," Egypt said of one of their latest residential systems that the tech team had designed.

"Yeah, it works just like the system at the office, just not as grand. There are two keypads, this one and the one on the top floor near my bedroom."

Egypt knew the basics, but Kenton went through some of the features anyway, pressing a button that brought up the security camera in the backyard, and then the one on the side of the house. For the next few minutes, he explained more than she'd probably ever need to know regarding the system.

Egypt released a noisy yawn then quickly covered her mouth. "Sorry." She gave him an apologetic look.

"No worries. It's been a long day. Come on. I'll show you where you're sleeping. They headed upstairs.

"How many bedrooms do you have?"

"Four, and three and a half bathrooms." They stopped at

the first bedroom at the top of the stairs.

"Pretty room," she said, moving farther into the space.

"My youngest sister, Chelsey, decorated it. She uses this room occasionally when she's not in school, but she won't be back until Thanksgiving."

"She's at the University of Georgia in Athens, right?"

Kenton nodded, surprised she remembered. Egypt had met his younger sister over a year ago, but not the other two.

He watched as she moved around the room. Chelsey had done a good job with the décor. She and Egypt had similar styles, preferring bold colors. The space was decorated in taupe, white, brown with splashes of orange with the throw pillows and pictures hanging on the wall.

"Feel free to change anything you want. If you need furniture moved around, just let me know." He wanted her to be as comfortable as possible, hoping that she'd forget about her situation, even if only for a little while.

"Everything is exquisite."

"If that's the case, you're going to love the bathroom." They moved to the en-suite. At first, Kenton had thought the lavishly decorated bathroom, in the same colors as the bedroom, with a sparkly chandelier, and an oversized soaking tub, were overkill. Now that Egypt would be using the space, he was glad he had agreed to the renovations.

"Wow, you're right. I *love* the bathroom, and I cannot wait to take a bath. This is my dream tub," she said, running her hand along the freestanding chrome faucet hovering over the tub.

"All right, then I'll leave you to it. Unless of course, you need me to wash your back...or any other part of your body," he said, leaning against the door jamb.

Egypt glanced over her shoulder, flashing him that playful smile she'd been tossing his way throughout the evening. "You have been extremely accommodating today. Tell you what. I'll holler if I need you," she said, batting those long eyelashes, her saccharine smile stirring something deep inside of him.

Damn, I've got it bad.

Hours later, Kenton lounged in his man cave, a beer in one hand and the TV remote in the other. An Atlanta Hawks preseason game covered the 55-inch screen mounted on the wall, but Kenton's mind was everywhere but on the game. Egypt had that type of impact on him. The woman already had a special spot in his heart, but tonight, how she flirted with him on a sly, had him thinking about getting her naked.

"That's the last thing she needs right now," he grumbled and took another long drag on his beer. What Egypt needed was for him to be a gentleman while she was under his roof and a friend she could count on. There were moments throughout the night that he couldn't believe she was actually in his house. Sure, she had been to his condo a few times when he had everyone over, but this was different. It was just the two of them, and all he had to do was keep his head and not think about all he wanted to do with her smoking hot body.

Kenton sighed and dropped his head against the leather sofa. It was going to be a long ass night if he couldn't go five minutes without thinking about her. It didn't help that he knew she was upstairs taking a bath. His dick twitched just thinking about her long sinewy body stretched out in the large soaking tub, bubbles gracing every inch of...

He shook his head. The woman had him horny as hell. "I'm so screwed."

Kenton finished his beer and turned off the television. It had been a long day, and he couldn't wait to fall face first into bed. While thinking about plans for the next couple of days, he went through the house, making sure it was locked up and the alarm system armed. Tonight had been about spending time with Egypt and taking her mind off the Pisano situation and the meddling FBI. Tomorrow he'd discuss with her how the protection detail would go.

Kenton shut off the light in the kitchen and headed up the stairs, inhaling as Egypt's scent of lavender and vanilla wafted past his nose. He stopped and released a low groan, a dizzying current of need soaring through his body. If her fragrance turned him on like this, he was in more trouble than he originally thought.

In the past when he needed sexual release, he'd call up Shelly, but he had ended their friends-with-benefits relationship months ago. Shortly after deciding that he wanted Egypt or no one. And since he was trying to be a perfect gentleman, Egypt was out of the question. He was going to have to get himself off if he planned to make it through the night.

Kenton sighed and continued up the stairs, but came to an abrupt stop when smooth, mocha legs came into view on the top landing. Long, shapely legs. Forever legs. His gaze roamed up her body, taking in firm thighs, tiny boy-shorts encasing shapely hips, and a thin V-neck T-shirt that failed to hide big breasts and perky nipples.

Mercy.

He stood gawking, his heart in his throat and his dick, hard as granite, pressing painfully against his zipper. Kenton knew she had an incredible body, but seeing it like this, barely covered, was almost too much to handle. If this was how she dressed around the house, his life was going to be a living hell for the unforeseeable future.

Egypt twisted her hands in front of her and bit her bottom lip, something she'd been doing a lot of lately. "Can I sleep with you?"

Kenton almost swallowed his tongue. "Is that a trick question?" he croaked.

She frowned. "No, it's just...I can't shut my brain off. I figured maybe if I...maybe if I slept with you then I'd be able to get some sleep."

Kenton just stared at her, trying to figure out if she was shitting him. She spoke the words with the innocence of a nun, but there was no way this intelligent woman didn't know what she was doing to him.

"I promise I'll keep my hands to myself," she added as if that was going to make this whole conversation any less strange.

"Sweetheart, it's not your hands I'm worried about." It was her breasts, her ass, her legs, his hands, his dick, and hell, his sanity. There was no way he could lay next to her looking the way she did without him wanting to strip her naked.

Kenton sighed and stomped up the rest of the stairs, knowing that if this was some type of test, he sure as hell was going to fail royally.

He walked past her toward his bedroom at the far end of the hallway but stop and said, "Yeah, sure, you can sleep with me, but not in those," he waved his hands up and down her tempting body, "not in those itty bitty clothes. I'm going to take a shower."

Once he was in his bedroom, he went into his oversized closet, the room that was the selling point for him. He yanked open a drawer in the large center island, grabbed a pair of boxers, then slammed the drawer shut. He hated sleeping in clothes, but one of them had to have clothes on. Otherwise, he couldn't be responsible for whatever happened once they climbed into bed.

Grabbing a shirt, Kenton marched to the bathroom. He was too tired for his self-control to be tested to the extreme by sleeping next to Egypt tonight. But he wanted to be supportive. Knowing that she trusted him, and felt safe with him, meant a lot. He just had to make sure he didn't accidentally roll on top of her, and slide inside of her, and...

Yep, I'm screwed.

After the longest shower he'd ever taken, Kenton took his time drying off. Maybe Egypt would be asleep by the time he got into bed. *If only.* He slipped into a black T-shirt and a pair of boxers and left the bathroom. He took two steps and froze.

"Egypt." The word slipped through his lips, but he wasn't sure if he actually said it out loud. All he could do was stare at the gorgeous goddess standing near the bed—naked.

"I was thinking," she said. "You might've misunderstood me when I asked to sleep with you. I mean, yeah, I eventually want us to sleep, but first…"

When her words trailed off, Kenton stood there dumbfounded. The lamp on the nightstand casted a soft light over her bountiful curves and bronze skin. The shyness radiating on her face, framed by her thick dreadlocks, didn't match the boldness of her actions. Egypt stood poised and confident as he took in her perfection. The woman was enticing in clothes, but without them, she was absolutely breathtaking.

Now, if only he could get his feet to move.

Chapter Twenty-Two

"Clearly, I'm no good at this seduction thing if I'm here and you're way over there." Egypt was way out of her comfort zone and too inexperienced to try and seduce Kenton. What the heck had she been thinking? It was Dakota's fault for putting those thoughts in her head about going after Kenton. All that BS about not missing out on life. Not having any regrets. What a load of crap!

She tried not to fidget under his intense stare, but this was the first time she'd ever stood naked in front of a man. Sure, she'd had a boyfriend in college, but the two times they'd had sex, the lights were off, and their trysts had been over before they started good. Heck, she couldn't even remember if they'd taken off their clothes.

I'm never listening to Dakota again.

Egypt picked up her T-shirt from the floor. "Maybe I shouldn't have—"

"Let me get this right," Kenton finally said, moving slowly across the room like a panther easing up on its prey. "You've been flirting with me all night with the intent of seducing me?"

Though he still looked larger than life at well over six feet tall and shoulders as wide as a doorway, he seemed less intimidating in the dark T-shirt that stretched across his broad chest. The last time she'd seen him in underwear, he'd had on boxer briefs that showed off how well-endowed he was and highlighted his tree-trunk like legs. Tonight, he wore striped boxers.

"You don't really seem like the boxer type guy."

Crap! Did I say that out loud?

By his raised brows, she had.

But she didn't miss the lust radiating in his eyes as he stood within an arms-length. "Yes," she finally said. "I was trying to get your attention."

Kenton chuckled. "Well, you have my attention.

His large hand slid around her bare waist, and Egypt's heart rate kicked up, anxiety pulsed through her veins. She was more than ready to take their relationship to the next level. Yet, she was still holding her T-shirt in front of her, like a shield, as if it was enough to cover her nakedness.

Kenton didn't seem to care, he pulled her close, smelling like fresh, clean laundry and kissed the tip of her nose, and then her cheek before he finally kissed her mouth. The T-shirt she held slipped from her fingers and Egypt gripped the front of his shirt to hold on for the ride. His tenderness melted her heart, and she molded against him. She loved how he made her feel special and desired while being thoughtful and patient. No man had ever made her want to give her all to him.

Without warning, Kenton released her. Tugging on the back collar of his T-shirt, he pulled it over his head, letting it fall to the carpeted floor.

Egypt's breath caught at the sight of his dark, muscular chest, thick biceps, and a six-pack that didn't look real. The man had a body that should be featured on the cover of *Muscle & Fitness* magazine. But it was when her attention went lower, witnessing the way his boxers tented, did Egypt's mouth go dry. She already knew he was packing, but when he dropped his underwear, heat spread through her body like a California wildfire, singeing everything in its wake. Nothing could've prepared her for the sight of his massive erection, proving that everything about the man was huge.

Egypt's pulse raced when Kenton stepped forward in all of his naked glory. He lifted her into his strong arms, and she gasped. She wasn't sure what she expected but hadn't considered him carrying her the short distance to the bed.

He laid her on the king sized mattress and stood above her, his gaze roaming down her body, and lingering on her breasts. Her nipples pebbled to harden peaks under his perusal. With the rhythm of her heartbeat revving up, Egypt couldn't take much more of his examination, and she fought to control the keen desire to beg him to take her fast and hard.

"You are exquisite," he whispered, finally climbing onto the bed. "I'm going to enjoy taking my time getting acquainted with every inch of this gorgeous body."

Kenton claimed her mouth. Crushing her to him in a sizzling kiss that promised so much more.

She'd had countless dreams about them being together like this, sharing a part of herself with the only man she ever truly wanted. And now that he was laying next to her, chest to chest and thigh to thigh, it didn't seem real. But Kenton was very real.

His hand slowly glided down her side doing a lust-arousing exploration as he caressed and his warm hands squeezed. Everywhere he touched, electric currents of desire shot through Egypt's body, and she couldn't get enough of the way his mouth worshiped hers, nipping at her lower lip, then the top one.

Egypt appreciated him taking their lovemaking slow, but she'd waited so long for this moment. Her deprived body couldn't wait much longer to feel him deep inside of her. In the meantime, she did her own exploring, her hands grazing over the sinewy muscles of his chest and biceps, loving how they contracted beneath her touch.

As if to prove his point, Kenton's lips traced a slow, sensuous path down the center of Egypt's body, lingering at every curve. Undeterred by her whimpers and her trembling beneath him, his tongue roamed over her nipple, pulling it into his mouth. Licking. Sucking. His teeth scraped over the sensitive bud and Egypt arched her back off the bed as a pool of potent heat charged through her body.

"Kenton," she breathed, squirming and squeezing her legs together, the sensational ache between them growing more demanding.

Without a word, he ran a hand over her flat stomach and didn't stop until he reached the V between her thighs. Egypt moaned, spreading her legs wider when he entered her first with one finger, then added another.

Kenton reclaimed her lips, kissing her passionately as his long, tapered fingers circled and slid in and out of her core. "God, you're so tight and wet," he mumbled against her mouth.

She couldn't speak, could barely think as she moved with each thrust, feeling her control slipping as deep pleasure swirled inside of her, mounting like a tropical storm.

Her breaths came in short spurts, and she gripped Kenton's arm, digging her nails into his skin while she rode his hand. Her head thrashed back and forth against the pillow as Kenton's pace increased, his fingers pumping deeper, and faster while the pad of his thumb massaged her clit.

She couldn't hold on. "Ke-Kenton, I'm com—"

"That's it. Come for me, baby."

As if his words had the power to make her do just that, a spine-tingling orgasm tore through Egypt hard and powerful. She fisted the bed sheet as wave after wave of pleasure roared through her body, and her world spun, careening out of control.

Oh. My. Goodness.

With her chest heaving, and her eyes closed tightly, she struggled to get air into her lungs. Never in her life had she experienced anything so erotically powerful. The release took her breath away, and she feared her heart rate would never level out.

Kenton moved away, and airbrushed across her damp

skin, but she was too spent to open her eyes.

Moments later, Kenton's hand was on one of her legs. His potent touch awakening something indescribable within her. When he placed a kiss on her eyelid, and then on the other, Egypt smiled at his tenderness, slowly opening her eyes.

"You okay?" he kissed her sweetly.

"Better than okay."

"Good, because that was just the first round."

*

Wedged between Egypt's firm thighs, Kenton hovered above her, unable to resist kissing her sweet lips. He was still blown away that she had come to him boldly and ready. And watching her climax moments ago was like witnessing a glowing image of fire for the first time. It had taken every bit of his self-control not to bury himself deep inside of her at that moment, but the next time she was hit with an orgasm, it would be around his shaft.

He reached over and grabbed a condom from the nightstand, and quickly covered himself. "I'll never be able to get enough of you," he murmured, kissing her lips and feeling her smile.

Egypt framed his face between her soft hands, forcing him to look at her. "Good because you're mine, and don't you forget it."

Where had that come from? Kenton had already considered her his, but hearing her say the words with such conviction did something to him.

"Staking your claim, huh?"

"Yep, so tell all of those women who be fawning over you at Dakota's dojo that you are *not* available."

Ahh, so that's what this is about. Dakota must have said something. Kenton didn't care what made Egypt finally admit her feelings and opened herself to him. He was just glad she had. "Sweetheart, I'm all yours."

Kenton hadn't been in an exclusive relationship since college. Even then he didn't feel the deep emotions he held for Egypt. She was in his heart, a part of him, and he had no intention of ever letting her go.

He sealed their agreement with a kiss that quickly turned fiery, and their tongues tangled as he ground against her. He had waited a long time to have her like this, and he planned to cherish and love on her until they were both sated. Besides that, kissing her was quickly becoming an addiction.

His pulse galloped as he caressed her, appreciating every dip and curve of her sexy body. His lips left hers to nibble on her earlobe before going lower and exploring her soft, sweetly scented flesh. Egypt moved beneath him, urging him on as her soft hands caressed his back, his arms. The heat from her touch and the taste of her skin had Kenton hard as stone. Soon he'd need to be inside of her.

With each peck of his lips, her body arched into him, and her breathing increased, sending Kenton's need to exponential levels. Nudging her legs, Kenton positioned himself, the tip of his length teasing at her entrance. But when she tensed beneath him, he glanced down, and her eyes were shut tight.

He moved some of her dreadlocks, pushing them away from her forehead and caressed her cheeks. "Relax, sweetie." Kenton teased her lips with gentle kisses as he eased into her sweet heat. "We'll take it slow, okay?"

She nodded, the hold she had on his arm loosened a little as her eyes drifted closed again and she moaned in pleasure. As promised, Kenton entered her slowly, allowing her tight body to get used to his size. Being inside of her felt incredible, and it was harder than he thought trying to take this slow when what he wanted to do was dive in and go hard. But he didn't want to hurt her.

Soon Egypt relaxed and boldly gripped his butt, increasing their connection as she pulled him in deeper. At this rate, there was no way in hell he'd be able to glide in and out of her slowly for long.

Next time.

Kenton braced himself on one elbow, grabbed her right

butt cheek and lifted her slightly for a better angle. "Damn, you feel good," he murmured, gritting his teeth as her inner muscles tightened around him. He slid in and out of her, marveling at how perfect they fit together. His pace increased, and Egypt matched him stroke for stroke as they moved in sync, creating their own rhythm.

His mouth covered hers, and he kissed her with an intensity that matched the pleasure building inside of him. The degree to which she responded was almost overwhelming as their moans blended. Kenton pushed deeper, harder, his pace increasing with each thrust. The way Egypt clawed at his back, she was as close to her release as he was to his, but he wasn't ready for this to be over.

Egypt ripped her mouth from his. "Kenton," she gasped, tightening around his length. He cursed under his breath when she wrapped her long, smooth legs around his waist, pulling him in even deeper and sending pleasure shooting to every nerve in his body.

His pace increased, and Kenton hoped he wasn't hurting her, but adrenaline pulsed through his body and he couldn't slow down. He also couldn't hold on much longer with the way she lifted her hips off the bed.

"Kenton!" Egypt cried, her nails digging into his arms again as she bucked and jerked uncontrollably.

The turbulence from her climax was like an igniter. Heat charged through him, exploding in a downpour of fiery sensation as the intensity spun him out of control. Erotic pleasure flooded his body, zapping what little energy he had left as he growled his release before collapsing on top of her.

"Damn, that was…" Kenton couldn't find the words as he panted against Egypt's neck until her ragged breaths met his ears. He quickly lifted up and rolled onto his back. "Amazing," he said.

"Yeah," Egypt rasped, her hand finding his and squeezing as they lay there for a moment.

Sated, Kenton pulled her against his body. He had no doubt they'd be good together, but making love to her had exceeded anything he could've imagined. Resting his chin on top of her head, his heart rate finally slowed and he basked in what they'd just shared.

Kenton cradled Egypt in the crook of his arm. This was where she belonged, right beside him.

"That was wonderful," she mumbled his same sentiment and slung her arm across his chest, while her soft, smooth leg draped over his thigh keeping him from moving. "For a few hours this evening, with dinner, laughter, and loving on me, you did what I didn't think was possible. You made me forget about my past. Thank you."

Kenton kissed the side of her head, glad he could help her forget. A few minutes later, he went to the bathroom to get cleaned up. By the time he returned to the bed, Egypt was sound asleep.

"There's nothing I wouldn't do for you," he whispered, his heart swelling as he thought about how important she was to him. Tomorrow they'd revisit her past, but right now, all he wanted to do was sleep with Egypt wrapped in his arms.

He turned off the lamp on the nightstand and reclaimed his spot on the bed, pulling her back into his arms. When Kenton closed his eyes, that same peace he usually felt whenever she was near, settle over him, and he drifted off to sleep.

Chapter Twenty-Three

With her eyes closed, Egypt snuggled deeper into the pillow, her mind relaxed. The pitter-patter of rain slapping against the windowpane lulled her into a peaceful state. It didn't hurt that she was completely satiated after a couple of rounds of mind-blowing sex.

Her lips kicked up into a smile as she recalled the night before and their 3 a.m. tryst when Kenton had awakened her, his erection pressing against her butt. The man had more energy than the Energizer bunny, but she couldn't complain. Muscles that hadn't been used in years ached, but oh what a delicious ache between her thighs.

Finally opening her eyes, she was surprised to see Kenton, propped up on his elbow staring at her. He smiled, and she couldn't help smiling back. They studied each other, grinning as if they held the world's greatest secret.

"Good morning," he said, his deep baritone washing over her like a tantalizing caress.

"Good morning." She yawned and stretched out her arms before snuggling back into the pillow. "How long have you been watching me sleep?"

"Not long. You looked so peaceful. I didn't want to wake you." He stretched out his long arm and pulled her closer, then kissed her sweetly.

Egypt could get used to this. Great sex, waking up to this handsome man, and feeling cherished like she was the most important person in the world. She had waited a long time to experience something this special.

"You make me happy," she blurted, the words flying out without much thought, but they were true. An overwhelming amount of happiness flowed through her like warm honey, and she never wanted to lose this sense of calm and joy.

"I'm glad, but if you would've started dating me sooner, you could've been feeling like this months ago."

Egypt rolled her eyes. She turned onto her back, holding the covers over her bare breasts. "Whatever. Can't you just accept a compliment or kind words without being a know it all?"

"I can't help it if I can see into the future as it relates to us."

"So what else do you know?" Normally, she wouldn't bother stoking this type of conversation, but she'd be lying if she wasn't curious about what he thought.

"We're going to get married, have a few children and then have a long, happy life together," Kenton said simply with all the confidence of a psychic.

Egypt turned on her side to face him, and a stab of longing gripped her. She hadn't been happy in so long, she was cautious to hope for more. "I like the sound of that, but I don't know enough about you."

"You know me better than most, but what else do you want to know?" He ran the back of his fingers down her cheek, and Egypt's eyes drifted closed at the tenderness of his touch. "I'll tell you anything, but not until I scrounge up something for us to eat. I'd be willing to guess that you either haven't had breakfast in bed or haven't had it often enough."

"You'd be right." Occasionally she prepared breakfast for herself and ate in bed, but no man had ever served her breakfast in bed. "So how are you going to do this if you can't cook?"

"Don't' underestimate your man. I'll have you know that

I can do a little somethin' somethin' in the kitchen."

Egypt laughed. She was pretty sure he was talking about more than cooking if the mischievous grin on his face and twinkle in his eyes were any indication.

"That may be, but can you cook?"

He planted a quick kiss on her lips. "You'll see. Be right back."

Egypt watched him slip into a pair of basketball shorts and head out the room. She leaped out of bed and put on the black T-shirt Kenton had discarded the night before. Bringing the collar of the shirt to her nose, she inhaled his scent and padded off to her bedroom. After quickly brushing her teeth and freshening up, she returned to his room, the smell of bacon flowing up the stairs.

Maybe he can cook.

A few minutes later when he returned with a tray, she got her answer.

"A banana, box of cereal, bacon, milk, and orange juice are not really cooking."

"I didn't say I would cook. I promised breakfast in bed, and here you have it." He set the tray over her lap and then climbed in on the other side. "Besides, I know how to microwave bacon. As far as I'm concerned, that's cooking."

They ate from the same tray, and Egypt hadn't realized just how hungry she was until she finished off her first bowl of cereal and two pieces of bacon. "Okay, I have to say, I haven't had cereal in like forever, and these Cocoa Pebbles are good. I can't believe you eat cereal."

Kenton shrugged. "I'm a bachelor. Cereal is a staple in my house."

"Well, if we're going to date, you're going to have to learn to cook more than just bacon."

"Well, if we're dating, you can do all of the cooking, since that's what you enjoy," he added quickly when she started to protest. "And I'll take care of everything else."

"Everything else like what?" she asked, pouring another bowl of Cocoa Pebbles, thinking that the sweet breakfast cereal might become a staple in her household too.

"Like cleaning up the kitchen after you cook, washing your back when you take a bath, and..." He thought for a long time, and Egypt couldn't wait to hear what else he would do for her. So far, she liked his list. "And I'll be the one taking care of all of your sexual needs."

"Oh," she said, unsure of what she expected him to say, but it hadn't been that. "Okay. I think I can get with that." She stared down at the bowl in her hand as heat rose to her cheeks, and she recalled all of the scandalous things he had done to her body the night before. Instead of commenting more, she said, "Tell me something I don't know about you."

He sat back, leaning against the headboard while he sipped his juice. "Well, you already know I have three sisters. But I don't remember if I ever told you that my dad raised us after my mother died when I was twelve."

"How did she die?" Egypt asked, thinking about her own family.

"She was killed during a bank robbery."

"Oh my, God." Egypt's heart thudded against her chest. "I didn't know. That's awful."

"Yeah, it was tough. My dad took it hard. She was everything to him, to us. For that first year, my oldest sister, who had just turned seventeen, kept things going around the house, at least until my father was able to get himself together. That was around the time she was getting ready to go to college. Both my parents insisted that education be a priority, and though my sister had offered to take a couple of years off, my dad wouldn't hear of it."

Egypt listened as he told story after story about his childhood and his father. It was clear that Kenton looked up to him, appreciating how his dad supported and encouraged all of them through school, their various extra-curricular sports and had even helped pay for college. Listening to him, she couldn't help but think about her childhood. Her family didn't have much, but she remembered the good times, the times before the trials.

"I've been wanting to ask you about your family," Kenton said. He moved the tray and set it on the bench at the foot of the bed. "Tell me about them."

"We were your typical, low to middle-class family. Both my parents worked, barely making ends meet most months, but made sure my brother and I did well in school. We went on at least one family vacation a year. Usually during spring break and to someplace warm and near water, like Florida."

Amusement bubbled inside of her, recalling one particular trip. "When I was about ten, and my brother was seven, we were in Orlando playing miniature golf. I can't remember exactly how it happened, but there was a hill near one of the holes and my dad's golf ball rolled down. Instead of going around and using the sidewalk to get to it, he went down the hill, somehow tripped midway and ended up tumbling head over heels all the way to the bottom. My brother and I fell out laughing. Mom joined in once she made sure he was okay."

Kenton laughed, his arm around Egypt's shoulder. It was amazing how being close to him made the memories, good and bad, not as painful.

"My parents used their sense of humor, and that helped us get through tough times, especially during financial troubles. For the most part, my childhood was good…until my uncle was killed and then the trial. When we went into WITSEC, it wasn't as hard on me and my brother as it was for my parents, especially my mom."

Her mother never liked change, especially when it meant leaving everything and everyone they knew behind. She hated the situation even more when they had to pick up and move without notice, twice.

Kenton pulled Egypt close and kissed the top of her head. "We don't have to talk—"

"I want you to know everything about me, especially since you plan on marrying me."

He laughed. Egypt might've been joking a little, but it felt good to share her past with someone, someone who

174

cared. Her life had been lonely for so long.

"For years I regretted being out that night, sorry that my thoughtlessness had destroyed my family. My father reassured me that I wasn't at fault; that everything happened for a reason. Deep down I knew he was right, but still some days guilt would eat at me." She paused for a moment, her painful reality too hard to absorb. "I thought I'd never recover when they died."

"When did they die?"

"A little over seven years ago in a boating accident. That's what the report said, but I never believed it was an accident."

"Why not?"

"After some digging, Nelson said that a fellow marshal thought that the investigation wasn't thorough and that it reeked of shadiness. My parents and my brother weren't boaters, knew nothing about boating, yet they were on a vessel by themselves."

"Yeah, I can see where that would be a little suspicious."

"The skipper of the boat contracts to take people out on Lake Washington all the time, but for some reason, he didn't accompany my family. According to the authorities, the owner said that my parents paid him double, so they could go out on their own. But two witnesses swore there were four people on the boat. Yet, only three bodies were recovered."

Egypt didn't know what was true, but she trusted Nelson's judgment. He'd dug into the incident on her behalf since no one involved in the case knew she existed. He never could get solid answers, running into one roadblock after another.

"Sometimes I wonder why my life was spared and theirs were taken," Egypt said. She was the only one left in her family, and despite the guilt, that had been her driving force to make something of herself.

"I hate what happened to your family, and all that you've been through, but I'm glad your life was spared. Call me selfish, but I believe you're on this earth for me."

Egypt knew by his tone that Kenton was serious, but she couldn't help laughing. When he frowned at her, asking what was so funny, she laughed even harder. Before he came into her life, she had never laughed so much. If for nothing else, she really did hope that his prediction of them being together for a lifetime was true.

"Okay, so now that you're done laughing at me, I have some questions." His hold around her waist tightened, and Egypt had a feeling she wasn't going to like this next line of questioning.

"How old are you?" he asked.

"You know it's not nice to ask a woman her age."

"I figured if it's *my* woman, it should be okay. Am I wrong?"

She started to tell him that she was thirty-six which would be in line with her latest identification. Yet, Kenton wanted to learn more about the real her, the person she was before she finally became Egypt Durand.

"I'll be thirty-three on my next birthday."

"So you're not thirty-six," he mumbled. "We usually celebrate your birthday on April 7th, I assume that's not your real birthday."

"It's January 17th"

Kenton shook his head. "So you've had two different identities?"

"Three, but I've had my current one the longest."

"Dammit. No one should have to go through what you've been through. It couldn't have been easy keeping the details straight."

"It wasn't too bad since I rarely let anyone get close. I might not think highly of law enforcement, but after the trial, whoever was responsible for changing our identities did a good job. We didn't have any trouble as far as getting jobs. And when I left WITSEC, Nelson took care of me and my new identity. I remember him saying, '*I know a guy.*'"

Kenton grunted. "Yeah, he's kind of like Laz and Myles in that respect. With the connections those fellas have, they could rule the country. So, what's your birth name?"

After a long hesitation, Egypt looked at him. She hadn't used the name in so long, it felt weird just thinking about it. "Paige McCurry."

He nodded. "Paige," he said the name as if testing it out.

Egypt could understand him being curious, but she had no intention of going by that name again. That was her past, and she planned to leave it all behind. Thanks to him, she was finally looking forward to the future.

Egypt scooted down in the bed and sighed. Snuggling into the pillow again, she was glad it was Saturday and that neither of them had to work.

Kenton laid facing her, his arm around her waist. "I think Egypt fits you. Regal and queenly. It's also fitting since you're the queen at Supreme."

Egypt smiled, not wanting to tell him the name actually meant *troubles*. She had chosen it anyway, feeling that it sounded strong and powerful, something she was trying to aspire to at the time.

"How many kids do you want?" she asked, more than ready to change the subject.

"Are you offering to be my babies' mama?" Kenton asked without missing a beat, and Egypt laughed. She loved how easily he rolled with things.

"Would you just answer the question?"

"Hmm…that wasn't a no," Kenton tease, rubbing his body against hers until she pushed against his chest still laughing. "Okay, seriously though. I want three. Two boys and a girl."

Egypt brows dipped, eyeing him suspiciously. "Really?"

"Yeah," he stretched out the word, "Why does it sound like you don't believe me?"

"It's not that I don't believe you. I'm just surprised because *one day* I want to have three also. Two boys and a baby girl."

Kenton studied her for a second. "See, that's just another reason why I know we're destined to be together. So when should we get started? You're not getting any younger."

Her mouth dropped open and then she punched him playfully. "You should talk. You're older than I am."

"True, which is why I'm thinking we need to quit messing around and get to work." He hovered above her and lifted the T-shirt she was wearing over her head and stared down at her. "I like your tattoo. I noticed it last night, but you were such a distraction, I didn't get a chance to comment on it."

"I got it to cover the stab wound."

He nodded. "I figured as much," he said before lowering his head and placing a soft kiss on the tattoo. Egypt felt the sweet gesture to her soul.

The laceration had been an inch and a half long and healed well, but Egypt hated seeing the small scar. It kept reminding her of that horrible day. The tattoo, a heart-shaped locket with a chain hanging from it, also reminded her of the past, but in a different way. She imagined a picture of her family locked away in the locket, and where she went, they were with her.

"We were talking about kids a moment ago, but what else do you want?" Kenton asked, hovering above her. "Do you have like a bucket list of goals that you want to accomplish?"

Egypt thought about that for a moment as she ran her hands up his hard chest. Her body suddenly stirred with need wanting nothing more than to make love to him. But instead of voicing that thought, she said, "I don't have a bucket list. All I've ever wanted was a normal life where I wouldn't have to keep looking over my shoulder, and I also hope to get married someday. What about you? What do you want?"

"Right now, all I want is you."

When Kenton lowered his head, he gave her a slow, drugging kiss and all thoughts of the past flew from Egypt's mind. All she could think about at that moment was how this incredibly sweet man gave her hope that her future would be better than her past.

Chapter Twenty-Four

Releasing Egypt's hand, Kenton yanked a shopping cart free from the long row of carts and followed her into the grocery store. The smell of freshly baked bread and fried chicken battled for first place, enticing his senses. Normally he wouldn't notice since he usually ran in, grabbed a couple of items and then left. This visit would be different in more ways than one. Based on Egypt's list, they would be there awhile.

After spending two days under his roof, loving on each other and getting to know one another better, it had been time to get some fresh air and food. They were down to a half a box of cereal and mostly empty shelves in the refrigerator. The moment Egypt had offered to cook him dinner was all the encouragement he needed to head off to the supermarket.

"Usually, I'd be more than happy to push the cart for you, but I'm going to need to be able to keep at least one of my hands free." At her questioning gaze, he bent close to her ear and explained. "Protecting you is my first priority."

"Oh, yeah. Actually, this is a first for me," Egypt said, bagging three blemish-free zucchinis and placing them in the cart. "In all of my adult life, I have never been grocery shopping with a man by my side."

"I plan on there being many more firsts for us. If it makes you feel any better, this is a first for me too, outside of going with my sisters, of course." He leaned down and pressed a kiss across her red lips. "Now, what can I do to hurry this along?"

Egypt smiled and shook her head. "Normally you're the most patient person I know. I think I just found the chink in your armor."

Kenton gave a slight shrug and stayed close as Egypt moved around the produce area, smelling, squeezing and picking over fruits and vegetables. He loved being with her, and even though he hated shopping, he had to admit that the domestic chore was a little more appealing with her by his side.

"Are you allergic to anything?" she asked placing a bag of onions in the cart.

"Nope. I'll eat anything if you're cooking."

"I'm going to love cooking for you. Not just because you're a big eater, but it sounds like you'll try anything at least once. How does steak, red potatoes, and asparagus sound to you?"

"It sounds great, especially if you leave off the asparagus."

She stopped. "You just said you would eat anything I cook."

"And I will, but asparagus wouldn't be my first choice of vegetables."

"So instead of asking if you were allergic to anything, I should've asked is there anything you don't like."

For the next thirty minutes, they roamed the store with Kenton sharing his food likes and dislikes. He'd been honest about eating whatever she cooked, but the fact that she wanted to make what he liked only made him love her more.

"A little help here," Egypt said, stretching for a bottle of lemon juice out of her reach on the top shelf.

"How many?" he asked.

"Just one."

Kenton put the juice in the basket, then placed his hand on the small of her back as they moved down the aisle. He found any excuse to touch her. He saw her almost every day at work for the last few years, but living with Egypt had taken his need to be close to her to another level.

"So, what do we have here?" came a familiar voice from behind them.

Kenton smiled, but Egypt stiffened and moved closer to him. He wrapped his arm around her waist, his hand resting on her hip before he turned to his long-time friend.

"Dang, they just let anybody in this store," he cracked, and Egypt relaxed her shoulders. Moving his arm from around her, Kenton extended his hand to Caleb, pulling him in for a man hug.

"Now I see why you've been avoiding my calls." Caleb's appreciative gaze took in Egypt.

"Sweetheart, this is a good friend of mine, Caleb Zander. Caleb, this is Egypt Durand."

Caleb extended his hand to Egypt. "Well, I'll be damn. I've heard a lot about you, but I was starting to think you were a figment of his imagination."

Egypt smiled and shook his hand, not moving from Kenton's side. If anything, she seemed to move closer. She had to know he wouldn't introduce her to just anyone.

"I'm a little surprised to see you grocery shopping." Kenton nodded toward the handbasket Caleb carried. He was also surprised to see how disheveled Caleb appeared, a wrinkled button-down shirt that was partially untucked, stained jeans, and muddy boots. That wasn't like Caleb.

"I'm not here by choice. The wife needed me to stop and pick up a few items on my way home."

"You doin' all right, man?" Kenton asked, still thrown off by Caleb's unkempt appearance. The scraggly beard was new, and so was the fading bruise on his left jaw.

"Oh yeah. I'm fine. I was at a buddy's house. A few of us helped him move and then headed over to Steve's place to watch the game. So, Egypt I hear you run things at Supreme.

Must be kind of hard keeping fellas like this guy in line."

They all stood around talking for a few minutes. Kenton and Caleb tossed verbal jabs back and forth and even got Egypt involved in the conversation. But she didn't seem as engaged as usual.

"Man, I'd love to stand around chatting with you," Kenton said sarcastically, "but we need to get going."

Caleb glanced down at his phone before holding it up and squinting. "Yeah, me too. Why don't we all get together sometime? I'll need to check with Dora, but let's plan for some time soon."

Kenton nodded. "Sounds good, man. I'll be in touch."

Kenton and Egypt continued down the aisle and up another. "What's wrong? All of a sudden you seem off."

Egypt grabbed a bag of flour, sugar, and cornmeal from the shelves and placed them in the cart. "Nothing really. I was a little um…what made you think I was uncomfortable?"

"You didn't move from my side, and your responses to his questions were stiff. I also could feel the tension bouncing off of you."

"I was a little uncomfortable with the way he kept looking at me."

Kenton stopped her from moving with a hand on her arm. He waited until a woman with a baby in the cart and a child holding onto the side passed. "Uncomfortable how?"

She shrugged. "I don't know, just uncomfortable. Like he was studying me each time he asked me a question. I know it sounds crazy. It was just a feeling. I'm sure it was nothing."

Kenton pulled her into his arms and kissed the side of her head. "It doesn't sound crazy at all. You should always pay attention to your intuition, your gut, or anything else that might keep you safe. Caleb was a therapist for the FBI. Now he has his own practice. I met him years ago when we both worked for the agency. He's a good listener, and the only thing I can say about his invasive behavior is that he listens with his eyes and ears. He pays attention to facial expressions, movements, and everything else. I wouldn't overthink it if I were you."

Besides his grubby clothes, Kenton hadn't noticed anything out of the norm with Caleb, but Egypt had been looking out for herself for a long time. He didn't want her to doubt or ignore any discomfort she felt with anyone. Intuition and gut feelings had saved his life more than once.

A few minutes later, and they were in the truck and leaving the parking lot.

"Do you mind if we go to my place after dinner? I want to check the mail and pick up a few items."

"Sure, unless you want to go now."

"Nah, later is okay. You mentioned you and Caleb meeting while working for the FBI. Did you guys leave the agency at the same time, for the same reason?"

Kenton maneuvered his vehicle down the highway, thinking about his time at the FBI. "No. I resigned after an op went bad. We were ambushed. I lost a witness and my best friend."

"Oh no. Kenton, I didn't know. What happened? Were you hurt?"

He told her about the trial, Santana, and how she'd been one of his confidential informants for years. Kenton's hands tightened on the steering wheel while he verbalized all that had happened the day he and his friends were attacked. But he left out the part about there being a traitor at their agency, someone who had given their location to the DeLevese gang.

"I'm so sorry for your loss."

"That time is a prime example of why you should trust your gut. Deep down I knew it was too risky. Yet, I put our lives in danger."

"Surely you don't blame yourself. You couldn't have known you guys would get attacked. Besides, you and Quaid were trying to do something special for Santana by honoring her *one* request." Egypt squeezed his hand. "You said that was the only thing she asked for before being carted off to God knows where. I didn't know her, but I'm sure she wouldn't want you blaming yourself for something you really couldn't control."

In his heart, Kenton knew Egypt was right about Santana, but he also knew he should've made different decisions that day. No, he couldn't have known there was a dirty agent in the FBI, but he could have declined Santana's request. Then she and Quaid would be alive.

"I know I blame the FBI and the U.S. Marshals for everything bad that happened to my family and me," Egypt said. "I also truly believe there were some instances they handled poorly. But if I'm honest with myself, I also know that sometimes crap happens despite the best-laid plans. The people who attacked you guys are to blame. Not you."

They drove the rest of the way in silence, but memories of all those years ago rattled in Kenton's mind. Yeah, he made mistakes back then, he just couldn't make them again. Egypt's life might depend on him.

Chapter Twenty-Five

Hours later, they pulled onto Egypt's street. As they drove passed one home after another, Egypt felt as though she'd been gone more than a couple of days. She was already getting comfortable at Kenton's place. When this nightmare ended, how would she be able to return to her quiet, little house and her lonely, empty life? Even though she and Kenton were now dating, chances were, she wouldn't see him every night. She'd fall back into long work days, eating alone, and everything else that composed her solitary life.

Egypt shook her head. *Think positive. No more loneliness.* She was going to get her happily-ever-after, with Kenton.

"Remind me to turn a lamp on before we leave," she said after Kenton stopped in front of the house instead of pulling into the long driveway leading to the detached garage in the back of the house. "Why don't you ever park in the driveway?"

"I like being able to see the truck as I approach. Fewer blind spots."

Egypt thought about that as he climbed out and walked around to the passenger side then opened her door. Kenton stayed close as they walked up the stairs.

"We need to install some floodlights in front of the bushes," he said. "Even if the inside of the house was

185

illuminated, it would still be too dark out here."

"Maybe I'll talk to the landlord. I don't want to put any more money in this place. I put up new blinds, changed the floor in the kitchen and had a security system installed. That's it for my improvements."

They stopped at the door, and Kenton glanced back at the street. "Remember what I said earlier. When we go inside, you stay near the door until I check things out."

Egypt nodded and let them in. Mail from the shoot in the door was on the floor in the front entrance. She stepped over the envelopes, turned on the hall light, and hurried to get to the alarm panel. Egypt started punching in the numbers when she realized the system wasn't beeping.

Her hand hovered over the buttons. "Kenton," she said quietly, glancing around the living room and dining area, but not seeing anything out of place. He had already started looking around and was heading down the short hall to the bedrooms.

Egypt didn't know what he heard in her voice, but he turned, his dark eyes locking with hers. His right arm was behind his back. No doubt his hand was on his weapon.

"What is it?" he said.

"My alarm system was disarmed. I'm almost positive I turned it on before we left."

He nodded. "You did. I saw you." He checked the front door lock then reached for her hand. "Stay close to me. We'll clear the place together," he whispered.

He had already looked into the coat closet, the kitchen and they headed down the short hall. The place was so small. It didn't take long to peek into closets, her office and then check her bedroom. No one was inside.

"Does anything look out of place?" Kenton asked while they stood in her bedroom.

Egypt didn't touch anything, but walked around, trying to remember how she left the space. She was a little OCD in putting things away, closing doors and drawers, and making sure everything was in its place. But she had been in a hurry before leaving. She hadn't left anything laying out but looking around, she couldn't be sure that she hadn't left the closet door ajar or the shower curtain pulled back.

Egypt pointed those things out to Kenton, panic swirling inside of her. Someone had disarmed her alarm and roamed around her house. She was trying not to freak out. When they returned to the kitchen, Egypt noticed a couple of other things askew. The notepad that she usually kept on the counter for her grocery list had been moved to the center of the counter. Usually it was kept near the wall. Also, the curtain over the small window that looked out to the neighbor's house was open. She never looked out that window.

There was something else.

"My favorite mug is gone," she said, unable to control the trembling in her voice.

"How do you know?" Kenton asked, his hand resting on her hip. He had no idea how much she appreciated his presence, offering a calm she didn't feel.

"After I use it, I always wash and place it back on the Keurig cup tray. It's not here."

"You think someone stole the mug?" Kenton asked frowning. "Why would they—"

"Why would someone disarm my alarm? If they can do that, I wouldn't put anything past them," she snapped. After a few frustrating breaths, Egypt realized she was lashing out at the wrong person. "I'm sorry. I shouldn't take this out on you."

Kenton held her close and kissed the top of her head. Something he'd been doing often. Then he pulled out his phone.

"Who are you contacting?"

Instead of telling her, he turned the phone around and showed her the screen.

Laz.

He put his finger to his lips for her to be quiet.

Oh no. He thinks the place is bugged.

187

He sent off the text, and Laz responded immediately. The former police detective was one of the best and would stop at nothing to get answers.

Egypt tapped her forehead with the palm of her hand as she thought of something else. Leaning in close to Kenton's ear, she said, "I have two surveillance cameras."

Kenton's brows lifted, and he directed her to the front entrance. She thought they were going to walk out, but they didn't. "Are they attached to the alarm system?" he asked in her ear, and she shook her head. They whispered back and forth.

"I bought them a couple of months ago. I rarely think about them." She pulled out her cell phone and found the app. While she did that, Kenton moved around the small space and then went to the back door.

"Sweetheart, come here." He directed his attention out the small window that overlooked the backyard. He pointed outside, and she saw that the garage door was partially opened.

"Is your car in the garage?"

Egypt nodded. She reached for the doorknob, but Kenton caught her hand before she touched it. "Whoever was here, came through this door. It's unlocked. Show me where the cameras are," he whispered in her ear.

Kenton followed her to the living room, and she pointed out the thin, six-inch camera that was on the book stand. No one would ever notice it amongst the books and a few knickknacks unless they were looking for the device. Then she led him to her bedroom and pointed to the heating and air vent.

Egypt handed him her cell phone. Part of her wanted to see the video, but a pulsating fear kept her from leaning over his shoulder. She really didn't want to know who'd been lurking inside of her home. While Kenton watched the footage, Egypt folded her arms across her chest and paced the living room, still disturbed that someone had gone through her stuff. She didn't have much, and there was nothing of importance in the house, but still.

"Sonof…" Kenton growled under his breath. Then wiped his hand over his mouth and down his perfectly trimmed goatee.

"Do I know the per…who is it? Just tell me."

Before Kenton could respond, there was a light tap on the living room window. He held onto her phone and went to the door, his gun at his side. After looking through the peephole, Kenton let him in.

Egypt's pulse pounded in her ear. Anxiousness roared through her body. Kenton either knew who broke in, or he saw something that freaked him out. Seeing Laz only doubled her anxiety.

Wealthy business people and crime families hired *fixers*, individuals who handle illicit situations and made them disappear. Supreme had Laz. The former police detective had connections in high and low places and didn't hesitate to use either when necessary.

Laz walked in looking big, bad and dangerous. Dressed in all black, including a black leather jacket and black skull cap pulled low over his head, he held up a listening device detector and put his finger to his lips. Egypt was surprised when Angelo strolled in behind him, dressed similarly. Where had they come from?

Angelo hugged her but didn't say anything. Dread clawed through Egypt's body while Laz checked the house. Between Kenton's reaction to the video, and Laz and Angelo showing up, the stakes were beyond serious. Next level serious.

When Laz returned to the living room, he held up three fingers.

Kenton cursed again. "Get everything you need, and let's go," he said to Egypt, and then pulled her solidly against his body, lowering his mouth to her ear. "I need your house and car keys."

She wanted to question him since he still hadn't told her what or who he saw on the video. Yet, the intensity in his eyes and the strong set of his jaw left no room for an argument.

While she hurried around her bedroom collecting her things, Angelo stood in the doorway. Were Kenton and Laz still in the house? At one point, Egypt thought she heard her car roar to life, but she wasn't sure. It didn't matter though. Whatever the guys were doing, she would go along with it. She trusted them.

Only having one suitcase, Egypt packed as many clothes and shoes as she could. There were no personal items in the house, like photos, a birth certificate or anything that could reveal her past life. Those few items were locked away in a safety deposit box on the outskirts of town. Egypt never expected for someone to break in, but she always kept the possibility in the back of her mind.

With shaky hands, she grabbed the last item—a dress bag that held a new evening gown for an upcoming fundraiser. Glancing around, only furniture she wasn't attached to was left. The day had started out filled with happiness and hope for the future, and now anxiety swirled inside her gut. What was next? And why did this feel like the last time she'd be in her home?

"Ready?" Angelo asked. He had the suitcase in his hand, along with another small bag that held her mail.

Egypt nodded and followed him out of the room, surprised to see one of Supreme's tech guys working on her alarm system. He nodded at her as Angelo led her outside to Kenton's SUV which was now parked in the driveway.

"Where is..." Egypt started to ask about Kenton's whereabouts when she spotted him and Laz walking toward her. "What's that guy doing to my car?" she asked.

"He's going to park it in Supreme's lot until we figure out what's going on," Angelo explained as he loaded her belongings into the back of the vehicle. "The tech guy working on your alarm is on the phone with Wiz, trying to determine how someone overrode the system."

"Okay," Egypt said, studying Kenton as he got closer. His dark eyes still looked lethal, and a muscle jumped near his jawline as he approached. He seemed even more pissed than earlier.

"I'll explain everything," he said, not giving her a chance to speak before he opened the back door of his truck. "Hop in. Angelo's going to stick around and lock up the house."

"Why is Laz driving?" she asked when Laz slid into the driver's seat and Kenton scooted in next to her.

"He thinks I'm unstable," Kenton murmured. As his grip made her hand numb, Egypt wondered if maybe Laz was right.

"I didn't say you were unstable. I said you have lost your damn mind."

"Well, will one of you tell me what's going on? What or who did you see on the video? Who was in the house?"

"Franklin."

"Franklin? I don't know any... Wait. The FBI agent? He was in my house?" she shrieked. "Oh no. What if he found som—"

"Don't," Kenton started, his finger under her chin forcing her to look at him. "Just listen—"

"No!" She jerked her hand away and pounded on the seat between them. "I will not listen. That man was in my house...going through my things. He can't just get away with breaking and entering. He invaded my private space." Even as she spoke the words, doubt raced through her mind. Jay Franklin was the FBI. Who was she going to tell? Who would do anything to him?

"I'm gonna find that asshole and make sure he thinks twice before contacting you again." Kenton's calm from earlier was gone. In its place was the same ferocity he had exuded when he came to her defense with Ross.

"And that's where we disagree," Laz piped in as he maneuvered seamlessly through the streets of Atlanta with ease. "We should sit on this incident and not show our hand just yet. Franklin might lead us to a bigger fish. But if yo ass goes half-cocked and beat the shit out of him, we won't get anything."

Kenton closed his eyes and pinched the bridge of his nose. He didn't challenge Laz's assessment.

"Kenton, maybe Laz is right. Don't do anything that'll get yourself in trouble. It's just not worth it."

"Anything involving you is worth it," he said with conviction, and for the first time that night, she saw worry in his eyes. Then something else dawned on her.

"Did the video show him taking my mug or anything else from the house?"

Kenton nodded. "He took what looked like an ink pen from the coffee table."

"But why? What could he possibly want with those items?"

"My guess would be for fingerprints. We just have to figure out why," Laz said from the front seat.

Egypt's heart slammed against her chest. One look at Kenton and she knew they were thinking the same thing.

Agent Franklin might be working for Pisano.

Chapter Twenty-Six

"Kenton!"

He could barely hear the sirens in the distance over the ringing in his ears and Egypt's screams. She ran toward him.

"Get down!" he yelled and fired off another round. "Stay down!"

Her body jerked. Her eyes grew large, and she grabbed the top of her bulletproof vest.

Blood.

No. No. No.

Kenton lunged, hoping to catch her, but she staggered then dropped hard to the grass. "Hang on, baby! Hang on!" Before he could get closer, he felt a pinch near his ear. Unbearable heat coursed through his neck, his shoulder, and his knees went weak sending him crashing to the ground. Pain gripped his body, clawing through him like a scalpel scraping across his bones.

Hang on. He couldn't lose her. He had to hang on.

Egypt stretched out her arm, reaching for him as tears flowed down her face, and her chest heaved. Kenton crawled toward her, his vision blurring as he fought to keep moving. He had to keep moving.

"K-Ken..." Her body shook. Once. Twice. And then...nothing.

No! No! No!

"Egypt!" he yelled, barely recognizing his gravelly voice as heavy darkness descended over him.

Hang on. I have to hang on. I have to save her.

193

Egypt! Egypt! Egypt!

"Kenton? Kenton, wake up."

"Egypt! Egypt!" Kenton shot up in bed, gasping. Blindly reaching for her, his heart hammering inside his chest. "Egypt."

"I'm right here, honey. I'm right here." She straddled him. "See, I'm right here."

Kenton's hands were all over her face, her neck, working their way down her body. "Are you hurt? Are you okay?" he rasped, his throat rough as sandpaper. He struggled to get air into his lungs as fear continued flowing through his veins.

"I'm fine." Egypt cupped his face, placing her forehead against his. "You had a bad dream." She littered his face with feathery kisses.

"Shit. I thought...I thought I had lost you." Kenton crushed her to him. He might've been holding on too tight, but he couldn't let her go. He squeezed his eyes closed, fighting to control the overwhelming emotion consuming him. God, if he ever lost her...

"I'm right here," Egypt crooned in his ear over and over, her arms secured around his neck as she rocked him. Kenton rested his head on her shoulder, the motion lulling his heartbeat slowly back to a normal rate. They stayed that way for the longest before Egypt lifted her head.

"Lay down. I'll be right back."

Kenton did as he was told. Exhausted, but still riled, he risked closing his eyes again while listening to her move around the room. Minutes later, she climbed onto the bed next to him. She placed a wet cloth on his forehead, and he released a long, steadying breath.

When he finally reopened his eyes, the bedside lamp was on, and he was staring into Egypt's worried face.

"That must have been some nightmare. Are you okay?" She kissed him, and dabbed the damp cloth across his forehead and then down the side of his face.

"Yeah, I'm all right," he said, really not wanting to talk, but knowing he had probably freaked her out. "What time is

194

it?"

"Almost four."

Good. They still had a couple of hours before they needed to get up for work.

Egypt wiped at the perspiration on his face a little more before dropping the small towel on the floor. "Do you want to talk about the dream?"

"Not really."

When he didn't continue, Egypt stretched out beside him and pulled the sheet over their naked bodies. She curled against him, her head resting in the crook of his arm, and her hand on his chest. A calm settled over Kenton as he thought about the nightmare. That dream haunted him more times than he could count, but this one was a thousand times worse. Scarier. Instead of the dream including Santana...it was Egypt in her place. He could see her so vividly, laying there, blood painting the ground around her.

Kenton closed his eyes again to block out the visual. His head was pounding, and his chest felt like someone had ripped out his heart and ran it through a shredder. Losing Santana and Quaid had rocked him, but he already knew if he lost Egypt, it would kill him. She had become such an important part of him, and he wouldn't be able to handle another loss.

"Talk to me, Kenton. You've been a rock for me during my situation over the last few days. Let me be that for you. Tell me about the dream. It might make you feel better."

He doubted that. If he could, he would wipe his mind free and never have the nightmare again. And right now, all he wanted to do was get some sleep. They had stayed up late, discussing whether or not to report Franklin to his superiors for breaking into Egypt's home. In the end, they decided to handle the situation Laz's way.

"Kenton, what are you afraid of?"

"Losing you." He couldn't think of anything at the moment that scared him more than that. What if he couldn't protect her? What if she suffered the same fate as Santana and Quaid?

Egypt lifted up on her elbow to look at him. "You're not going to lose me. I'm not going anywhere. You're stuck with me whether you like it or not."

Kenton's hand slid into her mass of locks, and he sifted his fingers through the strands. "I love being stuck with you, and you already know you can't get rid of me, but I'm concerned about keeping you safe."

She scooted up higher and traced the tip of her finger over his mustache and then his lips. "I trust you with my life. We will keep me safe. I'm not totally helpless. Yes, I wigged out when I saw Marco's photo that day at the office, but only because it caught me off guard. It had been a long time. Now, mentally and emotionally I'm in a better place, mainly because of you. Am I scared to come face to face with that monster? Yes, but I feel stronger knowing that you and the guys have my back."

He marveled at her internal and external beauty, and her resilience was second to none. She'd been through hell, yet she never gave up, only growing stronger with time.

"The nightmare is of the day Santana, Quaid, and I were attacked. The dream came frequently during the year after their deaths, but not as often after that, at least not until recently."

"Do you have a trigger? Did something happen to make it return?"

"The anniversary of their deaths is coming up, but this dream was different. Instead of Santana in the nightmare this time...it was you."

"Ah, honey, it was just a dream."

"A dream that felt way too real. I could even smell death. Feel the pain from the bullet to my neck, my shoulder. Every aspect of that dream was so vivid. It was as if I was right there."

Kenton met her gaze, surprised that it wasn't concern or fear he saw in her dark eyes, but love. He placed a kiss on the inside of her wrist. Her scented skin smelled like lavender and vanilla, stirring his desire and pushing out the melancholy.

"That's what I meant when I said I can't lose you. I want you to know I will give my life to protect you."

She shook her head and pulled her hand free. "Don't say that, because that would mean me losing you and that's not acceptable. You've already promised to marry me and give me three kids."

Kenton smiled at the conviction in her voice. He had seen her sense of humor often enough over the years, but he liked that she could make a stressful time feel a little lighter.

"That's right. I did tell you that, and I always keep my promises."

Except with Santana. His mind taunted, but he shook the thought free. He wouldn't let Egypt down.

"There's something I omitted yesterday about Santana and Quaid's death."

"And what's that?"

Kenton had debated all night on whether to tell her, especially knowing how she felt about law enforcement. But he didn't want there to be any secrets between them. This wouldn't affect their relationship, but he wanted her to know that some of her beliefs weren't off track.

Kenton sat up and put his feet on the floor.

"Where are you going?" she asked, holding the sheet up over her breasts.

"Nowhere."

He picked up the T-shirt he had discarded before they climbed into bed. "Here put this on." Her alluring, naked body was too much of a distraction for a serious conversation. While she put on his shirt, Kenton slipped into a pair of basketball shorts before climbing into bed and resting his back against the headboard. Egypt cozied up next to him.

"I didn't tell you the main reason I left the FBI. I wasn't originally responsible for Santana's protection, but one of her stipulations for testifying was that I be the one to guard her. While we were protecting Santana, our location had been compromised twice. After the second time, we figured either Santana had told someone where we were located, which she denied. Or there was someone in our circle of agents disclosing whereabouts."

"You guys had a mole." She pursed her lips and folded her arms across her chest. "And you wonder why I don't trust law enforcement."

"There are bad people in every walk of life, Egypt. Not all law enforcement is bad."

Kenton could say that now, although, after the death of his friends, he didn't trust anyone outside of his family.

"And yes, someone was leaking information. We just didn't know. Any information about the witness and her whereabouts was kept between our supervisor, and there was a backup team that assisted with the protection detail. The day of our detour to the cemetery, our backup team should have been in position before we arrived. It wasn't until we got there that we found out they got held up."

"And you guys stayed anyway. That's why you've been blaming yourself."

He nodded. "During the investigation, there was one excuse after another for why that team hadn't been in place. Ultimately, the decision not to abort was on me."

"Are you saying *the feds* blamed *you*?"

"No, but it was made clear that I didn't follow protocol. At the agency, they encourage us to use our best judgment in situations, but in that instance, they faulted me for putting the witness at risk. I should've aborted the detour or should've waited for backup."

"Is that why you resigned?"

"Partly. I was in a bad place up here." He pointed at his head, remembering how he had mentally shut down. Besides Caleb's help, it wasn't until Kenton's father had shown up at his front door that he started getting himself together. "I also didn't like the way the FBI was handling the investigation into what happened at the cemetery. They weren't working fast enough as far as I was concerned, and for a while, I lost faith in the agency."

"What do you mean?"

"I'll admit when I screw up, but there were some other misfires that no one took ownership of. They didn't support me the way that they should have, and where I come from, you always take care of your people, especially your witnesses. On top of that, the investigation was a joke. They didn't close that case until months after I left.

"It had taken months for them to find the traitor. It turned out that it was one of the logistics guys. His son had gotten in bad with the DeLevese gang, and they somehow found out his father was a fed. They snatched the son. They blackmailed the agent."

"Oh no."

"He gave them the information they wanted, and they still murdered his son. Two days later, the body was dumped in a junkyard. It took the feds months to get to the bottom of this. I question whether or not they would've figured it out at all if they hadn't gotten a tip from an anonymous source."

"Hearing stories like that...it's just awful all the way around."

"Even if there are some crooked agents, not everyone in law enforcement is bad. Sometimes there are individuals who end up in bad situations."

"Are you telling me all of this because you think that Agent Franklin might be in a bad situation?"

"I don't know, and I don't care what the hell type of situation he may be in. All I know is if he and I cross paths, or he comes anywhere near you again, he'll regret the day we ever met."

Chapter Twenty-Seven

Kenton woke with a start. He glanced around trying to determine what had awakened him but didn't see or hear anything. Egypt was fast asleep. Sprawled across him, her head rested on his chest and one of her legs entwined with his. The T-shirt he'd given her earlier to wear was bunched around her hips, giving him a good view of her perfectly round ass.

But unease swept through his body. Something was off.

As the sleep fog dissipated, Kenton heard a faint beeping. Several seconds later his house alarm blared.

He jumped. "Egypt." Kenton shook her several times as he reached into the top drawer of his nightstand for his Glock.

"Huh?" She bolted up, her head slamming into his chin.

"*Ow*, shit," he grunted, but didn't have time to dwell on the pain. "In the closet. Now."

He practically lifted her off the bed and hurried her across the room until she was walking on her own. They had discussed safety protocols the other morning, one being that the master closet would be her safe place. Though still a little dazed, she went in without question, closing the door behind her.

Barefoot, Kenton crept silently into the hallway. A sliver of illumination from the small nightlight plugged into a wall socket, guided his path. His pulse pounded erratically, and adrenaline rushed through his body. He moved quickly down the hall and didn't stop until he reached the top of the stairs where he stood silently, listening.

Not hearing anything, Kenton eased down the stairs, skipping the step in the middle of the staircase that squeaked. Then he heard movement. Someone cursed just as he got to the bottom of the landing.

"Chelsey! What the hell?"

His youngest sister let out a scream, her hand grabbing her chest. "God, Kenton. You scared me to death! What's wrong with this stupid thing?" She pointed at the alarm console. "I put in the code twice, and it didn't work."

The intense energy flooding Kenton's body moments ago slowed, but his heart was still beating faster than usual. He shut off the alarm and ran a hand over his low-cut hair.

"I changed the code last night."

"What's going on? You don't usually sleep this late, and what's with the gun?" she asked, worry marring her face. "Did something happen?"

"I thought you were someone breaking in. Sit tight, and I'll be back." He started for the stairs but stopped suddenly. "It's Monday morning. Why aren't you at school?"

He took in his sister's appearance. Her long, dark braids with a few blond strands, were pulled back from her face and gathered in a ponytail that went down her back. Dressed in a gray jogging suit that had UGA stamped across the front, and Nikes covering her feet, she looked every bit the track star. She was attending the University of Georgia-Athens on a full athletic scholarship.

"A friend of mine is in town and wanted to meet for breakfast before she flies out. I figured I'd beat the traffic and come early. But I'm only here for a couple of hours since my first class starts at twelve. Now, let's get back to you." She leaned a hip against the kitchen counter and folded her arms.

"There are only two reasons you'd still be in bed. Either you're sick or—"

"I'll be back," Kenton said again, ignoring anything else she had to say. His pulse still wasn't back to normal, but he needed to get Egypt. He took the stairs two at a time and returned to his bedroom, glad the door was still closed. If there had been an actual threat, he liked knowing that she took the possible danger seriously.

Kenton swung open the closet door, and his stomach flipped. Egypt stood on the other side of the island, a small pistol pointed at his chest.

"It's just me," he said slowly, his arms out to the side. Her intense gaze, nailing him in place, remained while she slowly lowered the gun.

Kenton stashed weapons in various parts of the house, including the closet, and had shown Egypt where to find them. One thing about her past that had benefited her, she knew how to protect herself, and she wasn't afraid of guns. He'd have to thank Nelson. The man had taught her well.

Still standing in the doorway, Kenton couldn't help the smile that spread across his face. Her locks were piled on top of her head with a few tendrils falling free. Her attractive face, with eyebrows dipped into a frown, was free of makeup, and there was fearlessness in her eyes. The sight of her was indeed a turn on. However, this wasn't the time for sexual energy to charge through his body, but damn if she didn't look like a total badass. And he wanted to lay her on top of the island and ravish her body.

Later. I'll do that later.

"What set off the alarm?" Egypt asked, her voice still thick with sleep. She returned the gun to the safe located under his row of suits.

"My sister. She stays here sometimes when she's not in school, and I had changed the code without telling her." Kenton stored his Glock back in the top drawer of the nightstand and slipped into a T-shirt. "Come downstairs and say hi."

Egypt glanced at the T-shirt that went down to her knees. "Let me shower and get cleaned up first."

"Not necessary. Just grab a robe. It'll only take a minute." He gave her a quick kiss. "Besides, a shower now will be a waste of time since I plan to get you dirty again."

Kenton stuck his feet into a pair of house slippers, while Egypt grumbled her way to the bathroom. On his way back downstairs, the smell of coffee greeted him.

"How's school?" he asked, expecting Chelsey to be in the kitchen. Instead, the lights were out, except the one over the stove, and Kenton didn't see her at first. Then he spotted her in the family room, kneeling on the sofa and peeking through the blinds.

He poured himself a cup of the dark brew. Steam billowed above the mug, and the rich, nutty aroma invigorated his senses. "What are you looking at?" he asked, taking a careful sip.

"When I turned onto the street, there was an unmarked car with dark windows sitting at the end of the cul-de-sac."

Kenton straightened and set his mug down. "What? Is it still out there?"

"Yeah, but the person inside might've seen me looking at him or her since they are pulling off."

Kenton glanced out the same window, needing to check for himself. It was still dark but daybreak, and the faint yellow and orange splash of sunrise was beginning to make an appearance.

If that asshole Franklin was sitting on his house, there was definitely going to be trouble. Kenton might've agreed to hold off on reporting the agent to his superiors, but he wouldn't tolerate stalking. What bothered him most about Agent Franklin was that he couldn't figure out the guy's end game.

Then again. It might not have been him.

Kenton released the blinds and turned to his sister. "Did you notice anything else out of the norm?" Chelsey was majoring in criminal justice and once told him that she eventually wanted to work for Supreme Security.

She shook her head. "Nah. The windows were too dark. I couldn't see the person inside, but I did see a light. Maybe they were on a laptop or cell phone. My first thought when I pulled into the garage was that they were watching your house, but I don't know for sure."

Kenton didn't speak, only tossed various scenarios around in his head. Did Franklin think they had something to do with Ross's murder? No soon as the thought entered his mind, he shook it free. If they were suspects, they would've been taken in for more questioning.

"Changing the security code. Roaming around the house with a gun. Sneaking up on me," Chelsey said, tapping her fingernails against the quartz countertop. "Is there something going on that I should know about? Is there a reason why someone would be sitting on your house?"

"Wait? What?"

Kenton and Chelsey turned toward the bottom of the stairs where Egypt was standing. Her locks hung loosely around her shoulders, and she had changed into a pair of burgundy lounging pajamas.

"Oh. My. God! Egypt!" Chelsey screeched and rushed across the room. "I haven't seen you in like forever. I was wondering who Kenton was hiding upstairs. Does this mean you guys are finally together?" The women hugged and Egypt, glancing over Chelsey's shoulders, looked at him with one brow raised.

Kenton grinned and pulled another coffee mug from the cabinet for her. "I might've mentioned my interest in you...a few times to Chelsey."

"A few times? Are you kidding me?" Chelsey said in exasperation and released Egypt. "For a while, I thought we were going to have to commit him for being delusional. I didn't know you two were *really* dating."

"I decided to put him out of his misery," Egypt cracked. Kenton chuckled and poured her a cup of coffee. Her sense of humor was shining through more and more these days.

"Now what is this about someone watching the house."

Damn, she's good.

There was a small tremor in Egypt's voice, but on the outside, she seemed cool and calm. Kenton filled her in on the conversation that he and Chelsey were having. "*If* someone was watching the house, they didn't stick around."

"You still haven't explained why you changed the alarm code, and why you were sneaking around with a gun," Chelsey said.

"I told you. I thought you were someone breaking in."

His sister looked at him through narrowed eyes, and Kenton almost smiled. She knew he wasn't telling her everything. That made him proud. Curious by nature, Chelsey had good judgment and had always been sharp, catching clues that others might miss. Any law enforcement division would be lucky to get her if Hamilton didn't snatch her up first.

"Chelsey, it's good to see you. Do you want to stay for breakfast?" Egypt asked, effectively changing the subject.

Kenton loved seeing his sister, but he needed to make sure she stayed clear of the house, at least until he knew what was going on with Franklin and the Pisano situation.

"Chelsey is getting what she came here for, and then she's leaving. And from now on, she's going to call before coming over. Besides, she's not welcomed here, and we need to get ready for work."

"*Kenton*," Egypt snapped, that motherly-chastising tone coming through loud and clear.

Chelsey laughed. "Don't worry, Egypt. My big brother is a jerk, but I'm used to it. Actually, I would love to stay for breakfast." She sat on one of the barstools and flashed her pearly whites at Kenton. "So, what are we having?"

Chapter Twenty-Eight

Egypt grabbed a navy-blue pantsuit and matching shoes from the closet in the guest bedroom. The visit with Chelsey had been nice, even though Egypt had been a little unnerved to know someone might've been watching the house. Would Franklin really follow her to Kenton's place? Or was someone else keeping tabs on her?

She didn't have a clue, and Kenton hadn't seemed concerned during breakfast. Or he'd been putting on a good act. Either way, she planned to question him.

A glance at the clock showed they needed to be on the road within the next half an hour. Even if she didn't have to be in the office until ten, traffic was unpredictable, and she didn't want to be late.

Slipping into a robe, Egypt went down the hall. "Kenton?" she called from the door of his huge bedroom.

When he claimed he didn't like anything small, he hadn't been kidding. The main part of the room held the king sized bed, two oversize nightstands, and a bench at the foot of the bed. The masculine color scheme of steel gray walls with black, beige and gray bedding, was dark for her taste but was perfect in the space. Off to the side was a spacious sitting area hosting two upholstered wingback chairs and a small round coffee table. Why one person needed so much room was a mystery to Egypt.

"Kenton?"

"I'm in here," he responded, the hum of an electric shaver coming from the bathroom.

"Are you still planning to..." Her words dropped off when she saw him standing in front of the sink in only a towel around his waist. Shutting off the shaver, he checked his handy work, moving his face back and forth in front of the mirror.

When he finally turned, his glistening, bare chest was on full display, and Egypt's greedy eyes ate him up. Her gaze did a slow glide over his dark, powerful body. His broad shoulders, muscled pecs, and rock-hard abs were a work of art. Her eyes went lower, and she licked her lips.

"Am I still what?" he asked.

Whatever Egypt was about to say flew from her mind. All of her attention was solely on his thick shaft, clearly outlined behind the cotton material. Her sex clenched with desire. It didn't matter how often she saw him without clothes, her body responded as if it were the first time.

So, so sexy.

"I guess you like what you see. Maybe I should show you more." The towel slid from Kenton's waist and tumbled to the floor. Egypt didn't even try to keep her gaze from going lower as Kenton moved toward her, his big dick seeming to grow with each step.

"I um...man. Each time I see you in all of your glory, I understand why you're so cocky."

He laughed and with a hand on the belt of her robe, pulled her against him. He smelled of sandalwood and soap, and unable to help herself, Egypt leaned into his neck for a better whiff.

"God, you smell good."

"You do too, and I think we have time for a quickie."

"Actually, we don't," Egypt murmured, but didn't stop him when he started untying the robe. When it fell open, her

207

lacy, blue bra and panties were exposed.

Kenton sucked in a breath. "We might be late because we're not leaving until I get my fill of you."

He had Egypt out of her underwear in record time then backed her against the linen closet door. Goosebumps raked over her flesh when his massive hands cupped her breasts, and he squeezed, pushing them together. His mouth didn't hesitate to devour her hypersensitive nipples, sending a stomach-dropping wave of desire surging to the tips of her toes. Egypt's knees went weak.

"It-it's good this is go-going to be a quickie. I don't know how much of this I can take." Heat rushed through her body, and she moaned. Desire nipped at each one of her nerves as his hot tongue flogged, and swirled over her hardened peaks.

Her pulse accelerated, and her body shivered as he worshiped her nipples. "Ke-Kenton," she breathed, gripping his arms tightly with her nails digging into his skin. She was barely hanging on. The sweet torture of his mouth as he paid homage to the other breast was almost her undoing. Need bounced around inside off her, and she wiggled under his hold, squeezing her legs together to control the throb at the apex of her thighs.

"Kenton," she said again with more urgency.

"I know, baby. I just can't help myself," he mumbled against her breast before lifting his head. "Let me grab a condom." He reached into the bottom drawer of the vanity and pulled out a leather travel case. Retrieving the foil packet, he ripped it open with his teeth and hastily covered himself. "Quickie, right?"

Kenton didn't give her a chance to respond. Egypt squeaked when he gripped the back of her thighs and lifted her off her feet. She marveled at his strength and how effortlessly he held her against the door of the linen closet. Wrapping her legs loosely around his waist, her arms circled his neck, and Kenton entered her without hesitation.

Egypt's eyes drifted closed, and she moaned as her

interior walls adjusted around his thick shaft. Together they moved as one, creating a lyrical rhythm that was all their own. She wouldn't protest to starting every morning like this.

When Kenton's lips sought hers, his tongue plunged into her mouth, swirling in sync with each rotation of his hips. In no time, the pace increased. Faster. Forceful. Deeper. With each thrust, Kenton took her to new heights. The harder he drove into her, the more frantic their kiss.

His ravenous mouth devoured hers, and Egypt held the back of his head, deepening their connection while matching him stroke for stroke. She couldn't get enough of this man, her man, and loved how good he felt buried deep inside of her.

Egypt squeezed around his shaft, and Kenton growled against her mouth and slammed into her with more vigor. A penetrating heat rippled under her skin and sparked a flame of need bursting from the top of her head to the soles of her feet. Egypt's hips rotated against him, moving like they had a mind of their own.

It didn't matter that the ridges of the door scraped against her back, and their pounding against the wood grew louder. She didn't want him to stop.

He pulled his lips from hers. "Hold on." Securing his grip on her thighs, Kenton took a step back. With raw power, he lifted her up and down his length as if she weighed nothing, and an intense storm roared to life inside of Egypt. Passion swirled, thundered, and stimulated every nerve, sending her heart rate to new levels.

Her breath came in short spurts as she clung to the control that was getting away. She couldn't hold on. Her legs trembled as she neared her release.

"Kenton," she whimpered, but then her eyes slammed shut with the next thrust, as an explosion of pleasure vibrated through her body and sent her tumbling over the edge of control. Egypt shook, riding the wave of ecstasy that continued pulsing through her until she had nothing left, and she wilted against Kenton.

He didn't stop. He held her tighter and continued driving into her. Chest to chest, Egypt could feel a low growl rumbling inside of him, and seconds later, his body stiffened, his hold tightened, and the turbulence from his release rocked them both to completion.

Totally spent, Egypt's body remained limp against Kenton. She hated being dead weight in his arms, but she couldn't move. Their deep breathing filled the air as their chests heaved against each other. Sweat-slicked skin stuck together as their high slowly waned.

Staggering, Kenton pulled out of Egypt and set her on the bathroom counter. With one arm wrapped around her waist, he dropped his forehead to her shoulder.

"Damn," he muttered.

Damn indeed.

Egypt never imagined she would experience such an intense connection with another human being. Each time they made love was more passionate than the last, and Kenton was quickly becoming an addiction she didn't want to break.

Chapter Twenty-Nine

Egypt sat at her desk, her mind still reeling from the quickie that she and Kenton shared in his bathroom earlier. Sex with him was like nothing she had ever experienced, and each time their bodies came together so intimately, Kenton raised the stakes. He was holding true to his promise of them having a lot of firsts together.

I had sex...in a bathroom...against the wall.

A powerful shiver shot through her body, and Egypt squeezed her thighs together just thinking about the intensity of the act. Each day with him, she realized how much she had missed out on in her adult life. Some people were sheltered by their parents. Egypt had been sheltered by the circumstances of her life. Now she planned to live like she should've been doing years ago, without fear.

Forcing herself to regain focus, she pecked away on her keyboard, finishing the letter that Hamilton had asked her to construct. The intercom on her desk squawked, and she picked up the telephone receiver. "Yes?"

"Hey, Egypt. Your 11 o'clock is here. Do you want me to put them in conference room A?" Kenton, asked, his deep, sexy voice pouring over her like sunshine.

Egypt had to get used to the security specialists managing the front desk. It was one of several changes that

211

Hamilton had put into place since the meeting with the FBI days ago. None of the guys were thrilled about the assignment. Most preferred staying busy and being a part of the action guarding their clients, instead of greeting visitors. But of course Hamilton expected push-back. He promised everyone scheduled to monitor the desk, during their shifts, additional compensation.

"Thanks, Kenton. I'll be down in a second to escort them to the conference room."

Egypt hung up the phone and pulled her small mirror from the top drawer of the desk. She checked to make sure none of her locks, that were in an intricate twist on top of her head, had fallen loose. Pulling out the neutral berry lipstick from her purse, she touched lips before returning the mirror to the drawer.

When Egypt stood and took a step toward the door, she was reminded of the cute ankle holster that Kenton had given her before leaving the house. He wanted her to be armed whenever possible.

She headed out of the office with a new client packet. Instead of taking the elevator, she hurried down the stairs, her heels tapping against the painted concrete steps. When she made it to the first floor, she headed to the front of the building. It didn't matter that there were two security specialists sitting at the long information counter, her gaze automatically met Kenton's. The mischievous grin he flashed sent heat rushing to her cheeks.

God, this man.

Part of her needed for their lives to get back to normal so that she didn't have to see him all day and night. He considered her a distraction, but in all truth, he was the distraction. She couldn't go more than a few minutes without her mind drifting to thoughts of him.

Egypt glanced around the modernly decorated waiting area. Rarely, did clients have to wait long, so the large room wasn't often used except for the occasional meet and greet events.

"Where is Mr. And Mrs. Wright?" Egypt looked from Kenton to Parker, another one of their long-time specialists, and they shrugged. The serious expression on their faces wasn't fooling anyone. They were up to something. She set the papers on the counter. "Okay, what's going on?"

"What makes you think something is going on?" Parker asked.

"Because I'm supposed to—"

"Hey, sis," came a raspy voice from behind her.

Egypt swung around, and her heart leaped. Standing in the middle of the long hallway was the man who had saved her life. "Nelson."

Tears welled in her eyes, blurring her vision as she rushed to him. His strong arms enveloped her in a bear hug, holding and rocking her like he always did when returning from a long trip. Hamilton and Mason had a few guys on the team who accepted extended assignments that sometimes took them across the country. Nelson was one of those guys.

"What's with the tears? It hasn't been that long," he said. His raspy voice sounded like a two-pack a day smoker when actually, he'd never smoked a day in his life.

Nelson kissed her cheek, the familiar scent of his woodsy aftershave surrounding her like a soft blanket. He was ten years her senior and considered her his little sister, but to Egypt, he was a father figure who had helped her navigate adulthood.

Egypt sighed, horrified that she had gotten emotional. Working with mostly men, she tried to maintain a tough exterior, but seeing Nelson always reminded her of a past shrouded in secrecy. Everyone had people in their lives who they couldn't imagine living without, and for her that was Nelson.

With the back of her hand, Egypt dab at her damp face, taking in the man who had been her only family for years. At six feet tall, Nelson was only a few inches taller than her, with mahogany skin, dark, soulful eyes, and a smile that rarely revealed his teeth.

"It's been almost six months," Egypt said. "I hate when you're gone that long."

"I know, but I can't stand to be in one place too long."

Egypt nodded. She learned that early in their relationship. At first, he didn't disappear for long periods of time, but once she had started at Supreme, Nelson agreed to handle some of their longer contracts. Over the past week, Egypt understood better why he felt comfortable leaving her behind. All this time, she never knew that he had Hamilton and Mason watching her back.

"What are you doing here? You weren't expected to return for at least two months."

"I had to come and check on you." He glanced over her shoulder and grinned.

When Egypt looked back, Kenton was leaning against the desk watching them, his huge arms folded across his chest. She rolled her eyes and shook her head.

"So, you and Kenton, huh?"

Instead of responding, Egypt couldn't fight the smile that broke free. Nelson had suspected a year ago, asking if they were seeing each other. Like usual when anyone asked about her feelings for Kenton, Egypt had played it down, claiming they were just coworkers. When in truth she had been secretly in love with him.

"Check him out. Looking all big and bad. Acting like he gon' do something to me for making you cry."

Egypt laughed. "Stop. He's been amazing."

Nelson draped his arm around her shoulders. "Honestly, if I had to choose a man for you, it would be Kenton. You guys are good for each other."

Egypt agreed. The more time she spent with him, the more he felt like her missing piece, filling a void that had been empty most of her life. "I take it Kenton had something to do with this surprise visit."

"Maybe," Nelson said, his eyes twinkling before turning serious. "I heard what happened, and I'm glad you didn't bolt. Why didn't you call me?"

"You're on assignment. I figured when you had a chance, you'd call me then I'd fill you in." When he was out of town, depending on the assignment, he would call at least once a week. It had been a couple of weeks since Egypt had heard from him.

Kenton strolled over. "I guess your surprise was a success."

"How long have you known he was coming?" Egypt asked.

"A few days, and I'll admit that it was hard keeping this from you." Egypt felt so blessed being around people who truly cared about her.

"That reminds me, Kenton. I ran into your FBI buddy a couple of weeks ago in North Carolina."

"Who?"

Nelson snapped his fingers a few times trying to remember. "What's his na...Caleb. I think that's his name. You know, the therapist."

"North Carolina? Where?"

"At a casino. Our client was performing in their nightclub, and I ran into your boy when he was trying to get into a restricted area. We talked for a second. He mentioned losing a shit-load of money on the tables, and even asked to borrow a few bucks."

"What did you tell him?" Kenton asked.

"I gave him a twenty, and told him to take his ass home."

Egypt studied Kenton, concern on his face. Days after they ran into Caleb at the grocery store, his wife had called Kenton, saying that her husband needed help. He'd been staying out late, drinking more than usual and had been emotionally distant. She thought he was in some type of trouble, but he wouldn't confide in her, and she wanted Kenton to talk to him.

"Each time I call the guy, I get his voicemail. I need to pay him a visit."

A buzzing sound caught all of their attention.

"That's me." Kenton dug into his front pant pocket and retrieved his phone. "I hate to break up this reunion, but Ham wants to see Nelson and me in his office."

"Well, since there's no real client, I guess I should be getting back to work. I'll walk up with you guys." Egypt wanted to talk to them about something that had been on her mind for the last couple of days. "Can I talk to you two before you go to your meeting?"

Kenton's hand went to the small of her back. "What's wrong?"

"Let's go in here." She stepped into an empty meeting room, and they followed. "I'm thinking about telling Laz, Angelo, Myles, and the girls about my past."

"Why?"

"That's not a good idea."

Kenton and Nelson spoke at once. Egypt valued both of their opinions, but ultimately it would be her decision.

Kenton shoved his hands into the front pockets of his dress pants. "Why do you want to tell everyone?"

"Mainly because they're my friends, and they're watching my back. Seems only fair that they know the real reason about my connection to Pisano."

Nelson squeezed her shoulder. "I know these years haven't been easy, but my opinion about your past is the same. Forget it. You are Egypt Durand, not Paige McCurry. She no longer exists so there's nothing to tell."

"Okay, well, I just want it all to be over. No more running. No more hiding. No more withholding the truth from those I love." Egypt wrapped her arms around herself. If only she could blink and make her past disappear. She regretted being a witness, and if she could do it all over again, she would've run the other way that night sixteen years ago. "I'm tired of having a *secret* past."

"I know," Nelson said. "But the people who know about your past, are the only ones who need to know. I told Ham and Mase because I wanted more than just myself watching your back. And I'm glad you told Kenton."

Egypt glanced at Kenton who hadn't said much, but he looked at her with an intensity that reached into her soul. Her heart swelled with love. Some days it was still hard to believe they were together, and he made her believe that she could have a normal life with a happily ever after.

"I trust our friends with my life...and your life, but it's still risky to tell anyone about your past, Egypt," Kenton finally said, and reached for her hand, pulling her closer to him. "It's a small world. You don't know who knows who, and someone could accidentally tell the wrong person about your past identity. Marco's father is not the only person you testified against. You might not ever have a problem with the Fed you help put away or anyone he knows, but that's not to say that you won't."

Egypt shivered at the thought. With numerous charges brought against him, the federal agent had received a life's sentence. But what if someone he knew, accused her of ruining their family like Marco had?

"Also, keep in mind. We don't even know for sure if you're on Pisano's radar. If you aren't, which I'm hoping, telling the guys your history doesn't serve a purpose. And whether or not they know your life's story, they will always have your back." Nelson put his arm around her shoulder. "I'm glad you're finally living your life, kid, but you still have to be careful. At least for now."

Egypt nodded, knowing they were probably right, but still thinking that if she shared her story with their friends, it wouldn't feel like such a dark secret. Then maybe she could move on and never look back.

"Nelson, can you give us a minute?" Kenton asked.

"Sure." He placed a chaste kiss on Egypt's forehead and walked out of the room, closing the door behind him.

Kenton's arms encircled Egypt, and she sighed, sinking into his loving embrace. How had she gone this far in life without him? Without his hugs, kisses, and the calm that surrounded him?

Pent-up energy flowed from her body as they stood

there in silence, and Egypt basked in the strength of his hold. Her heart was so heavy with love for this man. He comforted her in a way that only he could do.

"What brought all of this on?" Kenton asked.

After a slight hesitation, Egypt said, "You."

He leaned back and looked at her. "Me?"

She nodded. "My life has been cloaked in secrecy, and I've never had the pleasure of living freely. When you came to my house and stopped me from leaving town, you gave me hope. Hope that I could actually have all that I've dreamed of having. Marriage, kids…a family. *My own family.* You have no idea how lonely my life has been, or how unsure my future seemed before you came along."

I love you. The words teetered on the tip of her tongue, but fear or maybe it was insecurity kept her from saying them aloud. Instead, she said, "I'm tired of looking over my shoulders all the time. I'm tired of being afraid that someone will find out who I am and tell Pisano. And I'm tired of being alone."

"Sweetheart," Kenton framed her face within the palms of his hands and stared into her eyes, "as long as you have me, you'll never be alone again. You mean everything to me. I thought you knew that. This isn't some fling. I'm here for the long haul. Okay?"

Tears pricked the back of Egypt's eyes, but she batted them away and nodded.

Kenton lowered his head and warmth radiated through Egypt's body when their mouths touched. He'd kissed her a hundred times, but this kiss, this one she felt to the center of her core. Unhurried. Tender. Calming.

More importantly, she felt loved.

Chapter Thirty

I love you.

Three simple words.

Kenton wanted to kick himself. Why hadn't he been able to tell her? He wasn't some punk kid who wasn't in touch with his feelings. Yet, he let the perfect opportunity pass without saying those three simple words.

I. Love. You.

Sure, he had expressed how important she was to him, and that he was in their relationship for the duration. None of that compared to actually telling her how much he loved her. He wasn't only in love with her. She owned his heart.

Soon. I'll tell her soon.

After a quick knock, he pushed open the door to Hamilton's office.

"Good of you to join us. Must've been hard pulling yourself away from all the excitement at the front desk," Laz cracked.

Kenton sat on the sofa next to him. "Man, shut up. Your day of desk duty is coming, and I can't wait to see how excited you'll be."

Angelo and Nelson, who were sitting in the chairs in

front of the desk, laughed then went back to talking about the Atlanta Falcons game they had watched the day before. Hamilton was on the phone at his desk and nodded a greeting. The only other person scheduled to be in the meeting but hadn't arrived, was Myles.

"Before I forget," Laz reached into the interior pocket of his suit jacket, "everyone else has their tickets for the fundraiser gala next weekend. Here are yours and Egypt's."

"All right, thanks."

Kenton glanced at the tickets, noting the date and time before sticking them into his jacket pocket. Laz and Journey volunteered with Save Our Boys. The non-profit organization focused on young men between the ages of fourteen and twenty-five. Many of whom had endured some type of violence and abuse or had family members dealing with drugs and addictions. Kenton supported any organization that got kids off the streets and into programs offering apprenticeships and career training.

"Oh, and I found out that Franklin wasn't in your area last night," Laz said. "He's like…disappeared, but we'll find him. Right now, I'm not sure the car Chelsey spotted had anything to do with you, and without the plate number, there's not much I can do. And Wiz's team tried to tap into the street cameras in your area, but there aren't any on your block."

"What about your security cameras?" Angelo asked.

Kenton shook his head. "They didn't pick up anything. The car was outside of the scope. That'll be corrected before the end of the day though."

"Whatever Franklin is up to you guys are *not* to put your hands on him. Once we find out what he's looking for, or who he's really working for, we'll deal with him then," Hamilton said. Kenton hadn't realized he was off the phone.

"Ham, so what's the new development?" Angelo asked.

"Agent Griffith contacted me and told me that Gerald "Moot" Contrell confessed to the murder of Ross Hoakley. He used to be a foot soldier for the Pisano family up until about a year ago, at least that's what he's claiming."

"Yeah, right. Pisano probably felt the heat from the feds and went out and found some poor sap to take the fall for him," Kenton spat, irritation crawling through his body. "Did the guy say why he took out Ross?"

"According to Moot's confession, Hoakley sexually assaulted his girlfriend. He only planned to rough the guy up a little, but the situation got out of hand and..." Hamilton shrugged.

"Well, damn." Ross might've gotten what was coming to him, but unease crawled through Kenton he could've easily been the one sitting in jail for killing Ross.

"And before you ask, this doesn't mean that the FBI is taking their eyes off of Pisano. They still want him, and claim that they're getting closer," Hamilton explained but didn't sound too convinced.

There was a quick knock on the office door before it swung open.

"We have a situation." Myles strolled into the room with a tan fedora pulled low over his dark face. Unlike the rest of them, who were dressed in black suits, Myles sported a black long-sleeved Henley and khakis. "Last night, Mrs. Hoakley ended her contract with us, saying that our services were no longer needed."

"Yeah, I was getting to that," Hamilton said, rocking back in his desk chair. "But did something else happen?"

Myles handed Hamilton a manila envelope. "Guess who Mrs. Hoakley is dating?"

"Franklin?" Kenton tossed out.

"Nope."

"Then who?" Nelson asked.

"Marco Pisano."

"What?" Kenton hadn't known who he was going to say, but he hadn't expected Pisano. "You saw them together?"

Myles gave a slight shrug. "When she told me our services were no longer needed, I might've hung around her building for a while last night and this morning."

"Yeah, I bet you did." Kenton had always been impressed with how the former CIA agent was able to blend into his environment. Laz always teased him about being a ghost.

Myles leaned against the desk. "Pisano showed up at her place late and didn't leave until early this morning."

He passed pictures around the room, and Kenton studied each photo, one being of the couple kissing at the entrance of Hoakley's condo. The shot was taken at sunrise and considering the angle, Myles had to have been on a nearby rooftop.

"The FBI is supposed to be sitting on her place. Did you see them?" Hamilton asked.

"Yeah, one of their cars was parked up the street, but their asses are sleeping on the job."

Hamilton huffed out a breath and folded his arms across his chest. "So if she's with Pisano, and assuming the guy is responsible for Ross Hoakley's death, that means she hired us already knowing her husband was going to be killed."

"And she wanted to use Supreme as a front," Kenton added. He stood and moved around the room, unable to sit still any longer. "In a murder case, law enforcement always looks at the spouse as a possible suspect first. She played us."

"She has to be one bad bitch to be able to hang with a crime boss. Hope she's prepared to suffer the same fate as her husband," Laz said.

"If she used us, and was involved in her husband's death, the feds should have something on her by now," Angelo said.

Hamilton grunted. "They want a bigger catch. My guess is they think she can lead them to Pisano. What I don't get, though, is why Pisano wasn't more careful with being seen with her. He has to know the feds are still watching even if they *supposedly* have Ross's killer."

"And what I don't get is why they haven't been able to do a shakedown of his organization by now." Nelson tapped his fingers on the desk. "They should be able to get him on extortion, overseeing gambling operations, racketeering and probably a host of other crimes."

"Wait, do you know something we don't know?" Kenton asked. Nelson was in town partly to see Egypt, but Hamilton also wanted him to discretely look into the Pisano family and the numerous businesses they owned. He was confident they were a front for illegal activity.

"Not exactly, but Myles and I are following up on a few leads. We also heard rumblings about a turf war brewing. The LinKenzoy family don't take kindly to Pisano moving in on their territory."

The last thing the city needed was a turf war, Kenton thought.

"What if the Fed assigned to sit on Mrs. Hoakley's house has a connection with Pisano," Laz said. "We already know the man's reach is long. Chances are, he's like his father was and have agents in his pockets."

Kenton's stomach rolled. That thought made him sick. All of law enforcement took oaths, vowing to protect the country from enemies and not disgrace the badge. He hated knowing that some weren't honoring the pledge.

"Okay, we need to move this meeting along. I want all of you to continue handling what I've asked you to do regarding Pisano, but we're no longer working directly with the FBI on this case. I was never comfortable with our role, but even more so now since I think everything is not above board."

"You think Agent Griffith is shady?" Laz asked of the lead agent.

"No, he and I go way back. I don't know the rest of his team, but I trust Damien. He's doing all that he can, legally, regarding the case. He wants Pisano behind bars."

Kenton didn't care if Pisano spent the rest of his life behind bars or buried six feet under. He just wanted Egypt free to live her life without always looking over her shoulder, and he intended to do whatever it took to make that a reality.

Chapter Thirty-One

"Egypt, are you almost ready? We need to get out of here now if you don't want to be late," Kenton hollered up the stairs.

"Okay, I'll be right down."

They were heading to the fundraiser, and Egypt couldn't wait to see how everything turned out. The night before, she and Kenton were part of the volunteer team that had helped decorate the new, state of the art community center. By the time they had finished, the place had resembled the gala's theme—A Night at the Oscars. The committee had thought of everything. A red carpet, a roped off area for the paparazzi, movie posters and even several ten-foot Oscar statues were a part of the decor.

Excitement filled her. She sat on the bench at the foot of the bed and slipped into her four-inch strappy sandals. This would be the first time she attended a formal event with a man, and not just any man—her man. The last few weeks with Kenton had been some of the best in her life. They'd fallen into a comfortable routine and moved through their lives together as if they'd been dating for years. They were still vigilant about her safety, but they hadn't had any trouble with Franklin, and from what the guys could determine,

Egypt still wasn't on Pisano's radar. She hoped it stayed that way.

"Okay, I'm ready," she mumbled and took one last look in the full-length mirror, liking what she saw. The silk, black strapless gown hugged her breasts and cinched at the midsection where a band of crystals circled her waist. Kenton was going to swallow his tongue when he saw how high the deep split went and exposed her left leg. Egypt never thought of herself as a tease, but she couldn't wait to see her man's reaction.

Grabbing her purse from the bed, she headed down the stairs. "Kenton?" she called out when she didn't see him.

"In here, babe," he said from the powder room. Moments later, he appeared. Egypt's mouth went dry. Big, strong, and powerfully built, the man looked like a cover model for all things tall, dark, and sexy as hell.

They stared at each other, and Egypt liked what she saw. The perfectly tailored, black tuxedo jacket with satin lapels, molded around his muscular frame, highlighting his wide shoulders, and huge biceps. Her eyes slid lower and didn't stop until she reached the shiny black wingtips.

Talk about a total package. Jeez, can the man get any hotter?

Apparently, she wasn't the only one entranced. His heated gaze traveled the length of her, and a wave of desire spread through Egypt's body like a tsunami about to make landfall. The appreciative looks he often bestowed on her never got old.

"Damn, baby. You were definitely worth the wait." He reached for her hand, lifted it above her head and twirled her around slowly as he examined the gown. "You look so damn good. We should skip the event. I'd rather take you upstairs, throw you on the bed, and let you show me what's under the dress."

Egypt pulled her hand free, took a step back and pointed at him. "Don't even think about touching me. We've been late too many times because of you stripping me out of my clothes and pinning me against a wall. Not tonight."

Kenton chuckle. "You have to admit. We had fun."

"You're right, but we also ended up late. So don't get any ideas. You're going to have to wait until we get back to see what I'm hiding under all of this silk." She strolled to the hall closet and pulled out her long, dressy coat.

"Before we leave, I have something for you."

Kenton took the coat from her and set it across the back of a chair. Egypt's heart started racing when he pulled a small velvet box from his pants pocket, and he held it out to her. She eyed him warily. They weren't at the stage in their relationship for him to be giving her a ring, but any gift in a little black velvet box would be too much.

"You didn't have to buy me anything."

"I know, but I want you to have these." He flipped open the lid, and the pair of sparkling, diamond stud earrings, sitting on top of satin lining, twinkled under the bright lights.

Her breath stalled in her chest. "Wow. Those are gorgeous." Egypt fingered the stones. She wasn't up on diamond sizes, but they were larger than the 1/2 carat gems she currently had in the second hole in her ear. "Kenton, these are too much."

"Nothing is too much for you. I also had them...detailed."

"Detailed? What do you mean?"

"Don't be mad, but I had Wiz to outfit the set with a tracking device."

"Like what Journey has in her watch?"

He nodded, and Egypt prayed she never ended up in a situation like the one Journey had been in a year ago. "Why would I be mad? This is the most beautiful, and thoughtful gift I've ever received. Thank you."

"You're welcome, but just so you know, I didn't get them so that I can track your every move..." He stopped speaking and held up his hands. "What I mean is, the tracker is just a precaution. Unless you're in danger, missing, or something like that I promise I won't stalk—"

"I know," Egypt said softly, her hand on his chest.

Overwhelmed by his kindness, she tried focusing on her breathing to keep from crying and ruining her makeup but struggled. Her heart swelled and threatened to explode into a million pieces at how much she loved this man. The lavish gift was a sweet gesture, but then to enhance the jewelry in order to ensure her safety meant…everything.

"You have no idea how much this means to me…how much *you* mean to me. I'll never be able to thank you for all that you've done."

"Sweetheart, there is *nothing* I wouldn't do for you. Always know that," he said with conviction and brushed his lips across hers. "I love you. I love you so damn much it scares the hell out of me."

Egypt's heart split open, and she couldn't hold back the tears. "I love you, too." She sobbed and lunged into his arms, hugging him tightly around his neck. "I've loved you for so long. You just don't understand. I never thought I'd have someone in my life who made me feel the way you do."

Kenton pulled back and kissed a few of her tears. "I feel the same way. I absolutely adore you. The earrings are just a small token to show you how important you are to me. Now stop crying before you make me cry."

Egypt laughed, still a little overcome with emotion. "Now I have to go and fix my makeup."

Kenton swiped at his eyes. "Yeah, me too," he teased.

"You're so silly, but God, I love you." Egypt kissed him hard and then hurried back upstairs, taking the earrings with her.

A lightheartedness washed over her, reminding her that she could have all that she'd ever hoped for. If anyone had ever told her that she would ever be this happy, Egypt wouldn't have believed them. Now she felt like anything was possible, and she couldn't wait to see what joys the rest of her life brought.

*

Kenton stood in the hall mirror adjusting his bow-tie, thinking about Egypt's reaction to the gift and his profession of love. He liked seeing her smile and could even tolerate her tears if they were happy ones, but it was disturbing to know how much she missed out on. No one should have to walk through life without someone to love them. Sure, Nelson had been there for her as a protector and to guide her, but Kenton couldn't imagine how hard and lonely it must have been for her not to experience love.

She deserves so much more. He planned to spend the rest of his life making up for what she missed out on.

His cell phone vibrated in his pocket, and relief flooded through his body when he saw that it was Caleb.

"Man, where the hell have you been?" Kenton snapped. "You have your wife worried sick, and I've been calling you for the last two weeks."

"She le-left me," Caleb slurred, his voice raspy with emotion. "My wife took…"

When he didn't continue, Kenton glanced at the phone screen to see if the call had dropped, but it hadn't. "Hello? Caleb, you still there?"

"Took…kids and…never com…"

"Caleb, you're breaking up. I can't understand what you're saying. Where are you?" Again, nothing. "Caleb, you still there?"

"Yeah…"

Frustration clawed through Kenton. "Caleb? Can you hear me? Where are you?"

"Corner…ba…"

"Corner bar?" Kenton asked.

"Yeah…Cor…bar."

Kenton hadn't been to the Corner Bar in years. At one point it had closed down, but a few years ago someone else had purchased it. Kenton paced the length of the short hallway, trying to make out what else Caleb was saying.

"Caleb, I can't understand you. Sit tight. I'm coming to you."

"She left. What am…to do?"

"I'll be there soon." Kenton disconnected the call and

dropped the phone back into his pocket, hoping Caleb wouldn't do anything crazy.

"Is everything okay?"

Kenton turned. Again, a tug of arousal hit him at the sight of her in that dress. And the way she was standing, one hip cocked as if posing for a photo, he could see all of her shapely left leg and most of her firm thigh.

He shook his head. "Damn, that dress though... Hopefully, I won't have to kick some horny, bastard's ass tonight for looking at you too hard."

"Ha! There will be plenty of dressed-to-kill women there. I doubt you'll have to worry about anyone looking at me."

"I disagree. Sometimes I don't think you realize the impact you have on the male species." He placed a kiss on her cheek, and her familiar scent engulfed him. "But let's get out of here before I lose control and have my way with you. Oh, and we need to make a little detour."

Chapter Thirty-Two

Thirty minutes later, Kenton's truck bounced and rocked side to side as he drove over the gravel and crater-sized potholes of the Corner Bar's parking lot. Since only three cars sat in the lot, one being Caleb's, they had their pick of spots.

Kenton pulled into a space a few slots down from the front door, and his gaze swept their surroundings before shutting off the engine. The Corner Bar used to be his and Caleb's stomping ground when Kenton first moved to Atlanta. The little hole-in-the-wall bar had never been fancy, but now the brick, run-down building with glass block windows and a red door, was in drastic need of an overhaul.

"I should've had one of the guys pick you up from the house and take you to the fundraiser. I didn't realize the place had gotten this bad, and you look too pretty to take inside this dump."

"Nope, you did the right thing. You're my date for tonight." She held his hand. "I'm going to the gala with you, and I'm leaving with you, and that's final."

"You know it's a serious turn on when you talk all big and bad." Kenton leaned across the center console and placed his finger under her chin, pulling her close. His mouth covered hers and he drank in the sweetness of her lips. "I'm

230

glad you're here with me."

"Me too." Egypt ran her thumb over his mouth, wiping away lipstick. "So what's the plan?"

"We go in here, I talk to Caleb and get him to let us drop him off at home. If that doesn't work then…I'm not sure. I guess I can knock his ass out, throw him in the back of the truck, and leave him on his front porch."

Egypt shook her head and grinned. "Well, hopefully, the talking works. The other option sounds a little too caveman like."

"All right, let's get this over with. Let me shoot Laz a quick text first and let him know we might be a little late. We should get there before they serve dinner though." Kenton glanced at his phone and groaned. One bar. No wonder Caleb's call kept breaking up. "My cell signal is weak. Check your phone and see if you have any service."

"Not much. Mine is bouncing between one and two bars."

"Okay, send a text to Ham or Dee and let them know that we'll be a little late, and I'll text Laz. Maybe one of our texts will eventually go through."

"Why do you do everything on your phone when you can just use your watch?" Egypt asked, cramming her cell phone back into her clutch purse.

"The face of the watch is so small, and it's too much of a pain to text folks. And before you ask, I only wear the watch because Chelsey bought it for my birthday, and insists I wear it. Plus, it looks kinda cool."

"Oh, alright. I was just wondering."

Once he finished, Kenton reached into the glove compartment and pulled out a 9mm.

"Um, you don't think you're going to need that do you?" Egypt asked, concern in her voice.

"Nope, but better safe than sorry." His backup Glock was in his ankle holster, but since Egypt didn't have her weapon, he felt a little more comfortable with both of his. Once he stored the gun in the back of his waistband, he climbed out of the truck.

When they stepped into the dingy bar, the stench of fried food and spoiled beer greeted them at the door. Kenton glanced around, allowing his eyes to adjust to the darkness. The place was empty except for a bartender watching a basketball game, and Caleb. He nursed a beer at a small table in the back of the place.

Kenton gripped Egypt's hand tighter as they moved across the threadbare carpet and skirted around a couple of tables. The germaphobe in Egypt was probably cringing inside seeing discarded food, partially empty glasses and beer bottles littering the tops of tables. Kenton needed to make this conversation quick so they could get the hell out of there.

When they were within earshot, he cleared his throat and Caleb looked up. He stood suddenly, then extended his hand to Kenton.

"Man, good seein' you." His words were slurred, but Kenton could understand him better than he had earlier. "I shouldn't have called. I'm…I'm sorry. Looks like I messed up your plans. Hi, Egypt."

"Hello."

Caleb leaned in to hug her, but Kenton stopped him with a hand on his chest. "Have a seat, man. Tell me what's going on."

Kenton pulled out a chair for Egypt but shoved it back into place after realizing the plastic cushion was in shreds. After inspecting two other nearby seats, before finding one that was suitable, he waited for her to sit before taking the spot next to her.

"Sorry, the place ain't what it used to be. Y'all want somethin' to drink?"

"Nah, we're good." Kenton nodded at the three empty beer bottles on the table and the half-full one in his friend's hand. "It looks like you've had a few. What are you doing here, Caleb? You should be at home trying to work things out with Dora."

"She left me!" he snapped.

Egypt startled, and Kenton wrapped his arm around her shoulder.

"I messed up. Lost a lot of money, and my *wife* wants nothing to do with me."

"I know you play poker and hit the tables sometimes, but I didn't know you gambled enough to get caught up like this. How'd that happen?"

"Don't know. I was doubling my money and then... I just...I just started losing more. Checks started bouncing. Dora found out." He shook his head and banged his fist on the table. "Dammit! How did I get myself into this mess?" He looked at Kenton, his eyes red and glossy. "I'm in deep, man. I owe..."

"How deep?"

For most of the conversation, Caleb had been staring down at the table, until now. He looked at Egypt, for a little too long as far as Kenton was concerned.

"Hey." Kenton snapped his fingers. "Eyes over here." When his friend finally made eye contact, Kenton asked again, "How deep are you? How much do you owe?"

Kenton wasn't in the business of loaning money, but for Caleb, he'd do almost anything. After the incident in D.C, when Santana and Quaid were killed, Kenton owed his life and any bit of happiness he'd found to Caleb. He was the person who brought him mentally and emotionally back to life.

Instead of responding, Caleb took a long drag on his beer, then slammed the bottle on the table. He squeezed his eye shut and rubbed his forehead.

Kenton glanced around again. Where they were seated, he could see the front door and most of the bar, except the hallway that led to the bathrooms. Like the outside of the bar, the inside looked every bit as worn and neglected. Missing light bulbs, smelly and the grimy walls had him wondering how the owners passed inspections.

Movement across the room, in the right-hand corner, caught his attention. He straightened.

What the hell...

Kenton shook his head to make sure he wasn't seeing things. Shrouded in semi-darkness was Agent Franklin looking like a bum who'd been sleeping on the streets for weeks. The full beard and the wool hat tilted to the side distorted his features, but Kenton was sure that was him.

How had he missed seeing him? It was like he had materialized out of thin air. And what the hell was he doing there?

"I made so many mistakes." Caleb groaned, still holding his head and staring down at the table. "I have to fix this. I have to take care of my family."

Kenton said nothing, discretely watching Franklin over Caleb's shoulder. The man was like a damn statue, holding his position and barely blinking. Then, almost imperceptibly, he moved his head as if directing them to the back hallway.

Kenton's hand balled into a fist, and his gut stirred. At that moment, Franklin slipped from his seat with the stealth of a ninja. He disappeared behind the wall that was blocking Kenton from seeing the back hallway.

His pulse amped up, and he debated on whether to follow the agent or get out of there. Tapping his fingers on the table, his gaze swept the room again. The TV was on, but the bartender was no longer at the bar, and Caleb was still mumbling about Dora leaving him.

Kenton sat forward, the tingling across the back of his neck alerting him to make a move. Franklin was up to something. Or had he seen something outside that made him go to the back of the building? For weeks they hadn't seen or heard from the guy. Like he had fallen off the face of the earth. Now, out of nowhere, he makes an appearance, moving around like a damn ninja and looking like...

Wait. Is he undercover?

"Where's the lady's room?" Egypt asked, and Kenton could've kissed her. He knew her well enough that she would pee her pants before using the bathroom there. Had she seen Franklin too?

"I'll show you." He stood and held out his hand to her.

Caleb's head popped up. "You can't leave," he said in a rush. "Not yet. I-I need to talk to you. I need to tell you."

Kenton scrutinized his friend, and his bull-shit meter kicked into high gear. Had they stepped into some alternate universe? What the hell was going on here? "We're not leaving. Just let me show her to the bathroom, and I'll be right back."

Without another word, Kenton guided Egypt toward the hallway that led to the restrooms, mindful of her long gown and strappy four-inch heels. He pulled the gun from the back of his waistband and kept it at his side. He didn't know what was going on, but he planned to find out.

The moment they turned the corner, Franklin was right there. Kenton swore under his breath. Egypt gasped, but quickly put her hand over her mouth.

"What the fuck, man? What are you doing here?" Kenton said in a low growl and shoved Franklin against the wall.

Franklin pushed him back. "Get her out of here. Now," he said in a loud whisper, his gaze shifting back and forth from the front of the building to the back. "I'm undercover, and I know who you are—*Paige*."

Surprise gripped Kenton, and he reached for Egypt's hand again when she started trembling and backing away. Kenton's mind raced with this new information.

"Your boy is setting her up. He owes Pisano. Go. *Now*." Franklin moved toward his hiding spot.

With his heart pounding loud enough for the world to hear, and Egypt shivering against him, Kenton turned to head for the back door, but his watch vibrated, signaling a text. It had dinged a minute ago indicating a call.

He glanced at his wrist. *Myles*.

Then read the text. *Get out now! Bomb!*

Shit. "We gotta move."

POP! POP!

Kenton flinched and Egypt screamed.

235

The echo of two gunshots rang out, and Kenton shoved Egypt against the wall, covering her with his body. When he looked down the hall, Franklin lay on the floor, gagging, blood spilling from his chest, and Caleb stood over him.

"Let me see your hands. Now!" Caleb said, walking toward them, his gun pointed at Kenton. "I said now! I don't want to shoot you...but I will."

With Egypt shivering beneath him, Kenton slipped her his gun before turning slowly, his arms out to the side. With his wide body, she couldn't see Franklin and Caleb didn't have direct sight of her.

"I'm sorry, Ken," Caleb said, his gun hand shaking. "I can't let you take her. She has to stay here."

"Why?" Kenton asked, trying to sound calm despite the adrenaline pumping through his veins.

"When I saw her at the grocery store, I knew she looked familiar. Marco has a picture."

While he was talking, Kenton inched back but bumped into Egypt. Understanding what he was doing, she held onto his jacket, urging him to continue backing up.

"Stop moving!" Caleb screamed, his gun-hand shaking even more.

Kenton froze. He kept thinking about the text message. They needed to get out of there and were only a few feet from the door.

"Marco is coming to get her. I just called him. She's his."

"*No...No!*" Egypt cried, her voice trembling as it grew louder. "I'll die before I go anywhere with him!"

"Egypt!" Kenton snapped, forcing her to keep her attention on him. He needed her to stay calm and not freak out. "Stay with me, baby."

"You have to understand." Caleb inched toward them, fidgeting and sweat gleaming on his face. "If I don't deliver, Marco is going to kill me and my family. I *can't* lose my family."

"And I can't lose my woman," Kenton spat, his anger building to a boiling point.

While Caleb continued babbling, getting more flustered as seconds ticked away, Kenton lowered his arms and reached back. When Egypt set the gun in his hands, he could've kissed her. She was hanging in there, getting herself back under control, but he could still feel her trembling as they kept moving. He had to get them out of there before Pisano showed up.

Keep moving. We have to keep moving.

With each excruciatingly, slow step they took, Caleb moved with them. The only thing in Kenton's favor was how the man was rambling and sweating, anxiousness bouncing off of him. But when Mrs. Hoakley, Pisano and one of his men appeared behind Caleb, Kenton's stomach dropped, and panic roared through his body.

"I said stop moving!" Caleb yelled, and his gun fired. A bullet pinged off a light fixture, and chards of glass sprinkled around them. Egypt's ear-piercing screams filled the space, and all hell broke loose.

Kenton fired off several shots, then pushed Egypt toward the door.

"Run!" he yelled, still shooting and back-peddling, he glanced at the metal door. The moment Egypt was through it, he took off in a sprint behind her. Grabbing her around the waist, he held on tight as he practically carried her, running toward an open field.

Boom!

The earth shook.

Immense heat and a mass of debris plowed into them like torrential rain during a hurricane, propelling them twenty-feet through the air. Kenton crashed to the ground and screamed out, but didn't let go of Egypt who landed on top of him. Pain radiated up his back and down his leg, and he rolled, covering Egypt's body as much as he could. Her blaring screams mixed with the pounding in his head and the ringing in his ear.

Seconds ticked by before Kenton lifted his head. Through a blurry haze, he glanced back at the building. A cloud of dust, yellow-orange flames, and smoke touched the sky, while the stench of burning wood and wires filled the air.

His skull pounded like a jackhammer was hard at work, and he kept his head steady as he glanced down at Egypt. She was curled against him, crying, her head buried against his chest. He pushed back her long locks and she met his gaze. Scratches and blood were near her hairline.

"Are you okay?" he asked, his voice rough and his throat scratchy.

Tears streamed down her face and she swiped at them. "I'm alive, but God...I've never been so scared in my life. Are you hurt?"

Kenton started to lift up but gritted his teeth when pain radiated throughout his body. His back and his leg hurt like a son of a bitch. Instead of sitting all the way up, he lowered his head back to the hard ground.

"I'll live," he mumbled.

Sirens blared in the distance, and his mind raced with next steps, but as his adrenaline started to wane, so did his energy. But as long as Egypt was in his arms, nothing else mattered.

*

Kenton lounged on the sofa in his family room, a glass of Kentucky bourbon in his hand, and Egypt curled up next to him. The last few hours had been a damn nightmare, and all he wanted to do was take his woman and get as far away from Atlanta as possible. But running away never solved the problem. No matter how you try, you can't outrun memories.

"Maybe we should discuss this after you guys get some rest. It's been a long night," Nelson said. He sat in the recliner facing the sofa, and Myles leaned against a nearby wall.

After the explosion, Kenton and Egypt had to deal with a whirlwind of questions, and more pain than Kenton had experienced in years. Even now, his body throbbed like one huge muscle, but the physical aches were nothing compared to the mental anguish. To be betrayed by someone he considered a brother, rocked him to his core.

Why hadn't Caleb just come to him and let him know that he'd owed Pisano money? Kenton would've bailed him out of any situation. Instead, the man had chosen to betray him, try to take the one thing Kenton loved more than life. Egypt.

He took another sip of his drink, tempted to slam it back as anger and loss battled within him. Pisano had used Caleb to lure them to the bar, a bar that had been set to explode. Only a damn monster did shit like that.

"Did anyone ever find out why Franklin broke into Egypt's home?" Kenton asked.

"He thought she was somehow wrapped up with the Pisano family and thought she was keeping it from the feds," Nelson said. "When he received the results back from your fingerprints, Egypt, he did more digging and found the connection between you and Marco."

Kenton and Nelson still wanted to keep her true identity quiet, but Kenton wouldn't be surprised if the guys of Supreme already knew. He glanced at Myles, wondering if he knew the truth. If he did, he hadn't said anything.

"Before Franklin could let you guys know why he was digging deeper into Egypt, he was put on a different assignment. He was deep undercover and had infiltrated the LinKenzoy organization."

Egypt straightened and pinched the bridge of her nose as she released a noisy sigh. She hadn't said much since they'd gotten home but assured Kenton that aside from some cuts, bruises and achiness, she was physically all right.

"If Franklin knew about the bomb, why didn't he just tell us?" Egypt finally spoke. Kenton didn't miss the anguish in her voice. "And why didn't he get out of there?"

"We don't think he knew about the bomb. From what we've learned, Franklin was told to keep tabs on Caleb." Myles glanced at Kenton. "And we don't know if he initially knew your friend was setting you two up."

Friend. Real friends don't stab you in the back. Real friends don't lure you to a hell hole to die. And real friends don't try and hand your woman over to a damn monster.

Rage boiled inside of Kenton and he bolted off the sofa, immediately regretting the quick move when a pain shot down his spine. His irritation cranked up into high gear, threatening to blow at any minute. Just thinking about Caleb's plans sent Kenton's heart rate through the ceiling.

Myles toyed with the water bottle that was in his hands. "In the end, the agent became an unfortunate casualty in what went down."

Franklin might've been on Kenton's shit list initially, but he hated the guy had to die because of trying to help them.

Kenton paced the room, twisting and turning at the waist to stretch his back. "How did you guys even know the LinKenzoy family intended to blow up the bar?"

"I put out feelers weeks ago for any information I could get on Pisano," Myles said, rubbing the back of his neck. "I received a call during the fundraiser, saying something was happening at the bar tonight, and Pisano wasn't going to make it out alive. They didn't know for sure, but heard explosives would be involved."

"We're still not sure when or how the FBI found out what was going down," Nelson added. "And neither of us knew you were at the bar until Laz mentioned why you were going to be late."

Kenton's chest tightened as the realization that they could've died tonight hit him again. "God, I'm glad I texted Laz," he said more to himself than anyone else.

"And I'm glad this is over," Egypt murmured, hugging herself. "But I feel so bad for Caleb's wife and kids. Their worlds will never be the same."

If Kenton felt betrayed by his friend, he couldn't imagine what Dora was going through. "I'm going to reach out and do whatever I can to help her and the kids get through this."

"Let us know if there's anything we can do to help her," Myles said.

Kenton nodded. "Thanks, guys for having our backs

240

tonight. You really came through."

Nelson stood, and pulled Kenton into a man hug. "We're a team, a family. That's what we do, thanks for taking care of my girl tonight."

Kenton winked at Egypt. "Always. She's my top priority."

Nelson moved to the sofa, reached for her hand, and pulled her up.

"Ow," she groaned as she stood, grimacing in pain and rubbing her left hip.

"Oops, sorry. I forgot you're all banged up." Nelson gently wrapped his arms around her and whispered close to her ear, but Kenton couldn't hear what was being said.

"I'm glad you guys are alright." Myles pushed away from the wall and pulled his keys from his pocket. "Now, we're going to get out of here so you can get some sleep."

"All right, and thanks again for everything. I'll walk you out."

When Kenton returned to the family room, he dimmed the lights and put on some music. Within seconds, Coltrane's *In a Sentimental Mood* played through the speakers. The solemn melody fit Kenton's current disposition as he slowly lowered himself back onto the sofa. That's when he noticed Egypt wiping her eyes with the back of her hand.

"What's wrong?" he asked, then realized it was a stupid question. They'd been through hell. It was a wonder she'd been able to hold herself together as well as she had. He handed her a couple of sheets of Kleenex from the box on the table.

"I guess I'm just a little overwhelmed by everything. We almost *died* tonight." She sobbed, taking a moment to pull herself together. "Bits and pieces of the evening have been playing in my mind. I keep reliving those moments."

"I know what you mean."

Kenton laid his head against the sofa and stared up at the ceiling. There had even been a few times during the night that he had thought about Santana and Quaid. Trying to get him and Egypt out of that bar tonight triggered flashbacks of that day at the cemetery. A day he'd been trying to put behind him for years, but at least this time he hadn't failed the person he was protecting.

"You saved my life," Egypt said as if reading his mind.

"I can't take all the credit. We had help, but most importantly, we had each other's back."

"Yeah, you're right. We had each other."

Kenton glanced down at her. "Now that Pisano's out of the picture, you can stop running."

She gave Kenton a teary-eyed smile. "I had already stopped, but now I can start living."

Epilogue

Three months later…

"I thought Journey was going to wait a few months after the baby was born to have a housewarming party," Egypt said as she and Kenton strolled up the walkway to the large, two-story colonial. Laz and Journey's baby girl had been born seven weeks early, just days after the fundraiser.

"Since it was so last minute, Laz thinks she just wanted an excuse to have everyone over. That's why they told us *not* to bring a gift." Kenton held up the large box, a cookware set that Egypt had insisted they buy.

He also thought the gift was a waste of money since Journey didn't cook and Laz kept their meals simple, only needing a pot or two at a time. But Egypt had already started giving Journey and Dakota cooking lessons and knew the cookware would come in handy.

The door swung open seconds after they rang the doorbell. "Hey, y'all. Come on in," Laz said, yawning as he opened the door wider.

"What's up, man? You look like shit. Is our goddaughter keeping you up?"

"Man, don't get me started. I don't usually need much sleep, but that kid is not your normal infant. Seems she's awake more than she sleeps. What's with the box?"

"Egypt wanted to get you guys a housewarming gift."

Laz accepted the box. "Cool, thanks."

"You just don't listen, do you?" Journey strolled into the room carrying Arielle. "I told you no gifts."

"You know we couldn't come empty-handed. Well, I couldn't, but enough about us. Look at my little sweetie-pie."

The last few times Egypt had stopped by, Arielle slept through her visits. Today, her eyes were open, showing off the beautiful hazel-green color that was identical to Laz's. Egypt shook out of her coat and handed it to Kenton, who hung both of their jackets in the closet near the front door.

"Okay, hand her over so we can bond."

"All right, but you might want to wait until I change the little stinker. I was on my way upstairs when Laz mentioned you guys were outside. Actually, come and say hello to everyone and then you can go upstairs with me. I want you to see what I've done with the nursery."

"Sounds like a plan." They strolled down the short hall but stopped when they saw Dakota coming down the stairs with Dylan in her arms.

"Well, it's about time you guys got here."

"God, look at all of this cuteness," Egypt cooed, kissing Dylan's scented neck while he kicked his chubby legs. Dakota handed him to her, and Egypt marveled how big he was getting. Like Arielle, he had a head full of black curls. "It sounds like a lot of people here already. Are we that late?"

Journey waved the question off. "Nah, you're right on time. Everyone is in the family room, and those who are pretending that it's not chilly outside are sitting out back on the deck."

Egypt followed them past the home office and a powder room. "Mmm, something smells good. I guess those cooking lessons are paying—"

"Surprise!"

Egypt startled, her heart practically pounding out of her chest as she held the baby tighter. She glanced around at the

244

crowded family room, and at those who had spilled into the adjourned dining area and the kitchen. Most of Supreme Security was there, and it took her a moment to realize what was going on. Happy birthday balloons and decorations were all over.

"Happy Birthday," everyone yelled.

"Here, I'll take Dylan," Kenton said, lifting the baby out of her arms before kissing her lips. "Happy birthday, sweetheart."

Egypt smiled, tears flooding her eyes at the heartfelt love spilling over inside her chest. Her birthday wasn't for another two days, but the fact that they'd thought enough to celebrate her day, had her crying like a baby. She welcomed all the hugs and kisses.

Journey and Dakota hugged her at the same time.

"Happy birthday, sis."

"We love you."

They spoke at once, and Egypt thought her heart would burst. These women had welcomed her into their lives and were her best friends, her sisters. She swallowed a sob that bubbled up inside of her.

"Thank you…thank you all for this." She hadn't had a birthday party since she was twelve-years-old, and yet people who weren't related to her by blood thought enough to do this for her. It was almost too much.

"I thought this was supposed to be a housewarming party." Egypt pointed at the wrapped gift that she and Kenton had brought and everyone laughed.

"Let's eat!" Dakota yelled and pulled her into the kitchen.

Egypt thought she would burst from happiness. For so many years, she had spent her birthday alone. Now, she had an amazing man and friends, who were as close as family, to share her life with.

*

Kenton brought his beer bottle up to his lips as he glanced across the room at Egypt who was holding Arielle.

245

Over the last three months, Egypt had her good days and bad, but mostly good. The first few weeks after the bar incident, she had nightmares about the explosion and would wake up screaming. Now that she was seeing a therapist, the dreams had subsided, and she was back to her old self. Oddly enough, he hadn't had any nightmares about the night at the bar or the day he had lost Santana and Quaid. Maybe because he no longer blamed himself for what had happened to them.

"Have you heard from Angelo?" Laz asked, stopping at the patio door with a bag of trash. "He doesn't usually pass on a free meal. So he should've been here by now, especially since I lied and told him Egypt was cooking."

Kenton chuckled. "I called a couple of times, but haven't heard back. I'll try him again before we initiate a 311."

Hamilton and Mase had introduced a new safety protocol. That whenever one of Atlanta's finest didn't report in or didn't respond to calls, a search party would hunt them down.

"Okay, keep me posted. It's not like Angelo to be off the grid."

That was true. By nature, they were all overprotective, but since the bar bombing, everyone had been extra diligent in looking out for each other and checking in regularly.

"Dee said for everyone to come into the kitchen so Egypt can cut her cake," Dominic, Hamilton and Dakota's son, said.

"All right, let's do this." Kenton strolled over to Egypt, who was handing Arielle to Journey. "Hey, birthday girl. Ready for some cake?"

"I'm so full, I don't think I can eat another thing, but I don't want to stop anyone else."

When they arrived at the breakfast bar, Dominic walked up to Egypt. "Were you really surprised?" he asked, looking at her with narrowed eyes. "Or did Kenton tell you?"

"*Oh, God.* He's suspicious of everything. Just like his godfather," Hamilton grumbled, shaking his head.

Laz shrugged. "Hey, what can I say? I'm a good

influence on him."

Dominic was one of the smartest kids Kenton knew, and at eleven, he already had some of Laz's detecting skills. Hamilton might've been the kid's father, but it was Laz who Dominic seemed to worship. Their relationship was closer than some father-son duos.

"Actually, I was surprised, *Little Laz*," Egypt said, making Dominic grin.

Kenton playfully pulled Dominic into a headlock. "She was only surprised because we kept you away from her."

"I wasn't going to tell her. I know how to keep a secret," Dominic said with attitude. "I don't tell *everything*. I didn't tell her that you bought her a ring."

It was as if the world came to a screeching halt. Silence filled the room, and all eyes landed on Kenton. He turned and glared at the person who helped him pick the ring— Dakota.

"Oh no," she murmured, while others laughed.

Kenton shook his head. "Dom, man, you're like a wet paper bag, can't hold nothin'."

Dominic's eyes grew big, and then he stared down at his tennis shoes. "Sorry."

"No harm done, kid." Kenton held his large fist out for a fist bump, and Dominic brightened.

When Kenton finally looked at Egypt, she stood stunned, her mouth hanging open. He loved her more than any man could love a woman but hadn't planned to ask her to marry him until they were alone.

Now is as good of a time as ever.

He turned and moved a bar stool that was in the way. Then pulled the small, blue velvet box from his front pants pocket. He rarely got nervous. Yet, the steady thump of his heartbeat was picking up in speed as he reached for her hand and lowered himself to one knee.

When he opened the lid, revealing the two-carat princess cut diamond engagement ring, gasps filled the quietness of the room.

"Oh. My. God." Egypt lifted her shaking hands to her mouth.

"I had planned to do this later tonight when we were alone, but since the kid outed me, now is as good of a time as ever. Egypt, I knew from the first moment I met you that you were special. Since then our relationship has grown stronger by the year, and over the last few months, you have brought so much joy into my life. I love you, sweetheart. I don't want another day to go by without asking you… Will you marry me?"

"Oh, Kenton. I love you so much." She swiped at a tear that slipped through. "Of course, I'll marry you."

Kenton slipped the ring onto her trembling finger as everyone around them cheered, and he scooped Egypt up into his arms. He couldn't remember the last time he'd been this happy.

"How about changing your name one more time?" he whispered into her ear.

She cupped his face between her hands and kissed his lips before whispering back, "Actually, I think Egypt Bailey has a nice ring to it, and…thank you for loving me."

"Always. I'll always love you."

*

If you enjoyed this book by Sharon C. Cooper, consider leaving a review on any online book site, review site or social media outlet.

Join Sharon's Mailing List

To get sneak peeks of upcoming stories and to hear about giveaways that Sharon is sponsoring, go to **https://bit.ly/1Sih6ol** to join her mailing list.

About the Author

Award-winning and bestselling author, Sharon C. Cooper, is a romance-a-holic - loving anything that involves romance with a happily-ever-after, whether in books, movies, or real life. Sharon writes contemporary romance, as well as romantic suspense and enjoys rainy days, carpet picnics, and peanut butter and jelly sandwiches. She's been nominated for numerous awards and is the recipient of an Emma Award for Romantic Suspense of the Year 2015 (Truth or Consequences), Emma Award - Interracial Romance of the Year 2015 (All You'll Ever Need), and BRAB (book club) Award -Breakout Author of the Year 2014. When Sharon is not writing or working, she's hanging out with her amazing husband, doing volunteer work or reading a good book (a romance of course). To read more about Sharon and her novels, visit www.sharoncooper.net

Connect with Sharon Online:

Website: http://sharoncooper.net

Facebook:
http://www.facebook.com/AuthorSharonCCooper21?ref=hl

Twitter: https://twitter.com/#!/Sharon_Cooper1
Subscribe to her blog: http://sharonccooper.wordpress.com/

Goodreads:
http://www.goodreads.com/author/show/5823574.Sharon_C_Cooper

Pinterest: https://www.pinterest.com/sharonccooper/

Other Titles

Atlanta's Finest Series
Vindicated (book 1)
Indebted (book 2)
Accused (book 3)

Jenkins & Sons Construction Series (Contemporary Romance)
Love Under Contract
Proposal for Love

Jenkins Family Series (Contemporary Romance)
Best Woman for the Job (Short Story Prequel)
Still the Best Woman for the Job (book 1)
All You'll Ever Need (book 2)
Tempting the Artist (book 3)
Negotiating for Love (book 4)
Seducing the Boss Lady (book 5)
Love at Last (Holiday Novella)
When Love Calls (Novella)

Reunited Series (Romantic Suspense)
Blue Roses (book 1)
Secret Rendezvous (Prequel to Rendezvous with Danger)
Rendezvous with Danger (book 2)
Truth or Consequences (book 3)
Operation Midnight (book 4)

Stand Alones
Something New ("Edgy" Sweet Romance)
Legal Seduction (Harlequin Kimani – Contemporary Romance)
Sin City Temptation (Harlequin Kimani – Contemporary Romance)

A Dose of Passion (Harlequin Kimani – Contemporary Romance)
Model Attraction (Harlequin Kimani – Contemporary Romance)
A Passionate Kiss (Bennett Triplets Series)

www.ingramcontent.com/pod-product-compliance
Lightning Source LLC
Chambersburg PA
CBHW020826260626
47169CB00003B/856